"Ah, lass," he ⬛⬛⬛⬛⬛⬛⬛⬛⬛⬛⬛⬛⬛ s head. "A lifetime is ⬛⬛⬛⬛⬛⬛⬛⬛⬛⬛⬛ done. The time yo⬛⬛⬛⬛⬛⬛⬛⬛⬛⬛ life. It changed mine. You will not go back the same girl as when you left."

Already Heather felt different. Having him talk to her as if her ideas and plans mattered, as if her feelings were normal, not weird, made her feel wonderful. Back home, none of her friends understood her. Why, not even her own sister had caught on. How odd that here, a world away from all she had ever known, she had found someone who felt and thought the way she did.

·

From
ANGEL *of* HOPE

"I have a better idea, Mom." Heather leaned forward eagerly. "Come with me. Just for a few months. See for yourself. Chase your dream again—the one that inspired you in the Peace Corps. After we've worked in Uganda side by side, if you still can't see the value in what I want to do, I'll come home and enroll at the University of Miami. That's a promise." She settled back in her chair, her hands held out beseechingly. "What do you say? Will you come with me?"

Lurlene McDaniel

JOURNEY *of* HOPE

TWO NOVELS

Published by
Dell Laurel-Leaf
an imprint of
Random House Children's Books
a division of Random House, Inc.
New York

Visit us on the Web! www.randomhouse.com/teens
Educators and librarians, for a variety of teaching tools, visit us
at www.randomhouse.com/teachers

ISBN: 0-553-49451-1

Printed in the United States of America
First Dell Laurel-Leaf Edition October 2004

OPM   10 9 8 7 6 5 4 3 2 1

CONTENTS

To My Readers,

These books are close to my heart. A number of years ago, I accompanied a missionary team to Uganda. There, I met extraordinary people—missionaries, doctors, and American kids who were working in extreme conditions to help make a difference in the lives of others.

I would like to thank them all for inspiring me with their selfless courage. And I especially thank Dr. Henry Krabbendam of Covenant College and the Africa Christian Training Institute; my son, Erik McDaniel, a youth pastor in Anniston, Alabama, who regularly takes kids on mission trips to developing countries; Benjamin Jacobs, a student at Ole Miss, who served on the Mercy Ship Anastasis; and Dr. Monte Wilson, director of Global Impact Ministries, for their input in helping me create these works of fiction. I hope these books will enable readers to experience different cultures and different ways of looking at the human condition.

If you are interested in learning more about the Mercy Ship ministry, contact:

Youth with a Mission
MERCY SHIPS
P.O. Box 2020
Lindale, TX 75771-2020

Angel of Mercy

Then the Lord said to Cain, "Where is your brother Abel?"

"I don't know," he replied. "Am I my brother's keeper?"

Genesis 4:9
(NIV)

Therefore go and make disciples of all nations, baptizing them in the name of the Father and of the Son and of the Holy Spirit. . . .

Matthew 28:19
(NIV)

1

"I can't believe you're giving up your entire summer *and* fall instead of going to college, Heather. I mean, it's like forever! And just look where you'll be living. How can you stand it? There's no room to move, no privacy either!"

"I'll be home in time for Christmas," Heather Barlow reminded her sixteen-year-old sister, Amber. "And I don't care about the living conditions. As for college, I'll start in January. You'll hardly know I'm gone."

At eighteen, Heather was going off on a Mercy Ship to work in Africa, to try to make a difference in a place where children starved to death or died from terrible illnesses. She had grown up wanting to do something worthwhile with her life, but now that she was actually on board the ship, now that it was almost time to say goodbye to her family, Heather was beginning to feel the clutch of self-doubt. And Amber's reluctance to see her leave wasn't helping.

Amber glanced around the cramped quarters. "It's just so—so primitive."

Ignoring Amber's complaints, Heather opened her duffel bags and began putting her clothes into the narrow drawers of the dresser bolted to the wall. She would be sharing this old-fashioned small stateroom with a Swedish girl named Ingrid, whom she'd not yet met.

Across the narrow room, Amber seated herself on a bed attached by cables to the metal wall of the ship. "Ugh! This mattress is so thin, I can feel the springs."

"It's a hospital ship, sis, not a luxury liner anymore," Heather reminded her.

Years before, *Anastasis* had served as a cruise ship. But in the mid-1980s, it had been converted into a floating hospital, with three operating rooms, a dental clinic, a laboratory, and an X-ray unit. The aging ship, painted white from bow to stern, was more than five hundred feet long and nine stories high. Its staterooms, once luxurious quarters for wealthy travelers, now housed crew and staff—175 volunteers who paid their own expenses and agreed to serve a tour of duty as the ship sailed from port to port, bringing life-saving medical services to countries ravaged by disease, famine, war, and poverty.

Long-term crew members—missionary and medical personnel and their families who had signed up for extended tours of duty—were housed in the more spacious upper-deck staterooms, while short-term volunteers such as Heather were assigned the smaller rooms. The ship's once-elegant lounge and dining areas served as conference rooms and training centers. Children of the crew and staff attended school on board.

Once the ship dropped anchor in a port, engineers, carpenters, teachers, and evangelists took medical and dental services and supplies into remote areas and inland villages. They built schools, hospitals, and housing, all with donated goods. The Mercy Ship was a floating hospital. And a vision of hope.

"Well, I think it's a dumb idea to even be going on this trip, and I don't know why you want to go in the first place," Amber said, voicing her displeasure once again. "I'll bet there's no decent guys to date, and nowhere to go even if there were."

Heather sighed. It irritated her when Amber sounded so frivolous. Why couldn't she understand how important this trip was? Heather had spent so much time thinking about the trip, a whole year planning it, and ten days in May at a special boot camp preparing for it. She asked, "Are you trying to make me feel guilty? Because I won't. I've wanted to do this for a long time, and you know it."

Amber scuffed her fashionable shoes on the floor. "I'm going to miss you," she said quietly.

"I'll miss you, too." Heather saw tears shimmering in her sister's green eyes. "Hey, what's this? I thought you'd be glad to have the house to yourself. And no big sister to be in your way when school starts, either. You always said you couldn't wait until me and my friends were out of high school so that you and your friends could have the halls all to yourself." Heather sat beside Amber on the bunk and put her arm around Amber's shoulders.

"What fun is there in being home by myself? Mom and Dad won't have anything to do but go to work. And grouse at me, of course. You're the one they think is perfect in this family, you know."

"They grouse at you now," Heather teased gently. "So what will be different?"

"You won't be there to get them off my case."

"Then don't do anything to get them on your case." Heather gave Amber a squeeze. "Honestly, I really do think you go out of your way to provoke them sometimes."

"If you mean I like to have fun instead of trying to save the world, then guilty as charged." Amber sniffed and slumped lower on the bunk.

Heather did feel sorry for her sister. Their parents were both highly successful plastic surgeons—their father a wizard in facial reconstruction, their mother a respected specialist in body reshaping. True, much of their practice these days was given over to cosmetic facelifts, liposuction, and cellulite reduction, but they still were renowned for their ability to help the horribly deformed or tragically maimed. Their busy schedules left them with little free time at home. With Heather gone, Amber would be pretty much on her own. *She has tons of friends and her senior year coming up*, Heather reminded herself. Amber would be fine.

Heather scooted off the bunk. "Look, sis, Mom and Dad will be back from their tour any second now, so please help me out. No pity party, okay? I'll start to cry, and that wouldn't be good. I promise I'll write often. And don't forget, you all are going to spend a week touring Europe before you have to fly home. That should be fun."

The ship was docked in London, taking on supplies, and would sail in two weeks for the coast of Kenya. From there, Heather would accompany a special team to Lwereo in central Uganda, where she would work as an aide in the only hospital for the entire district—a hospital staffed by Irish missionary doctors. Heather's team would also build a dormitory for an orphanage run by Americans. In December, she was to fly directly home, arriving the week before Christmas.

"A week in Europe . . . whoopee," Amber said glumly. "My idea of fun isn't tracking through museums and art galleries. Mom's already got a list this long." She held her hand above her head. "Is there even one dance club on the list? I think not."

Heather laughed. "Can you see Dad moshing on a dance floor?"

A smile lit Amber's teary eyes.

Encouraged, Heather asked, "Or how about Mom fighting her way to the bathrooms? Both of them could get hurt twisting their way through such crowds. Who'd do surgery on the surgeons?"

Just then the cabin door opened and their parents stepped in. Amber quickly wiped her eyes, and Heather got up to meet them, not wanting them to see Amber's distress.

"Great tour," their father said. "You're in good hands. Excellent ORs—state-of-the-art—on a par with the ones I use in Miami."

"I'm glad you approve."

Her mother looked apprehensive. "Now I know how my mother felt when she was seeing me off to Guatemala when I was twenty-two." Heather and Amber's parents had met years before in the Peace Corps, and their stories of their adventures had inspired Heather all her life. The seeds of her desire to help the underprivileged had been planted early.

"It won't be easy, you know," her mother added. "You'll see things that will break your heart. It doesn't take much to have your idealism crushed."

"It's too late to turn back now. I'll be fine, Mom," Heather insisted, feeling more unsure than she sounded.

"Of course you will," her father agreed, sending her a confident smile. Still, she could tell by the look in her parents' eyes that they were nervous about sending her halfway around the world. "We're proud of you, honey."

A deep blast of a horn, followed by the command "All ashore" over the PA system, made them all jump. Heather's heart thudded.

"I guess that's us," her mom said. She hugged her daughter, then held her hand while they climbed the network of ladderlike stairs from the lower staterooms to the upper decks.

Topside, the June breeze felt cool. The open deck was crowded by other travelers, all in stages of telling families and loved ones good-bye. "This is it," Heather said, almost losing her nerve and following them down the gangplank to the dock below.

"You write," her mother said.

"And e-mail on that laptop I gave you," her father said, giving her a smothering bear hug.

She kissed the three of them one last time, then watched as they left. On the dock, they stood with a throng of people, waving and calling goodbye. Tears filled Heather's eyes. All at once, the six months away from home and from all she'd ever known loomed like an eternity.

The ship towered above the dock, making them look small and insignificant amid the hustling dockworkers and their equipment. Heather watched her parents and sister climb into a cab. Hanging out the window, Amber blew her a kiss. A lump the size of a fist clogged Heather's throat, while a breeze from the sea pushed her thick hair away from her face. Tears trickled unchecked down her cheeks.

Lost in sadness, she didn't realize that anyone was standing next to her until a deep male voice with a soft Scottish accent said, "It seems that your eyes have sprung a leak there, lass. Could I offer you my handkerchief to help mop it up?"

2

Heather swiped at her moist cheeks. She turned to face a young man with red hair and eyes the deep blue color of the ocean. He wore a sympathetic smile and held out a clean white handkerchief. Dazzled by his smile, she said, "I—I'll be all right."

"Here." He tucked the white cloth into her hand. "I've never met a lass who had a tissue when the waterworks started." His tone was gentle, his accent musical.

She dutifully dabbed at her tears to please him.

"Come, walk with me," he said, offering his arm. "It's better on the far side of the ship where you can look out over the water. Makes you forget your ties to the land."

She tucked her arm into his, and his large, warm hand clasped around hers. Together they strolled toward the ship's stern, away from the sight of her family's cab driving off.

"Your first trip over?" he asked.

"Yes." Heather was certain he thought her a big baby. Here she was bawling like a kid whose mommy had left her on the first day of school. "How about you?"

"My third." He nodded at her. "Ian McCollum, Edinburgh, Scotland."

She introduced herself.

"Heather . . ." He rolled her name around on his tongue as if tasting it. "Like the heather on the moors. And just as pretty, too."

She blushed, and he grinned. "In a few days you'll be so busy you won't have time to miss anybody."

"I know you're right. I didn't mean to get all sentimental. I've been wanting to do this for years, so please don't think I have any regrets about leaving."

"It's a good cause," he said. "I keep coming back to work between semesters at university."

"Where do you go to college?"

"I'm a medical student at Oxford," he said, then added, "Seminary student, too."

His soft accent fascinated Heather. She caught herself staring at his mouth as he spoke.

"Is something the matter with my words, lass?"

She felt her cheeks flush. "Uh—no . . . of course not. A doctor *and* a minister?" she asked quickly. "My parents are both doctors in Florida, and believe me, their practice keeps them busy all the time. How can you do both?"

"In truth, I cannot separate the two callings. To heal the body and not touch the soul—well, I could not do it. Physical healing is a fine thing, but to open the gates of heaven for a person . . . ah, well, that's the greater thing."

"I guess it's a little different for me," she said. "Mom and Dad were both in the Peace Corps—it's where they met, and they've always taught my sister and me that those who have been blessed by God should be generous. And I don't just mean by giving money away either. I think it's important to give of yourself, to do something worthwhile for others. I think of people as God's hands on Earth. A person shouldn't waste her life, or her blessings. You know what I mean?"

"Yes. It's more blessed to give than to receive."

"Ever since I can remember, I've wanted to make a difference in the world. I've wanted to go out and *do* something meaningful with my life. When I was a kid, at Halloween—" She broke off. "I'm sorry, I'm babbling."

"No. It's interesting. What did you do on Halloween?"

By now they had reached the far side of the ship, and they stood at the rail, looking out at the sea. "When other kids were out collecting candy, I collected money for UNICEF. It always made me feel really good to mail in that donation. I'd think about all the starving children I was helping. Kids in my classes thought I was crazy, but I didn't care. It was what I wanted to do."

"You have a sweet and gentle spirit, Heather."

She shrugged self-consciously. Sometimes she wished she were different. More like others her age. In grade school, she had been known as the school's do-gooder and was often teased about it. In high school, kids seemed more understanding, especially when she'd organized a food drive for a Miami homeless shelter and organized a clothing drive for hurricane victims and had been written up in the newspaper for her efforts. Two summers before, she'd been a candy striper at her community hospital and had loved it.

"I get sappy over a Hallmark card commercial," she confessed, then wondered if he even understood what she was talking about. "You know . . . I cry over anything that gets inside my heart. Sad movies, sad books."

"Don't think badly of yourself because you have a tender heart. Such hearts are needed in this world today. You will be touched many times when you go into the bush, Heather, lass. There are many in great need."

"I guess you'd know since you've done this before."

"Like you, I can't help myself. It's my destiny. To make people's bodies whole. To tell them about God and his love for them."

Ian McCollum's purpose sounded loftier than hers because it was double-edged. Once, when she and Amber were younger, in a fit of jealousy, Amber had hurled an accusation at Heather: "You just do this to get attention, you know. It's your way of getting Mom and Dad to take the time to notice you."

"And what's your way? To be as bad as you can be?" Heather had fired back.

Over time, she had often thought that there was a grain of truth in both her words and Amber's. She turned toward Ian. "What area of medicine are you interested in practicing?"

"Hands-on," he said with a grin. "I could

never be stuck in a stuffy laboratory, or even an operating room, day after day. Out in the bush, children die every day from things that are totally preventable. Stomach parasites, measles, whooping cough—illnesses that a simple vaccination or the right antibiotic can prevent."

"That bothers me, too. Knowing that kids die from things that are preventable. Mom told me how it frustrated her when she was in Central America to see little kids die from dehydration. They couldn't drink the water because it was contaminated. When they did, they died."

"It's a sad thing to see. When I've come before, I've stayed here on the Great White Ship—that's what the locals call the *Anastasis*—but this time, I'll be taking vaccines and supplies into Uganda."

"You're going to Uganda? So am I." The news pleased her. She liked this man from Scotland.

"Then we'll be seeing more of each other," Ian told her with a broad smile. "Once people in the bush know we're there, they'll come for miles, walk for days to see us."

"My mother told me not to expect to find much access to a phone. How does the news get around?"

"We're spoiled in the West. We think phones and computers and television are the only ways to communicate." He laughed dryly. "But news can travel in many ways, and in Africa, it travels quickly. Legend has it that the wind carries it along. And that only the ears of those born in Africa can hear it."

"I wish we could start tomorrow," she said impatiently. It would take a month to sail around the Cape of Good Hope and into the port at Kenya. "I can't wait to get there."

"It'll be here soon enough. In Africa time, as we keep it, doesn't exist. It drives Westerners crazy. No one sticks to a schedule."

She thought of her life in America, which ran by the clock. There were bells for class changes at school and schedules for planes, buses, movies, TV programs—the list was endless. She got tired of it. "Schedules are overrated," she said with a wave of her hand. "Maybe the people of Africa are on to something. The sun and the moon are the only clocks we need. Moontime—I like the sound of that, don't you?"

"You're smiling," Ian said, lifting her chin. "Makes your face even prettier."

She blushed. "You know, an hour ago my six months away from home seemed like forever.

Now, after talking to you, it hardly seems like enough time to get everything done."

"Ah, lass," he said with a bemused shake of his head. "A lifetime isn't long enough to get everything done. The time you spend here will change your life. It changed mine. You will not go back the same girl as when you left."

Already Heather felt different. Having him talk to her as if her ideas and plans mattered, as if her feelings were normal, not weird, made her feel wonderful. Back home, none of her friends understood her. Why, not even her own sister had caught on. How odd that here, a world away from all she had ever known, she had found someone who felt and thought the way she did.

She rested her elbows on the ship's railing and stared outward, her mind filling with a sense of purpose and commitment. "Thanks for talking to me, Ian. I feel much better now. All because of you."

He too leaned against the rail, his large, rough hands inches away from her soft, smooth skin. "It was my pleasure, Heather. We're all on the journey of a lifetime. God is our shepherd, and we have only to do what he asks of us. Kindness for one another, love for each other, that is what will change the world. Medicine can heal the body. But only God can make well the human soul."

His words touched her, and her heart swelled. "I think we're going to be good friends, Ian McCollum."

"You can count on it, lass. Yes, you can count on it."

3

Dear Amber,

We're out to sea a week now, and is it ever awesome. Nothing but dark blue ocean and gray sky. Seagulls followed us for two days, then flew away. I miss their sounds. Out here there's nothing but the sound of water, not a speck of land in any direction. This morning, the sun's come out, and it sure looks good. I can hardly wait until we get to Africa.

BTW, regular e-mailing is tough. The captain rations the time any one person can be on the special hookup, so I promise to write a long letter and mail it when I can. I'm so busy during the day that by nighttime, I just fall into bed and pass out.

My roomie, Ingrid, is truly cool! This is her second trip on the ship, so she's a real source of info for me. We're in the galley (that's the kitchen) together. Can you imagine me cooking? It's true. I can do scrambled eggs for almost two hundred in no time!

Most evenings, after all our chores are done, a bunch of us sit on deck and talk. The kids on board come from all over, and they're MAJORLY interesting. Plus, they're really knowledgable. They talk about world events like TV newscasters. They have opinions and ideas. I think of my friends at home who may know the hottest fashion trends but can't tell you what's going on politically in Bosnia, and I'm embarrassed. Yikes, did I just call my friends shallow? (Sorry.)

Miguel (he's from Madrid) has a guitar and after we finish talking and solving the world's problems, we sing while the stars twinkle down. I can hear the waves slapping against the hull of the ship and everything is so peaceful, it makes me want to cry with happiness. I've never been happier. And I haven't even gotten to the REAL work in Africa yet!

Hate to cut this short, but others are waiting in line for the modem plug. So, hang in there and try not to have too much fun without me. Hugs to Mom and Dad.

Heather hit Send and stared thoughtfully at the screen. She thought of all the things she hadn't written. She hadn't mentioned Ian. In other e-mails, she'd told Amber about meeting him, and about how cute she thought he was, but she hadn't confessed just how much she was liking him. No matter how long her day or how tired she felt, her spirits soared whenever she was around him. She couldn't call it a crush exactly—she'd had crushes on guys back in high school, so she knew what a sweaty-palms, racing-heart crush was like. This was different because *he* was different. She could hardly explain it to herself, much less to her sister.

Heather sighed and unplugged her laptop. She told herself that maybe she should give up sitting on the deck in the moonlight talking and listening to Miguel play the guitar. Maybe it would be best to turn in early rather than talking into the late hours of the night. Maybe staying away from Ian was the best thing to do.

She stood and shook her head decidedly. Then again, maybe it wasn't.

Each Monday and Wednesday morning, Heather met in the ship's conference room with Dr. Henry, the coordinator for her group, and the fifteen others assigned to the inland mission team. Dr. Henry, a surgeon and internist from Boston, stood six foot three and made a dramatic first impression. He was in his fifties, wore round, dark-rimmed glasses, and had a head of thick white hair. He was a veteran of the Mercy Ship and of Ugandan expeditions, telling the group that this was his tenth trip aboard the ship in twenty years.

"Uganda is a country that's been heavily influenced by the British," Dr. Henry said in his first lecture. "In fact, English is the 'official' language of the country, although you'll hear a lot of Swahili and Lugandan. Swahili has been spoken for over a thousand years in Africa, so it's good to know some words and phrases.

"When you meet an African, it's customary to open with '*Habari*,' which means 'What news?' And the standard reply is '*Mzuri*,' 'Good.' This formality is considered good manners, so try and remember to follow their protocol. All right, let's practice."

The group repeated the words, memorizing the inflections. "*Mzuri*," Dr. Henry said with a smile. "Another plus is that most Ugandans are literate. The best schools have waiting lists and are connected with the Anglican Church. The British influence in Uganda carried over into their schools. Children are sent off to boarding schools when they turn six. They live on campus year-round, partly because the roads within the country are so poor that it's impossible for children to return home daily. Kids have three traditional holidays a year. Formal education ceases in the seventh grade, but the brightest go on to upper-level schools. University abroad is for but a chosen few."

Heather knew two girls who'd gone away to private boarding schools, but each of them had a car and could come home when she wanted. Heather tried to imagine being a first-grader and not coming home from school every day. Or being cut off from her family for an entire school term.

Because Heather was to become a hospital aide, she also participated in basic first-aid courses, including CPR and trauma training. "Safety first," Dr. Henry told his team. "Double-glove at all times, especially when coming in contact with patients' body fluids. I know each of you has had basic inoculations, but we can't inoculate against HIV, so always be careful."

Before leaving the States, Heather had received an armful of vaccines, as well as a shot of gamma globulin to boost her immune system. She was taking typhoid and malaria medications by mouth daily. Her parents also had insisted that she carry a package of syringes in her luggage. Her father had said, "Medical supplies are at a premium in these countries. It isn't unusual for syringes to be reused, which runs a risk of contamination from other illnesses. Let's hope you don't need them, and when you leave, you can donate any of your leftover supplies to the hospital."

During a break, Heather turned to Patrick, a student of Dr. Henry's and an Ugandan. He had participated in their late-night gabfests. "Glad to be going home?"

"Yes. I have not seen my family for three years."

"Really? How come?"

He smiled. "It is a long way. And my father is not a rich man."

Of course. Why had she asked such a dumb question?

"My father is a teacher," Patrick said. "He has many children but only one wife." He laughed heartily, as if he'd made a hilarious joke. Heather didn't get it. "Because he teaches children, he has many," Patrick supplied, as if hoping she might finally catch on.

"One wife? Has he been married before?" That was the part that baffled Heather.

"In my country men take more than one wife," Patrick explained. "It is not unusual for a man to have two or three wives and ten, maybe fifteen children."

"But aren't there laws? Rules about bigamy?"

Patrick shook his head. "No. And that is one thing the Christian church is trying to change."

"I should think so."

Patrick regarded her with intense brown eyes. "Not for the reasons you may think. A man usually has only a small farm to grow food and make a living. If he has several wives and many children, how will he leave a proper inheritance when he dies? So then, the children are fighting over an acre of land. This is not good, brother against brother, woman against woman. The ground in Uganda is very rich, but how can an acre support a family of twenty when each is claiming a portion as his inheritance?"

"So if a man only has one wife, then he can pass his property down more efficiently," Heather said. "I understand." Patrick's logic was simple, but Heather was shocked to think of its being acceptable for a man to take several wives. Yet Patrick acted as if it were nothing extraordinary.

"This is true. And also, can you picture living in a house with many women, each thinking she is the best wife?" His expression was one of mock horror. "What man can stand the pressure? He might go off and meet another woman and marry her!"

She laughed.

Patrick sobered. "But there is even a far more serious problem with taking many wives. In my country, the HIV virus is spreading like a fire on the Serengeti. Dr. Henry will tell you, one in three Africans test positive for HIV. It is true. And when a man sleeps with many women, the virus is spread even faster. So my father keeps just one wife."

Heather had heard the lectures in school—unprotected sex and IV drug use were among the primary causes of the spread of HIV. Now she was hearing it again from a young man whose entire country was at risk. She looked into Patrick's eyes and said, "Your father's a very smart man."

"And my mother is a very jealous woman," he said with an impish wink.

One of the things Heather missed most of all was seeing green grass and bright, tropical flowers. The ocean world was beautiful, but the vast sea of blue sometimes depressed her. And some days, in spite of the bright sun, the sea air was cold. She stepped out on deck one morning to brilliant sunshine, but a northwest wind blew along the length of the deck, making her shiver.

"Would you like my sweater, Heather?"

Ian stepped up beside her. He wore a cream-colored cable-knit sweater of Irish wool, and his hair looked windblown.

"Thanks, but I'm headed down to the galley, and it's nice and warm down there. We're baking bread today. Maybe some pizzas too—food of the gods."

Ian laughed and rubbed her arms briskly. "That's a strange dish."

"You don't like pizza? That's un-American."

"I'm a Scotsman, remember."

She dropped her head dramatically onto his shoulder. "Of course you are."

"If it's bread you like, you'd better eat your fill on the ship, because Ugandans have no equivalent."

"What? A land with no bread? What do they eat instead?"

"Rice. *Matoke.* That's a cooked plantain, a kind of banana." She made a face. He added, "It's served in a mushy pile, like potatoes, but it doesn't taste like potatoes."

"Oh, the hardship of service." Heather placed the back of her hand against her forehead and pretended to swoon. "Well, you can't scare me. I'm still going to Africa—with or without my daily bread."

Ian laughed heartily. "Your enthusiasm is noted. And you will need it once we get there. When the power goes down and there's no hot water to bathe yourself or the patients, you may feel different."

Heather bristled. "I can take a little hardship. I'm not made of glass, you know."

"I'm certain that's true. But I don't want you to get discouraged."

"Then why are you trying to discourage me?"

His expression grew serious. "Because I don't want anything bad to happen to you. And I'm not just talking about your safety. Sometimes the dreams we hold in our hearts don't always measure up to what we must face in our life."

"You're afraid I'll become disillusioned? You sound like my parents."

"Is that who I remind you of? Your father?" He pulled back, pretending to be horrified. "I would hate for you to think of me as your kin."

"Then stop treating me like a baby sister."

His smile turned soft. "I have a sister, Heather. I don't need another one."

She gave him a grudging smile, not certain what to make of his teasing. Did he like her? Or was he just worried that she might weaken the team because of her inexperience? She was prepared to sacrifice her personal comfort. She knew her time of service in Africa wasn't going to be a picnic. She said, "Well, I feel sorry for your sister because you probably watch over her like a hawk and criticize every guy she brings home. You should give her the benefit of the doubt. She just *may* know what she's doing."

"Yes, maybe that's so."

Heather knew they weren't really talking about his sister, but it seemed the best way to get her point across. "Now, I've got to get down to the galley, or you'll be begging for your lunch and it won't be there."

"Then I'll see you later."

Neither of them moved. They stood looking into each other's eyes while Heather's heart hammered. Ian reached out and softly ran the back of his hand along her cheek. She shivered, but this time it didn't come from being cold.

4

Dear Heather,

I could go on about how boring it is around here without you this summer, but why put you to sleep? Mom and Dad are so busy that they hardly ever come home—except at night when I have something else to do! Anyway, we don't see much of each other (their loss). I print out your e-mails and stick them onto the fridge so they won't go snooping on the computer. That way if you ever want to tell me something personal and private, I can edit it out before I print it for general consumption. Smart, huh?

The only daytime company I have is Mrs. Lopez, who at least takes care of food for me (or I'd starve!), and the gardeners. There's a really cute guy trimming the hedges as I look out the window. Oh, BTW, I put a 2-inch blond streak in my hair. My friends think it looks cool. Mom says I look like Cruella in "101 Dalmatians." This from a woman who hasn't changed her hairstyle in 20 years!

One bright spot to report. Last Thursday, I came out of the mall to a flat tire on my car. (That's not the bright part.) I was freaking, when Dylan Simms came up to me. You remember him? He's on the basketball team and he's going to be a senior like me in the fall. Surprise! He's really cute—how did I fail to notice until now? Plus, we have something else in common— we both think I'm adorable.

Honest! He's had a crush on me for almost a year. Good timing, huh? I mean, nothing else is going on, so I might as well have a fling with a new guy. And BTW, I don't care what you say about you and Ian. I can read between the lines, and I know when my sister's got the hots for someone. Besides, what's more romantic than to be out on the high seas with a dreamy guy?

Well, got to run. Dylan's taking me to a movie.

Amber (who's tan and thin and looks like a goddess, or almost)

A pang of homesickness stabbed at Heather as she read Amber's e-mail. She pictured the screened-in pool and her sister stretched out on her hot pink bubble raft, floating lazily in the middle. Amber would have a soda can propped in the raft's cup holder. She'd be reading a hot, sexy novel and listening to music blasting from the poolside speakers. They'd followed this routine together for years growing up.

But Miami was more than two thousand miles away from the tip of Africa. The *Anastasis* had sailed around the Cape of Good Hope two days before and was now on the final leg of the journey. Soon the Great White Ship would anchor off the coast of Kenya and Heather would be bused into Nairobi airport, then flown to Entebbe, Uganda, with the rest of her team. If only she could communicate the grandness of her adventure to Amber. But she couldn't.

She closed her laptop with a sigh. Amber was right about one thing, however: Heather did have a thing for Ian. The more they talked, the better she got to know him, the more she liked him. But she wasn't going to let him see that. She hadn't come on this trip to have a romance. She'd come to help people have a higher quality of life. This trip wasn't about her, but others. Ian understood the concept perfectly. Amber might never get it.

* * *

One afternoon, Heather wandered into the refurbished lounge where school was held for the children of the crew and staff. Tables, desks, computers, and student artwork made the room look overstuffed. She found Mrs. Hoover, the teacher, busy scrubbing modeling clay off desks. "Can I help?" Heather asked.

The small, dark-haired woman straightened and flashed a tired smile. "Absolutely. What was I thinking to let them have clay and finger paints on the same day?"

Heather picked up a wet sponge from the bucket on the floor and set to work on a desk. "How many kids are on board?"

"Twenty—and a half, if you count Melissa Vanderhousen, who's due to give birth this fall." She chuckled. "But only fourteen come to school. The rest are too young."

"But you teach all of them? Even though they're different ages?"

"Yes, it's a real zoo some days."

"How do you do it?"

"Independent study for the most part, some group activities. And the older ones help the younger ones." Mrs. Hoover looked up. "You're Heather, aren't you? I'm Barbara. My husband, Bob, is in charge of the construction crew going into Uganda. Our kids and I will stay here on the ship."

Heather liked Bob Hoover and told Barbara so. "You know, I can't remember a time I haven't wanted to do this. How about you? It doesn't seem easy to uproot a family and stick them on a ship in the middle of the ocean." The trip was an adventure for Heather, but she knew it must be harder for families.

Barbara paused. "Actually, it was easier than I thought it would be. Four years ago, we lived in Atlanta. Bob was a partner in a large engineering firm. I was a teacher at a junior college. We had a gorgeous house, two cars, plenty of money in the bank. We were respected pillars of our church in the suburbs, and"—she paused—"we weren't happy. On the surface, we had it all. But in our hearts, frustration.

"The crowning blow came when our oldest, Todd, came home from school one day and announced that he wanted these sneakers that cost a hundred and fifty dollars. I told him no, and he pitched a fit. He was nine years old and ranting about sneakers that cost enough to feed a small country. That very night, Bob and I sat down and reevaluated our priorities."

Barbara dipped her sponge into the bucket and squeezed it out. "As timing would have it, that weekend missionaries came to our church and talked about their service aboard a Mercy Ship in the Caribbean. My husband and I looked at each other, and we knew what we wanted to do. We sold off most of our worldly possessions, and within nine months we were aboard this ship. It's been almost a year now."

She straightened. "We're the winners, you know. I've seen my kids become better for it. Without television every night, they read, they play with kids from many other countries, they've learned foreign languages. In short, they have an appreciation for life they never would have had back in Atlanta.

"As for Bob and me, we don't miss the rat race one bit. Some of our friends back home think we're crazy, but who cares? I've shopped in ports of call from Europe to Africa. Bob's helped build housing for some of the poorest countries in the world. We've traveled to the most interesting places. We love it. And you know what the Bible says." She didn't wait for Heather to answer. "It says that we must be doers of the Word, not only hearers." She looked down at the smeared mess on the desk. "And I can assure you, dear, I'm a real doer today."

Heather thought about her parents, about their medical practice and their lifestyle. They still had social consciences and continued to perform plastic surgery for battered women and abused children. She was proud of them for that. "You know," she said to Barbara, "I have some free time on Thursday afternoons. Why don't I come help you?"

"That's kind of you, and much appreciated. You're on." Barbara stacked some books. "I know this lifestyle isn't for everybody. And before making such changes a person must always count the cost."

"What do you mean?"

"Because we're doing this, there are things our family won't ever do. We've wondered how it will affect our kids when they become adults. Will they follow in our footsteps, or will they reject this kind of life?"

Heather shook her head. "I never went anywhere like this when I was growing up, but my parents talked all the time about their service in the Peace Corps. It seemed so much more interesting to me than what my friends were doing—worrying about who liked who, and stuff like that. My sister, she's different. I don't think she'd ever do anything like this. Not enough creature comforts."

Heather caught herself and reddened. "Not

that Amber isn't terrific. She'd do anything for a friend. But this sort of thing, taking care of people she doesn't know, well, it's just not her."

Barbara gave Heather a sharp look, then said, "We're not humanitarians, Heather. I've met many—United Nations workers, government relief workers. I know that the world has many good people who really care about serving their fellow man. But that's not why we do it. We do it because we want to see the Gospel spread all over the world."

She sounded like Ian. On a mission for a higher goal than simply healing people's bodies. Heather wondered again where she fit into the scheme of things.

"I'm sorry," Barbara said with a smile. "Here I am preaching to you and all you want to do is help me clean desks. I didn't mean to get carried away."

"No problem," Heather said lightly. But there was a problem. She knew she didn't feel the same kind of fire that the Hoovers and Ian felt. She was motivated, but not in the same way, not by the same force. Perhaps in Uganda she'd find such a fire. But for now, she was just going along to help—because children were dying and she was young and strong and committed to changing things for them. If God wanted something else from her, then perhaps, somewhere along the way, he'd let her know.

The *Anastasis* sailed northward toward Kenya, still too far from land to see either the island of Madagascar to the east or Mozambique on the African mainland to the west. The moon made a bright white trail on the calm waters of the Mozambique Channel as Heather relaxed in a deck chair, listening to Miguel singing in his beautiful tenor voice. Beside her, she heard Ian humming along, slightly off-key.

"Ian," she whispered, "why is there a ring around the moon?"

"Ice crystals," he answered. "Away up in the atmosphere."

"But it's not that cold."

"Remember, lass, you're below the equator now. It's winter."

"That's right. I forgot."

She felt his breath against her neck as he leaned toward her. "Did you see the sky this morning?"

"Sorry, it was dark when I headed for the mess hall."

"The sky was red."

"Meaning?"

"There is a saying from the sailors. 'Red sky at night, sailor's delight. Red sky in the morning, sailors take warning.' "

She turned to better see his face in the moonlight. He looked serious, all traces of teasing gone from his expression. "What are you telling me?"

"I read the bulletin that came over the navigator's telex. There's a storm coming. I fear we're in for quite a blow."

5

Pain woke Heather in the middle of the night. Tossed hard against the wall beside her bed, she seized hold of the bed rails to keep from being pitched to the floor. The cabin had turned cold and black.

"Ingrid!" she cried. "What's happening?"

"Storm," Ingrid said, after which Heather heard a thump and a yelp.

"Are you all right?"

"I hit my head."

Heather was disoriented—for a moment, she felt as if she'd been turned upside down. I—I think I'm going to be sick to my stomach."

"No! Try to sit up."

Terrified, Heather struggled upright. She swung her legs over the side of her bed. The floor met her, sending a jarring pain through her ankles and calves. She gasped and tried to remember emergency procedures.

"We should go topside," Ingrid said. "To the mess hall. It's worse here down below. My uncle owns a fishing boat and I've been in storms before. We'll have to climb and be quick about it."

Heather had no idea how they were going to make it. Their room was five levels below the top deck, in the interior of the ship. They'd have to weave their way down the narrow corridors and up many flights of ladder stairs. It was a long trek even when the ship was in perfectly calm waters. Heather swallowed her fear and groped toward Ingrid's bed. She took Ingrid's hand. "Come on."

The two of them started to the door, taking time only to tug on sweaters and sweatpants. The ship heaved and yawed, slamming Heather against the dresser. She cried out, and Ingrid groped for her arm. "Hold on to me."

In the corridor, emergency lighting glowed an eerie red beam. They merged into a group of their shipmates inching along the metal handrail. The smell of vomit made Heather gag.

A hand reached out to steady her. "Come along, follow us," Ian said.

Shaking, she eased in front of him, making sure that Ingrid got in front of her. "I'm scared, Ian."

"It's a good ship. She's come through storms before. We'll make it."

On the journey topside, they opened the doors and led others out into the serpentine of people, climbing ladders slowly, hanging on whenever the ship made an especially nasty heave or roll. It seemed like forever, but eventually they made it to the inside corridor leading to the giant ballroom that had been converted into the mess hall.

The air was chilling. Power was out, but a few flashlights and battery-powered lanterns broke the darkness inside the room. The wind howled, reminding Heather of a runaway freight train. She looked out the row of windows and cringed. The sea, white and boiling, sent plumes of spray crashing against the plexiglass. She froze, mesmerized. The ship was nine stories high and still the sea washed over the decks! She felt rooted to the floor, too terrified to move.

"Come this way. I've a spot for us." She felt Ian's arm around her waist.

He guided her and Ingrid around huddled groups of people to a place along an inside wall. Miguel was there, and so was Patrick. They covered the girls with blankets. Heather couldn't stop shaking. "Will we die?" she asked.

"No," Ian said, pulling her close to his side. "God will see us through. Have faith."

She struggled against the urge to vomit. "Wh-What if I get sick?"

"There's no shame in it. We have buckets; just ask for one."

She swallowed hard, forcing back her nausea. For certain, she didn't want to throw up all over Ian. "How long is this going to last?"

"The feeling in your stomach, or the storm?" he asked with gentle humor.

"It feels like I'm dying," she moaned into the blanket.

"No one's ever died of seasickness," he said.

"Are you sure?"

"Yes, lass."

Children cried and parents murmured to them in soothing voices from the surrounding dark. From somewhere, Heather heard a father quote from the Twenty-third Psalm. " 'Yea, though I walk through the valley of the shadow of death, I will fear no evil: for thou art with me. . . .' "

Heather gripped Ian's arm, and he tucked the blanket more tightly around them both, folding her closer, whispering in her ear, " 'Be strong and courageous. Do not be terrified; do not be discouraged, for the Lord your God will be with you wherever you go.' That's one of my favorite verses. I say it when I'm afraid. And it comforts me."

She couldn't imagine Ian ever being afraid of anything. "I've never been afraid this way until now. Not even when I was in a hurricane in Florida."

"Heather, the storm will pass. And the ship will weather it. We will get to Africa." He tipped her chin upward. "Talk to me. Tell me what inspired you to choose Africa from all the places in the world."

"I—I used to watch *National Geographic* specials on TV. I wanted to come for a visit, see all the wild animals. Then a few years ago, I read a book." Heather's voice trembled as she struggled to shift her thoughts away from her fear and the sick sensation in her stomach. "It was about Dr. Livingstone and his hunt for the source of the Nile."

"A Scotsman," Ian said with genuine pride. "He inspired a whole generation to come."

She nodded. "He came as a doctor and missionary. He fell in love with Africa and spent his whole life mapping it out. He never gave up, even when people in England ridiculed him. His story made me want to come even more."

"Many missionaries came to Africa in those days. It was a time of a great religious revival. Did you know that when those missionaries left Britain they packed all their worldly belongings in boxes six feet long, three feet wide, and two feet deep? The size of a coffin. That way, when they died—and most died within six months of coming—they could be shipped home for burial."

A chill went through her. "No. I didn't know that."

"Disease got them, mostly."

"How about you? How did you end up wanting to help in Africa?"

"My great-grandfather was a physician and a minister. And, like Livingstone, he chose Africa for his life's work. I read his journals and they made me want to go there too. That's why I keep a journal. It is not nearly so filled with hardships as his, but maybe one day it will inspire another generation of McCollums to do the same."

"Will you write about tonight?"

"Yes. And also of the bonny lass who shared it with me."

Ian could lift her spirits so easily. She cleared her throat. "What happened to your great-grandfather?"

"He served fifteen years in Africa as a doctor. He took a wife, the daughter of a British captain serving in Egypt. They had three children, and when they came of an age to be schooled, he sent his family home."

"Did he see them again?"

"That he did. He went home in 1916, caught influenza, and died in his wife's arms."

"He died of the flu?" She found it hard to believe.

"That flu epidemic killed over a million people. Remember, there were no antibiotics in those days."

She felt sorry for a family she'd never known, while her heart brimmed with emotion for Ian. He was six years older than she but a hundred years wiser. His heart was full of tenderness and compassion, and already she envied whoever would become his wife. "Did your father ever want to be a doctor?"

"No. But he is a minister. He's the vicar in a country parish. It's a small village and it's where I grew up. In the autumn, the heather stretches across the moor as far as your eye can see. And before the heather colors the moor, the lavender grows. Its scent hangs in the breeze like the breath of angels."

Her mental picture of rolling hills speckled with wildflowers under blue sky made the fierceness of the storm fade momentarily. "I'd like to see Scotland someday."

"And I'd like to see America."

Suddenly the ship dropped like a stone. Adults cried out and children shrieked. Heather stifled a scream and clung more tightly to Ian.

Hastily Miguel picked up his guitar and began playing "Kumbayah." Shaky voices joined in one by one, singing softly, " 'Someone's crying, Lord, Kumbayah. . . .' " And when the song was finished, Miguel played "How Great Thou Art," and they sang that. Hymn after hymn followed, voice after voice sang words of comfort while the storm raged outside.

It seemed like an eternity to her before the heaving of the ship lessened, before the waves no longer crashed against the windows and the howling wind died down. Slowly, as the storm grew less intense, exhaustion made Heather's eyelids droop. In the warmth of Ian's arms, she drifted in and out of sleep. She dreamed she wore a long, dark dress, high-necked and long-sleeved, and a bonnet of midnight blue. She saw Ian leaning against a wall, wearing an old-fashioned suit. He held a medical bag in one hand, a Bible in the other. The wall grew transparent, and she saw Amber sitting by the ship's pool in a bikini. Heather turned and saw her parents anxiously peering through the windows of the mess hall. Fearful they'd be washed overboard, she cried, "Watch out!" and woke with a start.

The cold gray light of morning filtered through the salt-smeared windows while the ship rolled from side to side like a cradle rocked by some giant's hand. All around her people were stretched out, covered with clothing and blankets, sleeping. Her first thought was, *I'm alive!*

The horrible queasiness was gone, and she realized that soon all these people would wake and need to eat. But eating was the last thing she felt like doing! She turned and saw that Ian was no longer beside her. As quietly as possible, she stood, tucking her blanket around the sleeping Ingrid, then threaded her way to the door. On deck, she was hit by a stiff, damp breeze and the briny smell of wild ocean. The world looked gray, heavy with thick fog. The deck was wet and slippery, strewn with seaweed and a few broken planks. Long strings of sea algae dangled from the railings like thick bands of rope. Carefully she edged closer to the rail to look over the side. The sea was listless now, as if tired from being driven by the wind.

"Not too close, lass," she heard Ian say through the mist. "Couldn't have you falling in, now. We'd never find you in this soup."

He emerged from the fog like a ghost.

"I'm not about to fall overboard," she told him. "I worked too hard last night to keep from dying of fright."

"You should be inside."

"I woke up and missed you," she confessed. "Where'd you go?"

"Up to the bridge. Most of the crew's been up all night, making sure we didn't wash overboard. We lost some deck chairs, and a mooring on one of the lifeboats broke loose, but they were able to secure it again. The captain says that according to the radar, the storm's well west of us now. All in all, we weathered it well."

Heather sagged with gratitude. "I'd hate to go through that ever again."

He hooked his arm around her shoulders. "Yes, thank God for bringing us through."

"I—I was so scared, Ian. Weren't you?"

"Yes. But if I had died, then this morning I would have waked in a far better place for having crossed over."

"Well, I'm not ready to 'cross over,'" she told him. "I've still got a lot of living to do."

He laughed as if she'd just told him a funny joke. "Lass, we don't choose when we get to cross over. God does. And for those who believe, it doesn't matter which side of time we live on. This side, we do God's work and spread his word to others, waiting for when he calls us home to heaven, where we will spend eternity with him. We lose our life in order to gain it."

Heather longed to share Ian's faith and self-assurance, but the storm had left her bruised and badly shaken. Until the previous night, it hadn't occurred to her that she could actually die—that all her plans and dreams, her very future, could have been swept away by the wind from an angry sea.

6

Hi, Sis—

I survived a storm at sea! I'm not kidding, it was the scariest thing I've ever lived through—waves as high as downtown buildings. Believe me, it's sure changed my take on the ocean! Back home, the beach is a cool place to spend the day, and waves are swoopy heaps of water to ride our rafts on. But out here, with nothing but a few tons of metal between me and the bottom of the sea, I saw the ocean in a whole new light. It's strong and violent. And nothing can tame it. It makes a person feel helpless and insignificant. And it's made me wonder why people ever wandered off dry land in the first place.

It also makes me glad that I'm flying home straight from Uganda and not sailing again on the ship. One thing's for sure, I DON'T want to become fish bait!

BTW, the storm also set us back a few days. Now we're not due to reach Kenya until the first of the week, so there's been a little change in plans. Evidently, planes don't fly in and out of Nairobi each and every day. We have to wait until Thursday to fly into the airport in Uganda. That means me and the rest of Dr. Henry's team will help for a few days at a special World Health Organization project about half a day's drive from Nairobi. We'll be taken in buses to the compound, where Dr. Henry's told me that hundreds of people are already gathering for medical help. He says some of these people have walked for days, even weeks to be there when the doctors from the Great White Ship come to treat them. The worst cases will be bused back to the ship.

Ian tells me that it can get pretty crazy, and that I should be prepared to see some awful sights, diseases, open sores, malnourished kids. I've told him that I can take it, that I'm familiar with gross medical things. Honestly, he worries about me and it isn't necessary. I can do this, Amber. I can make a difference!

Heather signed off after reminding Amber that this would be her last chance to e-mail until she reached Uganda. She wished it weren't so, because she didn't like feeling totally cut off from her family and everything familiar. Still, she was glad to finally be getting to do the work that she'd come so far to do.

The storm had left a mess that had to be cleaned away before the boat docked. The ORs needed special attention, and it seemed to Heather as if she would never get out of the galley. She'd spent long hours packing the food and other supplies her group would need for the days they were to stay at the World Health Organization compound. She entered the galley, asking, "What's cooking?"

"Rice," Ingrid answered. A huge pot simmered on the stove.

Heather made a face. She was sick of rice and longed for a helping of french fries. "Yummy," she said without enthusiasm.

Ingrid laughed. "There's dried herring, too."

"Double yummy."

"I'd kill for a peanut butter and jelly sandwich," a boy named Boyce said. He was from Alabama, and his heavily accented Southernisms usually sent Ingrid into fits of giggles. As for Boyce, he'd taken one look at the stately Scandinavian girl and proclaimed her "cuter than a sackful of puppies."

"I stashed a couple of jars in my backpack," Heather said.

"I stashed some myself," Boyce admitted. "But I ate it during the storm."

"You're kidding."

"I was nervous. Eating it made me think of home."

"Thinking of food turned me green," Heather said.

Boyce leaned on his elbows across the counter. "So, what do you want for one of your jars? How about an Alabama football sweatshirt?"

"Dream on. I'm not parting with my peanut butter."

Boyce dropped to his knees and folded his hands in supplication. "Please. Pretty please with sugar on it. I'll be your slave for a day."

She poked him playfully. "Not for anything."

He begged all the harder, making them laugh. Heather ignored him but later that day did send him a small container with a scoop of peanut butter inside. When she told Ian about it, he said, "Yes, it's hard to come by some of these Uganda things."

"Are there any grocery stores?" she asked. They were standing on deck, watching the sun set over the water. The evening sky was streaked with pastel colors, and a few puffy clouds had turned bright pink, as if they were blushing.

"There are some small stores, but without refrigeration there's little that can be kept except what can be housed on the shelves in boxes and in cans."

"Where do the people get their food? Their fresh food, I mean?"

"They grow it. It's said that if you poke a stick in the ground, it'll sprout; the soil's that rich. And the wealthier people, they own cows and chickens. A man who has many cows is very rich indeed."

"I have no cows. Does that mean I'm poor in their eyes?"

He laughed. "You are an American. They believe all Americans are rich. But without a cow, what man will ever marry you?" His eyes danced mischievously. "A dowry of cows can get you a husband, you know."

"Is that the way a girl gets engaged? Her family arranges it with cows?"

"Sometimes. But men and women fall in love and get married without its being pre-arranged. Television has shown them the way we do things in the West, and so they want to follow in our ways. Yet tribal customs still remain. A man's tribe is his pride."

"His tribe?"

"In Africa, it matters which kingdom or tribe a person belongs to. It is a source of much fighting in this country. One tribe hates another. They go to war and many die. It's one of the things the church is trying to change.

To help men see each other as brothers in God's eyes.

"In Kampala, on Kasubi Hill, is the palace tomb of the kings of the Buganda Kingdom, still maintained and guarded by the Buganda clansmen. Their palaces are made of reeds and thatch, not like the palaces of the kings of Europe. You must remove your shoes, though, for it is sacred ground."

The ancient African world seemed mysterious and exotic, and it captured Heather's imagination. "Will you take me there? I'd love to see it," she said.

He sighed. "If there's time. There will be much to do, and we haven't much time."

"We have plenty of time," she chided. "Four whole months."

He smiled and brushed a wisp of hair away from her face. "It will pass in the twinkling of an eye. But we will be together, and that will make it happier for me."

"I like being with you, too," she said, feeling warm all over. "Even if we are from different tribes and I have no cows."

His laugh sounded rich and full. He hugged her shoulders. "Lass, you're a wonder. A blessing from the Lord. I will never forget you."

And then and there, she decided she would never let him.

Two days later, she saw her first glimpse of the Kenyan coast. "Look!" she cried, pointing to the west. "There it is!"

Ingrid and Boyce, who were with her swabbing down a deck, dropped their mops, and all three of them hurried to the railing. "That's it, all right," Boyce whooped. "We have arrived!"

"Not quite," Ingrid said in her practical way. "Two more days, I'd say."

Boyce hooked his arms through the girls' and together they stared out to the land rising on the edge of the sea. "My feet are begging to hit solid land."

"Mine, too," Heather said. Her lifelong dream of going off to other lands was coming true. She was more than five thousand miles from the sun-kissed shores of Miami, far from America and her way of life. All the plans, all the effort, all the work was about to pay off for her. And as a bonus she had never expected, she'd met Ian. Life didn't get any better than this!

7

Dust. In her hair, in her mouth, in her nose, in her very pores. Heather was choking on dust. She'd been in Kenya two days but had barely had time to do anything more than help unload supplies and food from the ship and reload it all into two decrepit buses, two vans, and a Jeep. On the third day, the convoy pulled away from the dock, away from the Great White Ship and through the city of Nairobi toward their destination, a World Health Organization facility a hundred kilometers to the north—into the grasslands, and into clouds of clinging red dust.

They left paved roads behind in the city and struck out on rutted dirt roads that jarred her teeth and kept her from taking a much-needed nap. The grasslands were flat and yellow with wild grass, broken only by an occasional gnarled tree. Far in the distance, she saw a range of mountains, but the mountains never seemed to get any closer, no matter how far the group traveled.

"How're you doing?" Ian asked, squeezing into the bus seat beside her.

"I think this is worse than the storm," she said, half shouting over the noise of the engine and the voices of the others. "Are my teeth loose?" She bared them, making him laugh.

"They look fine."

"Hey, I thought it was winter here. How come I'm sweating?"

"It's cooler at night. It's really quite pleasant, you know. In the summer it's over a hundred degrees."

"No complaints," she said, throwing up her hands. "I'm here, and I can't wait to get started."

He gave her an amused look. "You can't be faulted for lack of enthusiasm, lass. But get some rest if you can. We'll be there in a few hours, and then there'll be no time for resting. No time for anything except seeing the sick."

To oblige him, and because she was exhausted, Heather closed her eyes. The bus hit a pothole and tossed her hard into Ian's shoulder. She yelped. He caught her. Silently they stared into each other's faces. No need to apologize. No need to say anything. He steadied her, then returned to the back of the bus.

The WHO compound rose out of the flat land like an old-time fort. Several portable buildings were clustered behind a tall wire fence that stretched around a large open area, with a gate made of wire and timber. Guards dressed in military uniforms were positioned at the gate. Heather didn't need to ask why guards were needed. One look at the mass of humanity camped around the gates explained everything.

As they drove up, people surged forward, surrounding the bus and forcing it to slow to a crawl. Heather stared out at an ocean of dark faces. Men crowded against the bus. Women held up babies and small children, as if imploring the workers to take them through the windows.

"What do you think?" Boyce asked, leaning across Heather to peer out the window. "Think they're anxious to see us?"

"I—I've never seen anything like it," Heather answered, immediately consumed with pity for the children.

"Then you've never been to a 'Bama game," Boyce joked, but Heather could see by the expression on his face that he was taken aback too. "Looks like half the country's showed up."

"How will we ever help all of them?" The bus inched forward. Packed along the fence were makeshift shelters of cardboard and other tattered material. Small cooking fires dotted the ground, and the smell of charcoal hung in the hot, sticky air.

"We've got four days to find out," Boyce said. "Then it's off to Nairobi airport and on to Uganda."

Ian's words came back to her. How would they ever take care of so many people in such a short time?

By now, the convoy was through the gates and parked inside the compound, where order prevailed. Heather stood, slapped the dust off her arms, and filed off the bus with her group. Dr. Henry led them inside a small building adjoining a larger one. There they were greeted by a Dr. Greeley from England. He shook hands with Dr. Henry, then turned to the new arrivals.

"Welcome," he announced in a booming, rapid-fire voice. "As you can see, we've got our hands full. A few of the peacekeeping soldiers will help offload supplies, and nurses will direct their disposal. The OR schedule is already full for the day, but we will need some of you to help organize tomorrow's group. It's important that each patient understand that they can't eat or drink eight hours prior to their surgeries. Interpreters are available.

"The mess hall is the building on your right. We have a small refrigerator because we have our own generators. We store vaccines and medications in it, so it's off limits for anything else. There are bottled and boiled water available too. Those of you on construction, follow Private Luswa. We need more latrines dug."

Heather stood wide-eyed. She had thought she'd have more time to get instruction, more time to become acclimated to the hurly-burly, circuslike atmosphere.

"This way," Ingrid said, taking hold of Heather's arm. "We'd better get our tents up, because once it's time to go to bed, you're going to want to pass out. We'll come back for our assignments."

Heather followed her friend to the housing area. One-person canvas tents sat in orderly rows, looking to Heather like a Boy Scout farm. Quickly she found her gear in the pile already stacked by the soldiers. At boot camp, she'd learned how to erect a one-person tent and bed down in it. Now, in the wilds of Kenya, the tent would be her home.

Beyond the tent city, she saw rows of portable toilets, where the construction crew was already digging a long, narrow pit to accommodate the new arrivals. Attached to the outside of another building were outdoor showers with plastic walls just high enough to conceal a person's torso. A large tank hung over the unit, with open-ended pipes aimed downward.

"The tank collects rainwater," Ingrid said. "The sun heats it all day, so it is not too cold to bathe in."

Heather unrolled her tent and set to work adjusting the center pole and hammering the stakes into the hard ground. Inside the tent, she rolled out her sleeping bag and squeezed her two duffel bags to one side. She had stuffed everything she could into the bags, making them almost too heavy to lift. Her laptop was wedged safely inside, but it was useless without a place to plug it in. She itched to read her e-mail, longing to hear news of home and to tell Amber everything that had happened since the storm.

As soon as their things were stashed, Heather and Ingrid returned to the main building,

where the clinic was operating at full capacity.
A nurse directed Heather to a long line of
women and children whom another nurse,
Josie, was interviewing.

"Hello, luv," Josie said in a British accent.
"This is the screening area. I'll need you to take
a history, then send them over there"—she
pointed—"where they'll be examined by a
physician. These are the less serious cases—
scabies, bronchitis, diarrhea . . ." she rattled off
a list of ailments.

"We give out antibiotics and inoculations
and make very sure the mothers understand
how the medications are to be given. Sometimes they give it all at once instead of over the
days prescribed, which, of course, brings on a
new set of problems."

Heather nodded, feeling nervous. She wanted
to do a good job, but it looked overwhelming.
The line stretched outside the door, seemingly
endless, while mothers juggled sick and crying
children with resignation. She couldn't even
guess at the children's ages, but many were just
tiny babies. She set about taking names and filling in forms, surprised at the number who bore
familiar names, such as Harriet, Joseph, Ruth,
and Michael. She could not even begin to spell
their African names, but many of them helped

her, for most were literate. They seemed like gentle people, stoic about the long wait, even jovial when talking among themselves.

She was also surprised at how young they were. Girls of fifteen and sixteen were mothers, and women who told her they were in their thirties looked worn out, as if their lives had been too heavy for them. She thought about her parents' patients, who came in for expensive cosmetic procedures to keep them looking young. Here, getting fed was the focus of everyday life.

Heather had no idea how long she stood taking down information, but when she finally took a water break, she noticed shadows encroaching across the floor. Evening was near, and the end of the line of people could be seen, cut off at the gate, hours earlier, by the soldiers.

"That's it for the day," Josie said, still cheerful, when the last woman and child stepped up. "You look exhausted, child. Do sit down before you fall over."

"Thank you." Gratefully Heather eased onto a wooden bench. Her legs ached from standing, and her fingers were cramped from writing. "Is that it for today?"

"For today," Josie said. "It will begin anew tomorrow."

"How'd we do?"

"The doctor saw one hundred and fifteen patients." Josie smiled broadly. "And most were treatable."

Startled, Heather asked, "Most? Which ones weren't?" She racked her memory, trying to conjure up the faces of those who had passed in front of her. There had been so many.

"Two babies were placed in our hospital ward. Dysentery has left them barely alive."

How could that be? Heather had seen each child with her own eyes. How could she have not been sensitive to the few who were so critically ill they had to be hospitalized? "Will they be all right?"

"Hard to say, luv. You know, the baby gets sick in the village, the mother walks for days to get here, they wait outside for a turn . . . by then the child is pretty far gone. We put them on IVs to replace the fluid, but it's often too late."

"Gosh, I'm sorry. Poor little babies."

Josie patted her hand. "Brace up, dearie. We can't save them all."

Josie came across as almost flippant, and Heather hoped she herself would never grow indifferent to the suffering.

"Run along, now," Josie said. "You should be

having your dinner, then to bed. Lots more to do on the morrow."

Outside, night was falling and the temperature had dipped. Heather glanced toward the mess hall, lit by electricity, fueled by gas generators. The smell of charcoal fires from the encampment filled the air, and stars were winking on. That night she would fulfill a childhood dream—she would sleep beneath the skies of Africa.

From somewhere in the outer darkness, a baby cried. Heather shivered, then hurried toward the lighted building, toward a warm meal, toward the company of friends.

8

Heather woke in the middle of the night, and in spite of her bone-deep exhaustion, she couldn't go back to sleep. Gone were the familiar drone of the ship's engines and the squeak of metal plates and bolts. In their place, she heard the faraway howls and yips of night-hunting wild animals, which sent shivers up her spine. And she heard the forlorn crying of babies from the camp outside. She kept thinking about them, the babies and children too little and too sick to fend for themselves.

She thought about their sweet, round, dark faces when they'd come for treatment. Some had clung to their mothers. Others had simply stared out with blank expressions, seemingly resigned to whatever was going to happen. She realized that her house in Miami would seem palatial to most people. Her allowance alone could probably feed a family for weeks. Guilt stole over her. Guilt because she had so much, while these people had so little. But that was why she'd come, she reminded herself. To make a difference in other's lives. After all, wasn't she supposed to be God's hands on Earth?

She lifted the flap of her tent and stared out into the compound. The silhouettes of other tents hunkered down in the darkness. Overhead, a million stars glowed. The sight took her breath and lifted her spirits. Surely God was in his heaven and knew the suffering of the people. How could he turn an indifferent ear to them?

She remembered that she had packed hard candies in her bags. Tomorrow she would stuff handfuls in her pockets and give a piece to every child who passed through the clinic doors. She vowed to work twice as hard, twice as long. After all, she would be returning to Nairobi with her group in a few days. She'd have time to rest on the trip to Nairobi and on the plane ride to Uganda. Now it was time for work.

Out of the darkness, she heard the plaintive notes of Miguel's guitar. She followed the sound. Behind one of the buildings, she found Miguel, Boyce, and Ian sitting on the ground together. "Is this a private party?" she asked.

"We're praying," Ian explained. "Come join us."

She sat cross-legged on the ground beside him. "I didn't mean to interrupt."

"No problem," Boyce said. "Can't have enough prayers, can we?"

"Is there something you want to ask God for?" Ian wanted to know.

"Success," she said. "I guess that's what we all want, isn't it? I want the people who come here to get well."

Ian asked God to be merciful to those who were sick, and the rich sound of his voice comforted Heather. She'd never heard anybody pray with such devotion.

After the group broke up, Ian walked her back to the tent area. "That's me," she said, pointing. "Fifth row, fourth tent."

"I should have known. It's the prettiest tent of the lot."

She giggled. "It's dark and they all look alike."

"No, yours is different. Just because it's yours."

She felt a warmth spread through her. She looked at him, and by the light from the sliver of moon in the sky, she saw that he was watching her intently. For a moment she thought he might kiss her, and her heart pounded in anticipation. But he squeezed her hand and stepped away. "You should be in bed. Tomorrow will come quickly."

Disappointed, she nodded. "Thanks for letting me join you tonight. It was good to have all of us together again."

"You can join us anytime. We will meet to pray every night when things quiet down." He turned, then paused. "Are you making a difference, Heather? I know how much you wanted that for yourself."

"Not yet. But I've only just begun."

He smiled. "Yes. You've only just begun."

She watched him walk away, wondering what was going on in his mind. Wondering if he ever thought about her as anything other than just some idealistic high-school girl. Wondering if she could ever find a place in his heart.

By midday, she had almost lost her resolve of the night before to work twice as hard. Heat seeped like steam from a hot faucet through the metal walls of the hut used for a treatment room. Heather mopped her forehead and tried to tune out the sounds of people in pain. Today she was doing more than taking histories. She was assisting two nurses as they dressed a young woman's wounds. The woman had fallen off a truck, had gotten her foot caught, and had been dragged over hardened, rutted ground. Her ankle was badly sprained, and all the skin had been scraped off her back. Heather's stomach had lurched when she saw the pulverized flesh, but she'd fought off the nausea and quickly gathered the items the nurses needed.

"Sterile water," one nurse ordered.

"We're out," Heather answered.

"Go to the supply room and get two bags. And do hurry."

Grateful to get away from the pain-racked woman, Heather jogged to the next building, where supplies were kept in a locked room. Martha, an older woman who'd been with Heather on the ship, was responsible for the key. Heather told her what she needed, and Martha entered the room, emerging minutes later with two clear, plump fluid-filled bags. "Supplies are dwindling."

"Already?"

"They go fast when there are so many to use them."

Heather was dismayed. The ship had spent weeks taking on donated supplies in London. "When I get home, I'm going to do a fund-raiser for the ship," she announced firmly. "My parents' friends have wads of money. They can donate some of it to help buy medical supplies. I'll make sure they do."

Martha grinned. "That's the spirit. I can't imagine any of them refusing you."

"They better not." Heather knew she could persuade these wealthy people to give money to the cause. She'd work on a community fund-raiser too. Maybe she could get coverage in the newspaper and on TV.

Excited by her idea, she rushed back to the treatment room. But when she arrived, the atmosphere had grown chaotic. A child, badly burned from a fall into an open cooking fire, had been brought in. "Best to take a break," one of the nurses told Heather, taking the water from her as she stepped inside the door.

The child was screaming, and two other nurses were busy helping one of the doctors hold him down. His anxious mother hovered nearby.

Heather stepped back without argument. The child's cries were almost unbearable. She went to the mess hall, where she grabbed a bottle of drinking water. From there, she retreated to the back of the compound, near the tents. Shaking, she leaned against a scrub tree and forced herself to breathe deeply. The doctor would help the child, she told herself. The child would be all right. She slid to the ground, bracing her spine against the tree.

Back home, a child with such burns would go into a special burn unit. Out here, there was no such thing. If he was in bad enough shape, they might take him into Nairobi to be hospitalized, but she could hardly imagine such a trip for a child already in agony from bad burns. She wished there were something she could do to help.

Someone shouted, *"Rafiki, rafiki!"*

Heather looked up to see a group of women and children gathered outside the fence not too far from where she was sitting. She acknowledged them with a wave.

"Rafiki," they called out again. *"Njoo!"* They beckoned to her.

Did they want her to come over to the fence? Heather glanced around, but there was no one else. "Me?" she asked.

"Njoo. Tafadhali."

She recognized the Swahili word for "please." Dr. Henry had taught the word to her group. Slowly she stood, and with her pulse racing, she edged to the wire fence. The women all talked at once. "I—I can't understand you," she said. "English?"

The women kept talking in Swahili.

"I—I'll go get someone—" Heather turned, but the group let out such cries that she turned back.

She heard a wail from the back of the group and saw an object wrapped in a piece of dirty cloth being lifted. It was passed quickly overhead, from woman to woman. Mesmerized, Heather watched, and as the bundle came steadily toward her, she caught a glimpse of a face. Suddenly she realized that the object was a baby, and that the women meant to pass it to her over the top of the fence. Except that the fence was eight feet high.

"No! No!" she cried, stepping away. "I'll get some help."

But the crowd ignored her. The baby, bundled in rags, continued to be passed. At the barrier, the last woman to take the baby hoisted it over the top. Heather ran back to the fence, frantically begging her not to drop the baby over. But there was no stopping the woman's momentum. Heather positioned herself to catch the baby.

Please, God, don't let me drop it, she pleaded silently.

Time passed in slow motion. The bundled baby balanced on the woman's fingertips, teetered, then tipped. Heather stood on tiptoe, reached up, and felt the infant slide into her outstretched hands. "Got it!" she cried. She eased it down, clutching it to her breast.

Her heart hammered and her arms and legs trembled, but she felt jubilant. The baby was safe in her arms. She felt it wriggle and heard it let out a weak cry.

She flashed a relieved smile at the women, but they had stepped back and were dispersing. "Wait!" Heather called. "Don't go! I need the mother. Who's the mother?" She racked her brain for the Swahili word for "mother" but couldn't remember it.

The women continued to melt away. Heather watched until only one very young woman was left standing far back from the fence. She stood tall and wore an expression of hopelessness. Then she, too, began to walk away.

"Wait!" Heather shouted. She watched as the woman picked up her pace and headed quickly away from the camp, off into the tall grass. Heather glanced down at the baby in her arms and pulled aside the tattered material covering the tiny face. The baby lay quite still. Its eyes were wide open, and its skin was the color of ash from a burned-out fire.

A cry rose in Heather's throat, strangled, and died on her lips.

The baby was dead.

9

In Heather's eighteen years of living, nothing had prepared her to look into the face of death. Not her education, not her upbringing, not her experiences, not any of her training for the Mercy Ship program. Nothing.

Death was final. Death was irrevocable. Life was flutterings and tremblings. It was warm breath and soft sighs. It was flesh that felt warm and didn't look waxy. In her arms, the dead baby felt almost weightless, as if its bones were hollow, like a bird's bones. Just minutes before, its lungs had filled with air and it had looked up into her face. Now those same eyes stared fixedly, their pupils dilated. They would never see again.

Heather began to shake, and despite the intensity of the noonday sun, she felt icy cold.

She didn't know what to do. She couldn't abandon the baby. She couldn't dig a hole, put the baby in it, and cover it over as she and Amber had done for their goldfish when they'd been kids. She couldn't go too far away, either. What if the mother returned? What if she wanted her child back?

Somehow Heather made it to the tree. She slid down the trunk and sat on the hard ground, carefully balancing the dead infant on her lap. And slowly she unwrapped the soiled cloth. The baby, a girl, lay naked within. Her belly looked distended, and her ribs bulged through her thin, dark skin. Heather counted each rib, running her finger along the ridges that no longer heaved with breath.

The tiny girl's forehead was wide and smooth as glass, and she had only the barest beginning of black fuzz covering her head. Her arms and legs were no bigger around than sticks—skin wrapped around hollow bones, Heather thought. The baby's face looked skeletal, like an old person's. She had no fat, round cheeks like those of other babies Heather had seen.

As she held the small body, Heather felt the infant's limbs growing rigid—rigor mortis was setting in. A fly buzzed past Heather's hand

and settled on the baby's cheek. "No!" Heather cried. "No. No. No." She quickly flipped the cloth over the little body and sent the fly whizzing away. Vermin would not take this child. No way. She'd see to that. Heather felt her shoulders heave. Her vision blurred as tears filled her eyes, and she wept as if her heart were breaking.

Heather didn't know how long she sat crying. She had no sense of time passing. But it must have passed, because the shadow of the tree grew longer over her, and her back and legs grew numb from not moving. She sensed someone coming up to her and crouching down. She didn't look, couldn't bear to look, because life had no rapport with death. And inside, Heather felt as dead as the child in her lap.

"Are you all right, lass?"

Ian. She didn't look at him, but she shook her head.

"People are asking for you. No one's seen you for hours. They're worried."

She couldn't find her voice.

"What have you there in your lap? Will you show me?"

She wanted to, but her fingers wouldn't move.

"Let me have a look-see." His fingers moved deftly to the edge of the cloth and gently pulled it aside.

She heard his breath catch. He was looking at the baby, at death, just as she had. Now he knew. He had seen. Finally she could answer him. "I don't know who she is. I never heard her name." Her voice sounded thick and foreign to her own ears.

"Can you tell me how you came by her?"

"They gave her to me. The women at the fence. They passed her over the top this noontime, and I caught her."

"And you've been sitting here alone with her all this time?"

"I couldn't let the flies land on her," Heather said matter-of-factly. "You understand, don't you?"

"We should be taking her to Dr. Henry. She should have a Christian burial."

"And flowers. She should have flowers, too."

"Come, Heather." Ian slid his arm around her waist and urged her to stand.

Her legs wouldn't work at first. He massaged her calves until a prickly sensation began to radiate through them. Then, with Heather pressed against his side and his hand cupping hers beneath the bundled baby, they walked slowly to the main building, while the long shadows of afternoon made dark, joyless smudges on the parched African earth.

"Whooping cough and dysentery would be my guess," Dr. Henry told Heather after he had examined the infant. "She didn't have much of a chance. Both are preventable, but her case was too far advanced. It's doubtful we could have saved her."

If his words were supposed to comfort Heather, they didn't. "Her mother left her. She left her with me, a stranger."

"She probably knew she was dying," the doctor said kindly. "You were her last hope."

"How could she do that? Just hand her over and walk away?"

"It was an act of desperation."

It was dark now, and the clinic had closed down for the night. The baby had been cleaned up and wrapped in plain white cloth, a shroud for burial. Ian had not left Heather's side since he'd found her.

Dr. Henry put his hand on Heather's shoulder. "Don't judge her harshly, Heather. People see death differently in other cultures. In America when a mother loses a child, we prescribe medications, she sees a grief counselor, maybe even a psychiatrist. There's a complete social service system to help her over her loss. But over here, these mothers can't afford to fall apart. They must get on with life quickly. Too many things are depending on them—food, care of other children, survival.

"Does that mean they don't grieve? Of course not. But in a country where the infant mortality rate is almost fifty percent, mothers have a different perspective on a baby's death. Some see it almost as a form of rescue from a harsh life."

"She shouldn't have left her," Heather murmured. "She shouldn't have."

Dr. Henry sighed. "You can't change what's happened. Please tell me, will you be able to continue with the work you came here to do? Because if you can't . . ."

Could she? Her lip trembled, but she said, "I can."

"Get some rest, then," Dr. Henry said. "Tomorrow the fight begins all over again. And, Heather, stay away from the fence. We have a system for patients to get into the facility for a reason."

Chastised, she nodded. She'd brought this on herself. "Will we have a funeral for her?"

"In the morning," Dr. Henry said. "Early."

Outside, Ian took her hand. "You haven't eaten all day. Let's get you some food."

"I can't eat."

"You can't let yourself get sick over this. It won't help."

"I'll be all right tomorrow," Heather said, without meaning it.

In the distance, she saw the glow of camp-fires lit by all the people still waiting to be treated. How long had some of them been there? Days? Weeks? How many had babies who wouldn't make it through the night?

"The first time I saw a person die, it affected me too, lass. Death is never an easy thing to accept. Doctors are supposed to chase death away. So we always feel defeated when it wins a round."

"I should have done something for her," Heather said quietly. "All afternoon, while I sat there with her, I kept thinking, *Why didn't I go get help sooner? Why didn't I grab the baby and run for help?* Maybe the doctors could have given her CPR. Maybe they could have gotten her breathing again. If I'd acted faster, maybe we could have saved her."

"You heard Dr. Henry say she was too far gone."

"He was trying to make me feel better."

"Heather, listen to me, you cannot let this defeat you."

"You tried to warn me, didn't you?"

"Warn you about what?"

"On the ship, every time we talked about my 'enthusiasm,' you tried to tell me that dreams and reality are two different things. You tried to tell me that we can't save everybody. I feel stupid. And I'm sorry I didn't listen to you." She thought back to the girl she'd been just a short time ago, when she'd first climbed aboard the Mercy Ship. Naive. Starry-eyed. Confident. So sure that she could make a positive contribution to the world. And today she had been powerless to get one tiny baby to medical help. So much for saving the world.

"I don't think you're stupid. And I think your dreams are good dreams. You cannot see yourself as a failure. We cannot come over here and heal every person who's ill. Why, we can't do that even in our own countries. We can only help one person at a time. And then another. And another. You *will* make a difference, Heather Barlow. Just maybe not in the way you once thought."

Ian could not take away the shame she felt, but his words had reached inside her and soothed the gnawing pain of self-doubt. She was grateful. "Thank you for being so nice to me."

He smiled tenderly. "It's not a hard thing to do, lass. We have months ahead of us on this trip. We have Uganda next and work there waiting for us. You cannot give up now."

Wrapping her arms around herself, Heather drew in a long shuddering breath. "I'm not giving up, Ian."

"That's the spirit."

No, she wasn't giving up. But she wasn't the same person she'd been when she'd first climbed aboard the ship. Or even the same one who had lain looking up at the stars the night before, believing that she was God's hands on Earth. Yesterday she had faced a long line of people whom she could help and had felt good about herself. Today she'd held a baby she could never help again. It had been life-changing.

"Will you come to the funeral with me?" she asked.

"Yes. I'll be there. And think on this, Heather. Perhaps at this very moment, that little one is in the arms of angels, near the throne of God. Could there be a better place for her to be?"

"No, I guess not."

"Then let her go in peace."

Before dawn the next morning, Heather gathered with her friends to pray and to watch Dr. Henry put the shroud-wrapped infant into the ground. "We are all saddened by the loss of this little one," Dr. Henry said to them. "We cannot understand why the Father has taken her home to be with him so soon. But take her he has. And all we can do is trust in his wisdom, which is far above ours. Let me read from Isaiah forty-one, verse ten:

'So do not fear, for I am with you;
do not be dismayed, for I am your God.
I will strengthen you and help you,
I will uphold you with my righteous right
hand.' "

Heather felt Ian's hand slip into hers.

Dr. Henry continued. "This promise from God was given thousands of years ago, as a comfort to his people. And this next promise was given several thousand years later. I read now from Revelation twenty-one, verses three and four.

'Now the dwelling of God is with men, and he will live with them. They will be his people, and God himself will be with them and be their God. He will wipe every tear from their eyes. There will be no more death or mourning or crying or pain, for the old order of things has passed away.' "

Dr. Henry closed his Bible. "I read these two passages because I want you to understand that God is faithful from age to age, and that his Word can be trusted. And now, *we* entrust the soul of this little one to the arms of a loving, faithful God. In the name of the Father, the Son, and the Holy Ghost."

In the silence that followed, Heather struggled against the lump clogging her throat. It was over. The baby was gone. Now dirt would fill the grave, and once it was trampled down, no one would know the hole's secret. For they had buried the baby deep to keep animals away once the facility was dismantled.

Heather had no flowers to give, but she had shaped a crude cross from a branch of the tree that had sheltered her and the baby the day before. She bent and placed it on top of the freshly turned soil. Then she stepped away. As the group dispersed, she watched the sun break over the horizon. It rose over the dry, grassy plain like a great orange ball, larger than a mountain, older than life itself.

10

The airport in Entebbe, Uganda, was less than an hour's flight from Nairobi, and from the air Uganda looked lush and green, different from Kenya's stark plains and grasslands. At the airport, Heather's group was met by two Ugandans sent by Paul Warring, the missionary in charge of the Kasana Children's Home. After they had cleared customs, the men drove them into Kampala, the capital. As they wove their way down the crowded streets, Heather was struck by the vivid contrasts between the rural and the modern in the teeming city.

Vans and late-model cars, high-rise buildings under construction, rows of shops and bazaars lined the streets, while cattle roamed the median strips along thoroughfares where makeshift tents and cardboard dwellings had been erected. The cattle, large, reddish brown animals with expansive horns, looked more like Texas longhorns than the docile milk cows she was familiar with and seemed oblivious to the noise of city life. "So those cows are what I need to find a good husband?" she asked Ian as she pointed out the window.

"Yes, there's your dowry."

"I guess I'll stay single, then. All Daddy has is cars."

He grinned. "That's a pity, lass."

"Do people really *live* on the median?"

"People live wherever they can. Kampala is home to a million Ugandans, most of whom have come to the city hoping to find a better life. But there's little work here, so they have nothing to do. They get up, grub for a day's living, sleep wherever they can."

The city didn't appear crowded. It was noon, and traffic flowed smoothly. In Miami, downtown would be filled with workers heading off to lunch, and traffic would be thick on the freeways. Here the people moved in no particular hurry. Many sat on benches or in front of stores, reading newspapers and sipping coffee. Most were dressed in Western clothing, but Heather saw several women wearing colorful Ugandan dresses and carrying large bundles balanced on their heads. Blaring radios poured sound through open shop doorways. She wondered how so many survived without jobs, how they got along from day to day.

The vans climbed up a winding, rutted road into hilly terrain. The sun shone brightly under a canopy of bright blue sky, and the air felt warm, but not steamy as it was in Miami. Banana trees and thick hedges, bright with exotic flowers, dotted the roadside, where the earth had a reddish hue.

"If I didn't know better, I'd swear I was back in my home in Alabama," Boyce drawled from a seat behind Heather's. "We have red dirt too."

The vans turned down a dusty road and pulled inside a compound surrounded by a low concrete wall. A large sign announced Namirembe Guest House. The L-shaped building was made of cinder block, painted white and bright blue, with a porch that ran its length. The vans parked and everyone piled out.

Ugandan women emerged from the building and greeted Dr. Henry warmly. He turned to his group and introduced the women as friends who would show them to their quarters. Once the vans were unloaded, Heather scooped up her bags and followed a woman named Ruth into a room that she would be sharing with Ingrid and two others, Cynthia and Debbie. The room's concrete floor was painted gray and the walls a pale green. A window with wooden shutters that could be closed at night let in warm sunlight. The beds were covered with clean sheets and old British army blankets. A wooden cross hung on one wall; a photo of an African Anglican bishop dressed in red robes hung on another.

Ruth pointed to a lone dresser and said, "You each have a bottle of boiled water. Use it for everything, even for brushing your teeth. The water closet is down the hall and turn right."

"Water closet?" Heather whispered to Ingrid.

"Bathroom," Ingrid whispered back.

"You should shower early because the water from the city is turned off every day to conserve, and sometimes it stays off for many hours. Hot water is scarce, so use it with care." Ruth smiled. "And there is water in buckets by the door you can use to flush the toilets when the water is off."

Heather had learned at boot camp about the primitive conditions she would face. She told herself that taking a warm shower and washing and blow-drying her hair every day were Western luxuries she'd willingly forgo in Uganda. It was a small price to pay for helping children who had never even seen the simple pleasures of life she and her friends took for granted.

"Dinner is from five until six o'clock in the dining hall," Ruth added. "And breakfast is served from seven until eight each morning. We wish that all of you have a pleasant and joyful stay at the guest house. I will help you, whatever your needs."

Once Ruth had gone, Cynthia said, "I'm crashing."

"Me too," echoed Debbie.

"I must write home," Ingrid announced. "Better to do it now."

Heather was in no mood to rest. She wanted to explore. She walked outside and took a stroll around the grounds, stopping at the perimeter wall to gaze down at the city below. She remembered Dr. Henry saying that once, Kampala had been pristine and beautiful— "the pearl of Africa." But after decades of military rule, it looked dingy and ruined. Heather heard a whooshing sound and turned to see two men cutting hedges and grass with long, thick-bladed machetes. Their swinging, singing blades glinted in the sunlight, mowing and pruning as machetes had done since ancient times.

"Beautiful, isn't it?" Ian asked, coming up beside her.

"Yes, it is. And it sure beats being blasted awake on a Saturday morning by a lawn mower." She closed her eyes and inhaled. The air smelled of freshly mown grass, tinged with lemon and charcoal.

"You smell lemon grass," Ian said. "It mingles with the scent of the charcoal cooking fires. It's a perfume that belongs only to the air of Africa."

She saw that his eyes wore a distant, longing look. "Do you like it as much as the smell of Scottish lavender?"

"A hard question, lass. Both are beautiful. Scotland is my home, but Africa has slipped inside my head and heart, and I have come to love it."

And she realized then that despite all that had happened to her in Kenya, she loved Africa too. "I'm glad I came," she said.

"Are you all right?"

Both of them knew what he was asking her about. "I still feel terrible about the baby," she said. "But I make myself think of something else whenever the bad thoughts come. I think about the look on the children's faces when I gave them candy after their shots. I think about how their smiles break out. I think about trying to make a difference in their lives."

She turned toward Ian. His red hair ruffled in the slight breeze. "On the road from the airport, I saw women walking with huge bundles on their heads," she said. "Some had babies strapped around their waists and little children following behind them. And I saw the cows walking around with only ropes around their necks to keep them from wandering off. And I wondered why the cows weren't carrying the bundles instead of the women. Why is that, Ian?"

A brightly colored bird landed on a tree branch and sent a shrill whistle into the sky.

"Perhaps you know the answer to that already, lass."

She nodded slowly. "It's because the animals have more value than the women, isn't it?"

"Maybe not more. But a different value, surely. Do not judge them for this difference, Heather. The animals are their livelihood, and a family without a cow has no milk to feed its children. Yet they want for their children what every parent wants—an easier life, a gentler way to take a living from the land."

Remembering what Patrick had told her on

the ship, she said, "I guess a man can get another wife, but another cow . . ." She let the sentence trail off.

"You can't measure their world by our standards. These people have lived for centuries with war, famine, pestilence, and death—the Four Horsemen of the Apocalypse in Revelation. In our countries, we believe we have conquered them, but we haven't. It's just that over here, we see them more clearly, more violently. That's what frightened you so in Kenya, Heather. You saw the baby in all its beauty. You saw death in all its ugliness. You saw how the two things do not go together, and it broke your heart."

She thought again about her parents, about how their medical skills went to fix people's physical imperfections and make them lovely once more. But people like Ian and Dr. Henry saw beyond the outside of a person. They saw with eyes of compassion to the inside, to the dark places. Places where hate and murder and sickness dwelled. Where the Four Horsemen wielded their swords as deftly as the workmen wielded their machetes on the grass.

She bit her lower lip. "I thought I could come and work and feel good about it and go back home and put this away in my scrapbook like I do other things in my life. But I don't think I can, Ian."

He grinned and touched her cheek. "That's the way it happened for me, too. I came once. It changed me. And now I come again. But this time, *you* have come."

"And that makes you happy?"

"Yes. Because you see Africa not only with your eyes, but with your heart. Coming here is not about bringing people medicine and supplies. It's not about doing good deeds for needy people. It's not even about taking a man's land and showing him how to plant it so that his crops grow tenfold. We do all these things, for sure. But that's not what it's all about."

He took a deep breath. "It's about changing lives. And the first life that changes is your own."

She couldn't deny anything he'd said. At the moment, all her reasons for coming seemed shallow and incomplete. They had been good reasons, but somewhere along the way, they had begun to grow roots. She didn't know how deep the roots would go. Nor did she know how she'd ever rip them out and return to the life she'd once lived.

*   *   *

On Saturday, Dr. Henry took a group into the city, and while he met with friends and church leaders, the group was free to wander. The first place Ian took Heather was Kampala's post office. "It's the only place that has a phone line outside the country," he explained. "If you want to call home, you'll have to wait in line along with all the other foreigners and make your call."

A foreigner. That was what Heather was in Africa. She hadn't thought of it that way before, until he'd said it. But she *was* a foreigner— one who wanted to hear her family's voices very much. "I feel like ET," she told him wearily after an hour's wait in line. "You know, I want to phone home, but I can't."

Ian grinned. "I know what you mean. And then if no one's home, it's a letdown. It's my father's habit to prepare his sermon for Sunday on Saturday, so I know he'll be in."

Heather wasn't sure anybody would be at her house, since it was seven hours earlier in Miami. Her heart sank as she realized that Amber was probably out. "Well, I don't care if all I get is the answering machine. I want to hear a familiar voice."

When it was finally her turn, Heather stepped into the old-fashioned wooden booth and closed the door. The air hung stale and sticky. She dialed the string of numbers that would get her into the United States, then Florida, then Miami. Because of the daily power failures and lack of phone lines, she could no longer use her laptop to e-mail, so this might be her only chance to reach home for a long time. The phone rang until she was almost ready to give up.

At last she heard a breathless "Hello."

"Amber? It's Heather."

"Oh my gosh! Is it really you? I can't believe it! How are you? Where are you?"

Emotion clogged Heather's throat. "I'm in Uganda. It's the middle of the day and I—I have so much to tell you, but not much time to talk." She explained her e-mail problem, then asked, "Are Mom and Dad there?"

"No, they're out," Amber said.

Heather felt the keen edge of disappointment. "Since I can't e-mail anymore, I'll have to start writing letters. Tell them—" Her voice cracked with emotion. "Tell them I love them and miss them."

"We miss you, too."

"I almost hung up. I thought you'd be out too."

"I'm grounded. Dylan and I stayed out past

curfew last weekend and Dad blew a gasket. Jeez, you'd think he could cut me a little slack now and then. I'm going stir-crazy around here." Amber paused. "Promise not to tell a secret?"

"My lips are zipped."

"I sneaked Dylan in. We're watching videos and swimming in the pool."

"You shouldn't—"

"Don't lecture me. Dad is such a pain these days. Let me tell you what happened yesterday. And it wasn't my fault either."

Heather held on to the receiver, listening but wanting to yell, *"Stop! Don't you know children are dying over here? Don't you know that there's something more important going on in the world than you being grounded?"* But she didn't interrupt.

"Mom and Dad hate me, Heather," Amber said, her voice suddenly low and sad. "I'd give anything if you'd come home. Can you? Can you just leave Africa early and come home right away?"

11

"Amber, I can't just pick up and leave. People are counting on me."

"But I need you," Amber wailed. "Things are impossible around here."

"How impossible?"

"Just yesterday, Dad took away my car keys."

"Why?"

"Because he's mean. And he hates me."

"Amber . . . ," Heather said in her best tell-me-the-rest-of-the-story voice.

"All right, so I'd gotten a parking ticket."

"And . . . ?"

"A speeding ticket too. But it wasn't my fault. Marsha was driving my car, and she got stopped for speeding, not me. But Dad says it's my responsibility because it's my car."

Heather sighed. Would her sister ever grow up? "Well, you can't make Dad change his mind once it's made up, so you'll just have to live with it."

"But school's started and I can't even drive to school! And he won't let Dylan take me either."

"School's already started?" Heather couldn't believe it. It seemed as if only yesterday she'd set out on the Mercy Ship. She had less than three months left in Africa.

"Hell-o," Amber said, drawing out the two syllables. "It's September. Don't you have a calendar over there?"

"Life's a bit different over here. . . . So, tell me, how are you getting to school?"

"The housekeeper's taking me. Can you imagine the humiliation of getting out of our housekeeper's car every day? I'm the joke of the senior class!"

"I can't change things for you, Amber. Even if I was stateside, I wouldn't be at home. I'd be in college and I couldn't come running home over every crisis." She heard Amber sigh.

"I know . . . but I can ask, can't I? Oh, before I forget, Joanie stopped by last week. She's on her way to college and wanted to make sure I told you she'd see you at Christmas."

"I appreciate the message. Listen, the line for the phone is growing, so I've got to go. But do yourself a favor and get Dylan out of there after we hang up. If Mom and Dad catch you, you'll be grounded until Christmas."

There was a moment of silence. "Okay," Amber said glumly. "But only because *you* asked me to. Before you hang up," she added in a rush, "are you all right? Are you having fun?"

There were a thousand things Heather wanted to say, but she was out of time. "Sure. Things are fine with me. Busy, but fine. I'm glad I came."

"How's Ian? You still revved about him?"

"Still revved," Heather said. "Tell Mom and Dad I'll write when I get to Lwereo. And take it easy on them, sis. They're old, you know."

Amber laughed. Once they'd hung up, homesickness swept over Heather. Her friends were going off to college, just as she would have been doing if she'd been home. But she wasn't home. She was where her dreams had taken her. She was in a world more different than even she had realized was possible. She loved her sister dearly, but Amber was a child—a petulant child who had no clue that two-thirds of the world did not have the luxury of a car. Or a home. Or food on the table every day.

Heather slipped from the phone booth, back into the world she'd come so far to see.

* * *

"Where are we going now?" Heather asked as she walked with Ian down a long, narrow sidewalk.

She had waited for him to finish his call home, and then he'd taken her by the hand and said, "Come with me."

Now he said, "We're going to the Delta. That's where all the cabs in Kampala wait for their fares."

"You mean the cabs don't come to the passengers?"

"How can they? Few phones, remember? The cabs wait in this one area and so you come to the Delta and find the cab that's headed out to where you want to go. When people want to come back into the city, they wait at special cab stops. The cab comes along eventually and picks them up. No buses here. Cabs and walking are the way people travel."

"They could ride their cows," Heather muttered under her breath.

The Delta was a half-block-wide dirt parking arena filled with minivans, the cabs of the city. Ugandans milled around, some hawking their services, others waiting patiently for their vans to fill so that they could be on their way. "No van moves until it's packed," Ian explained. "And each van holds fourteen to six-teen people."

Heather wondered how Amber would man-age under such conditions, then decided she probably wouldn't. She hung close to Ian as he wove through the parked vans, asking a ques-tion or two in Swahili before moving on. Even-tually he found the cab he was looking for, paid the driver, and ushered Heather inside. The space was cramped, but at least she had a window seat. Again she asked, "Where are we going?"

"To the Nalongo Orphanage. I want you to meet Mother Harriet."

The ride to the western outskirts of the city was bumpy and accompanied by clouds of dust. By the time they reached their destination, they were the only two left in the van. Ian asked the driver to wait, and the man parked under a nearby tree and turned off his engine. Immediately quiet descended.

"There it is," Ian said. They walked toward a midsized brick building with a tin roof sitting in a large field, shut off by a metal fence. He opened the gate.

"Can we do this?" she asked, half expecting guards to jump out.

"The gate means little. It's only a way to mark

the property," Ian told her. As they walked inside the fence, he added, "I met Mother Harriet when I was last here. She takes in street orphans, kids whose families have disappeared or been killed. I send her money to help out. Every little bit helps here."

They entered the building, and Heather stopped cold. The place was absolutely empty. She saw a dirt-smeared concrete floor and dirty, unpainted, peeling walls. Curtainless windows let in light, and a single bare bulb hung from a long cord in the center of the ceiling. She saw not one piece of furniture. "Have they moved?" she asked.

"No. This is the home of twenty-five children. This is their main activity room."

"B-But where do they live? Where do they sleep?"

"Their sleeping quarters are in the back. I'll show you, but first let's find Mother Harriet."

They found her in a small room off to one side, sitting behind a decrepit wooden desk piled with papers. She sprang up as they entered, a wide smile of recognition lighting her dark face. She was a tall woman, thin as a rail, and she wore a faded skirt and plaid top. Her hair was wrapped in a scarf.

"Mr. McCollum!" she cried. *"Habari."* She

greeted him in Swahili. "How good to see my fine Scottish benefactor. Why did you not tell me you were coming? I would have kept the children here, instead of sending them off to school."

"*Mzuri*," he answered, then said, "I did not know myself if there would be time to come by, so please excuse us dropping in unannounced." He introduced Heather.

"I will make us tea," Mother Harriet said. "Look around, then hurry back. Oh, and please see the fine dining table I was able to buy with some of the money you sent."

She hurried off into another room, and Ian took Heather by the elbow. "This way," he told her.

On the other side of the empty main room, they walked into a smaller room. There an old table stood, its top scratched and marred. It was quite long and fairly wide. "Where are the chairs?" Heather asked.

"I'm guessing that she couldn't afford chairs too."

"You mean the kids stand to eat?"

"Chairs are a luxury. It's better to buy food than a place to sit. And the table's used for many things besides eating. It was a good purchase."

"I—I can't believe they have so little." She thought of homeless shelters back home— she'd been in a few during her fund-raising efforts. Even though the kids who lived in the shelters were often destitute, they still had a recreation room with TV and toys.

"They have safety here. That's the best gift of all." Ian took her hand. "Come. There's more."

He led her down a corridor with a series of doorways. She stopped at the first one and saw six wooden beds covered with thin, colorful woven blankets. "A dormitory?" she asked.

"Yes. The kids are separated by age. The older ones stay here."

The walls were starkly bare, except for one window covered by aged striped curtains that fluttered in the faint breeze coming from outside. The window had no screen, so Heather knew there was no way to keep out mosquitoes—the main carriers of malaria and other diseases. Over one bed, someone had hung a tattered poster of Michael Jordan. Written on the walls surrounding the poster were threatening words about what would happen to anybody who touched it. On another bed, half stuffed beneath a thin pillow, she saw a ball of aluminum foil.

"They don't have much to call their own," Ian explained, following her glance. "So what they do have, they guard."

"But a *foil* ball?" Heather asked incredulously. "How can that be valuable to a kid?"

"It's all that's his," Ian said. "You have to understand that before coming here, they lived on the streets, begging or stealing food. Possessions, things a child can call his, are valuable indeed."

She wanted to slip something under every pillow, but she had brought nothing of value with her. No candy, very little money, and a bottle of water.

Next Ian took her outside, and Heather was glad to feel the warmth of the sun. The dormitory had depressed her and left her feeling cold.

"Over here is the garden," he said, walking her out to a large patch of cultivated land. She recognized rows of corn and cabbages. "They grow what food they can. Mother Harriet scrounges for the rest."

"How?"

"She begs local businesses. She writes letters to church groups in Europe and America. She's inventive and hard to refuse. But she's got a big job. It's not easy feeding twenty-five mouths two meals a day, three hundred and sixty-five days a year."

"She said they were in school. Where do they go to school?"

"They hold classes at a church in town with volunteers as teachers. They walk there and back every day. It's about ten kilometers—six miles."

"A long walk for a child," Heather said. She looked off into the distance and saw bedding—sheets and blankets—lying on the ground. "What's that?"

"It's an alternative to doing the laundry. Every few days, the children spread their sleeping things outside to catch the sun and kill the creepy crawlers in their pallets."

"Bugs? Ugh—don't they ever wash their clothes? How do they keep stuff clean?"

"They have no washing machines, you know. No running water, either. Water must be hand-carried up the hill from a pumping station almost a half mile away. When they do wash clothes, they boil water in pots and throw in the clothes with lye soap to get them clean. Then they hang them in the sun to dry." He grinned. "Our ancestors did the same thing. Unless, of course, they had servants to do the work."

She felt her cheeks flush as she realized that she had sounded judgmental. She must seem like a pampered princess to him. In truth, she could not dispute the impression. She did live a life of privilege. "You make me feel guilty."

"Heather, lass, you're curious. It's fine to ask questions. And you can't help where God saw fit to give you birth. He has blessed you, and it's nothing to feel shame for." His tone was kind, gentle. He pointed to a large metal tank on wooden stilts. "Recognize that?"

She'd seen one in Kenya. "It catches rainwater."

"Right. Good until the dry season comes, then it's down the hill for water."

A call from the building made them turn to Mother Harriet waving them inside. "Tea's ready!"

Back in her office, a wooden tray had been set with three cups and a china teapot. There was also a small plate holding three peeled, hardboiled eggs. "Eat. Our hens laid these just this morning," Mother Harriet said proudly.

Heather nibbled on her egg, feeling guilty, thinking that this was one less egg an orphan would get to eat. But she knew better than to refuse. Dr. Henry had told them in one of his sessions aboard the ship how insulting it was to refuse African hospitality. She sipped her tea from the chipped china cup and said, "Thank you. It's delicious."

The woman beamed at her. Then she turned to Ian and outlined her efforts to raise money. Heather listened, amazed—not by her efforts, but by the refusals she spoke of and the indifference to all Mother Harriet was trying to do to help children survive. Didn't the government care? Couldn't she get help from politicians? Heather wanted to ask a hundred questions but didn't. Ian was closing the conversation and standing. It was time to leave.

He reached inside his shirt and pulled out a wallet. "Take this," he said, and handed Mother Harriet a stack of folded money.

"Bless you," Mother Harriet said. "This will help us buy food. And I will be taking the youngest ones into the clinic for shots and medicine next week. The medicine is free, but they are too young to walk so far. Now I can take them by taxi."

She shook hands with Ian, and he and Heather walked to the van. The driver folded the newspaper he'd been reading and opened the door. Once they were on their way, Heather asked the questions she'd kept to herself before.

"The government is overloaded," Ian answered. "Almost half of the Ugandan population is under fifteen years old. The country is awash in orphans. Only a handful get taken into places like Mother Harriet's."

Heather's heart ached. She felt overwhelmed by what she'd seen that afternoon, impotent. She turned to Ian. "Why did you bring me here?"

He clasped his hand over hers and looked deep into her eyes. "We're going to Lwereo tomorrow, to the Kasana Children's Home. It's run by missionaries, with a thought for feeding both body and soul. They do things differently, and to my way of thinking, they do things better. I want you to judge for yourself, lass. I want you to see the children as I see them. Not through the eyes of men, but through the eyes of God."

12

The city of Lwereo was little more than a bump in the road. A few buildings, a town square, a soccer field—all clumped together within short walking distance of a village of thatched huts set back in the countryside. A turnoff onto a rutted dirt trail eventually brought the vans into a clearing. On one side was the Kasana mission hospital, on the other a gate with a sign: Children's Home.

Two young boys waved and opened the gate, and the vans drove through, stopping in an open area between several thatch-roofed buildings and a cinder-block ranch-style house. A young couple, surrounded by three blond boys, greeted Dr. Henry's group with hugs and smiles. The woman held a baby.

"I'm Paul Warring," the brown-haired man said. "And this is my wife, Jodene, and our sons,

Kevin, eight, Dennis, six, and Samuel, four. The baby"—Jodene waggled the baby's arm at the group—"is our eight-month-old daughter, Amie. Welcome."

Heather had not expected to see so young a couple here in the African bush. Paul was tall and trim, his wife petite and dainty, with shoulder-length blond hair and wire-rimmed glasses. The three boys kept jockeying for a position closest to their father's side, until Samuel fell and began to wail.

"Stop it, boys," Paul admonished. "We have guests. Who will show them to their rooms while I take Dr. Henry and Mr. Hoover inside for tea?"

The boys jumped up and down, begging for the job. Minutes later, Heather and the other girls were following Dennis into a dormitory-style building, where they found a living room furnished with a sofa and two chairs, and a small kitchen table and chairs. There were also two bedrooms, each with two beds.

"Wow!" exclaimed Ingrid. "This is wonderful! I thought we'd be pitching our tents again."

"Look," Cynthia announced with a grin, "indoor plumbing."

Heather was equally pleased. They had all

been expecting communal latrines like the ones they'd had in Kenya.

She went out for her bags and saw Ian sorting through the pile for his. "I didn't expect the place to be this nice," she told him.

"Yes, they've made some improvements since I was here last."

"And the Warrings . . . well, I thought they'd be old. And they're Americans, aren't they?"

Ian laughed. "They're from your North Dakota."

"Out west," she told him. "Wonder how they ended up in Uganda?"

"We're having a meeting in an hour. Why don't you ask them?" He tapped the end of her nose playfully. "See you there, lass."

The meeting was held under one of the thatched pavilions while the smell of grilling chicken wafted through the evening air. The kitchen was really a separate small hut set away from the other buildings but close to the house. The chickens cooked over open coals, watched carefully by a couple of Ugandan kids—residents of the home, Heather learned. Several enormous cast-iron pots filled with beans and corn sat atop a cement-and-brick stove, fueled by wood and charcoal.

"Before we eat," Paul began once everyone

had sat down on long wooden benches, "I want to thank each of you for coming so far, for giving up months of your real lives, to help out. I first came here on a mission trip when I was twenty-two, and returning to Uganda was a dream of mine for years.

"I'm a contractor by trade, and when I learned what my church organization planned to do over here, well, I begged Jodene to pull up stakes and come with me." He patted his wife's shoulder. "Thankfully, she agreed. That was three years ago. Jodene and I are the current overseers of the children's home, and we plan to remain here two more years.

"You see, Uganda is a country finally at peace after years of a military regime that killed over one million citizens before it was toppled. Thousands of people, mostly children, were left homeless and parentless. And it's these children we're hoping to help."

Heather listened with her heart. Here were people doing what she wanted to do. Here were people who were realizing their dream, in spite of the sacrifices they had to make. And by now, she understood what a sacrifice it was to leave family, friends, and country and come halfway around the world to help better the lives of strangers.

Paul continued. "We came here with a different philosophy. We base it on the old proverb. 'Give a man a fish and you feed him for a day. Teach a man to fish, and you feed him for a lifetime.' It wasn't enough to just take in orphans and care for them. We wanted to return the concept of fatherhood to these children's lives. First, we wanted them to see God as their heavenly father. To do that, they need an earthly father as a role model. Most of these kids don't even remember their parents or village life.

"Our goal is to train the oldest young men to become heads of families. The younger children are placed in these family groups, where they learn to live together much as they may have before they lost everything. With our supervision, the 'father' of these families is taught how to be responsible for his unit. Under his headship, his family learns to farm and raise livestock, which we supply; they learn a trade, such as carpentry or ornamental ironworking, sewing, or basket making—all the trades that their Ugandan forefathers learned and taught before the wars came. Eventually, the family members will grow up, move out, and create new villages. And, ultimately, marry and give birth and train up another generation.

"Everyone attends school daily here on the grounds, then spends time gardening or doing assigned chores. Our goal is to teach the youth skills and leave them self-sufficient and self-governing and able to fend for themselves once we return stateside.

"No one is forced to stay against his or her will. The door is always open for residents to leave. But if they stay, then they must obey the rules, which are mainly to work and go to school and live within one of our families."

Paul paused. "In the past three years, not one person has left." He looked over his audience. "Your being here is a blessing. Some of you will help build a new classroom. Some of you will begin teaching in our school. Others will work at the hospital on the other side of the road. None of you will be idle. You will never work harder, but you will never feel more useful.

"Now, if you want to ask questions, come to me during dinner. Right now, it's time to eat. That is, if you're hungry."

A deafening cheer went up. Heather stood, found Ian's gaze, and smiled. He winked, and she blew him a kiss.

Early the next morning, Heather showed up at the hospital along with Dr. Henry, Ian, and her roommate Cynthia. The hospital grounds were neat and well kept, the flower beds ablaze with pink and red blossoms. Patients who were ambulatory sat outside under banana trees in old-fashioned wooden wheelchairs and on benches positioned along the porch. They played cards, read newspapers, or talked with family and friends. Heather saw none of the high-tech equipment she was used to in American hospitals. IV stands held glass bottles rather than soft plastic bags, and rubber rather than plastic tubing. Traction for a man with multiple broken bones was a system of ropes and wooden pulleys instead of stainless steel and slim cables.

Inside, the hospital smelled of antiseptic and soap. The walls were painted yellow; the floors were bare concrete, still damp and shiny after being mopped. Banks of windows allowed morning sunlight to flood the wards, where white metal beds lined the walls. The beds reminded Heather of ones she'd seen in old war movies.

She learned that she and Cynthia would work with the nurses, while Dr. Henry and Ian would see patients and help in the operating room. The doctor in charge, Dr. Gallagher, was Irish, and he and his family lived in a small house on hospital property. The other two doctors were Ugandan—second-year residents on loan from hospitals in England, where they were getting their medical training. There were also six full-time nurses, three of them nuns, all of them Ugandans. Dr. Gallagher's wife was also a nurse, but she worked only when there was a crisis.

Dr. Gallagher walked them through the facility, showing them the women's and men's wards—two wings of the building, connected by a central receiving area. Rooms off the central area contained the lab, the clinic, a small lounge where cots were set up for night personnel, and a room for sick infants. The babies were kept not in plastic Isolettes, but in hand-carved wooden cradles. There was no neonatal intensive care unit.

"The operating and recovery room is off the men's ward," Dr. Gallagher explained in his heavy Irish accent. "The building out back is the isolation wing. That's where we keep the tuberculosis patients, the contagious cases that come in, and AIDS victims in the final stages of their disease."

His words sent a chill through Heather. In America, AIDS victims had an arsenal of drugs that often kept their disease at bay; here there was no such hope. The treatments were simply too costly. Dr. Gallagher explained that the best they could do was to keep the patient as comfortable as possible until he or she died.

Heather recalled what Patrick had told her on the ship—multiple wives, multiple sex partners had spread the disease quickly through the population. And when Dr. Gallagher explained that part of their work as aides would include counseling women in the clinic on family planning and HIV awareness, Heather realized that her job was going to be more than cleaning bedpans and keeping track of paperwork.

She and Cynthia went straight to work with Sister Della, tackling a maze of jobs that included changing patients' bandages and dispensing medications. The morning passed so quickly that Heather was shocked when Ian stuck his head in the door and reminded her that it was time for a lunch break. "I don't know if I can take a break," she told him.

"You must. We can't have you dropping over the first day on the job."

He took her outside to a bench beneath a graceful old tree and spread a white napkin between them. He opened a small canvas bag and took out two bottles of water, a few bananas, a pile of cooked rice wrapped in a banana leaf, two boiled eggs, and a baked sweet potato.

Heather hadn't realized how hungry she was until she smelled the food. "Tastes good," she said, eating a sweet, finger-sized banana in one bite. "Where'd you get it?"

"Jodene sent it over. She knew none of us had thought about lunch. I gave a bag to Cynthia and Dr. Henry, too."

"I guess there's no cafeteria or vending machines around here," Heather said. "When I worked in the hospital back home, food was never a problem."

"They prepare food in a cookhouse out back for the patients. For some, it's the only time they eat regular." He took a bite of sweet potato. "How was your morning?"

"Busy. How about yours?"

"Stitched up a man who'd fallen in a ditch, and assisted Dr. Henry in the OR, setting a broken leg. Greenstick fracture—bone came clear through the skin."

She grimaced.

She saw that a bandage had been taped to the inside of Ian's elbow and asked about it.

"Gave blood. I'm O negative, the universal

donor. The man needed a transfusion, and the lab had no blood, so I rolled up my sleeve."

"You gave blood right there in the OR?" She couldn't imagine her parents stopping an operation to give blood to one of their patients, although she knew that her father donated blood on occasion to the hospital's blood bank.

"A person does what he has to," Ian said matter-of-factly.

The news unsettled her, making her wonder if the man would have died if Ian hadn't been there. "I guess I could give blood too," she said.

"If you can spare a pint, the lab can use it. Dr. Gallagher said some should be coming next week, but in the meantime, we may have an emergency. All the doctors and nurses give blood regularly. It's part of the job."

"I have some syringes my dad made me bring."

"Smart thinking," Ian said. "Dr. Gallagher runs a good hospital. He never reuses needles."

She was glad of that—she didn't want Ian running any unnecessary risks.

"Lass, I believe lunch is over," he said looking past her shoulder. "Here comes an ambulance."

Surprised because she hadn't heard a siren, Heather turned. She saw no vehicle, just four men carrying a litter attached to long poles that rested on their shoulders. A woman covered by a blanket lay on the stretcher. A man and a small child tagged along behind. "*That's the ambulance?*"

Ian stood, scooping up the debris from their lunch. "Yes. They probably walked all night from the bush to bring her. I'd better go see to her problem."

She watched him trot toward the stretcher bearers, move alongside, and take the woman's wrist, feeling for a pulse.

Something bad had happened to the woman, of that Heather was certain. But there had been no 911 emergency service to call for help. For her there had only been the men of her village to carry her to the nearest hospital. For her there had been hours, maybe days of pain. And maybe, like the baby Heather had held in Kenya, the woman was already beyond help.

A chill ran through Heather as she watched the men walk into the hospital, followed closely by the other man and the child, who began to cry for his mother.

13

Heather's days quickly fell into a routine. Six days a week, she worked at the hospital. On Sunday, she joined everyone in the compound for church services, where Miguel's guitar music was added to the African flute and drums. Sunday afternoon was free time, and Sunday evening, the entire camp came together for dinner and prayer.

She loved her work. She and Cynthia shared stories from the hospital with Ingrid and Debbie, who had their own stories about teaching in the school. "The children are bright," Ingrid often said. "And so eager to learn. At the end of the day, I feel like a dried-out sponge."

Under Bob Hoover's direction, the construction project took shape, and by the middle of October, a concrete slab had been poured and cinder blocks had risen to form walls.

Boyce, Miguel—all the kids working on the building had turned nut brown under the African sun, and their bodies bulged with well-toned muscles.

Ian spent long hours in the OR or sitting by the bedsides of critical patients, adjusting IVs and doling out pain medications, always in short supply. Once every two weeks, a Red Cross truck arrived with supplies, but the hospital never knew if it would be the supplies they desperately needed or an overabundance of something they didn't. Every day was an adventure.

One Saturday evening, Paul and Jodene invited Dr. Henry, Bob, and Ian to the house for dinner. Ian asked Heather to join them, and she found herself frantically sorting through her duffel bags for something pretty to wear.

"Wear my silver hoops," Ingrid offered, dangling the pretty earrings under Heather's nose.

"How about my long skirt?" Cynthia said, shaking out a lovely aqua skirt with lace insets.

"I have one unstained white blouse," Debbie said. "It's yours for the night."

"I love you all," Heather said, tying up her hair with a white ribbon and dabbing a few drops of perfume behind her ears.

Just before she was to leave, Ingrid pulled

her to one side. "You are very pretty. Ian will be moved."

Heather blushed. Was it that obvious that she was dressing for him and not for dinner? She'd told no one except Amber, thousands of miles away, how she felt about Ian, and even then she hadn't expressed the depth of her feelings. "He's been nice to me," Heather said to Ingrid. "But I know I shouldn't read too much into it."

Ingrid shrugged. "He is a fine person, and yes, handsome too. It is not hard to see why you care for him."

"It's not a dumb crush. It—It's different."

"*Ja*," Ingrid said with a matter-of-fact nod. "This I can see by the look on your face."

"Oh, great," Heather moaned. "Don't tell me that."

"But it is true. And tonight you are beautiful for him." Ingrid smiled and patted Heather's arm. "He will be—how do you say it?—bowled over."

When Ian arrived to fetch Heather, the look on his face told her that Ingrid had made a good call.

Jodene served dinner at a long, narrow table that had been hewn from a single log. The underside was still rough and curved, the top sanded smooth. Kerosene lamps and candles lit the room. "We have a gas generator," Paul explained, "but we try and make do without it because gasoline is so expensive."

Heather didn't mind. She found the atmosphere charming.

Jodene served an egg "pizza," the crust formed from crackers. There was a bowl of pilau—rice mixed with spices—and the ever-plentiful *matoke*, which Heather had never developed a taste for. But she found the conversation wonderful, surprised at how hungry her ears were for sounds of English words pronounced with American accents.

She was helping herself to a dessert of pineapple and mango when she caught a movement out of the corner of her eye. On the other side of the room, peeking from under a cot beside the sofa, she saw the dark face of a child. Startled, Heather set down her fork and turned for a better look. "Who's that?" she asked.

Jodene gently pushed back her chair and crossed to the cot, knelt down, and held out her hand. "Kia, would you like to come out and meet our friends?"

The child crawled farther under the cot.

"They won't hurt you, Kia." The child refused to budge, and Jodene returned to the table. "Sorry, she's not coming out."

"Who is she?" Heather asked.

"It's a sad story," Paul said, hunching over the table. "She came here about three months ago with her mother. They were Sudanese and somehow had made it out of a refugee camp into Uganda. Problem was, Kia's mother was desperately sick. She died within a couple of weeks, and we took in Kia."

"Poor little girl! How old is she?"

"We're guessing four or five. Poor nutrition has left her small for her age, but Dr. Gallagher checked her over and that was his guess. The boys have tried to befriend her, but she won't have anything to do with them. She's fascinated with Amie, however."

At this point, Jodene took up the story. "Her mother had a photograph with her. Here." She fished in a desk drawer and pulled out a Polaroid snapshot of little Kia and a woman holding a baby—a baby whose face was tragically deformed.

"Cleft palate," Dr. Henry said studying the picture. "We can correct that with surgery. Where's the infant now?"

"A health worker took the photo. It helps

keep relatives together when they come into the camp. According to the mother's story, a worker took the baby to the infirmary. Somehow, she was able to get herself and Kia out of the country, but in the turmoil, she had to leave the baby. By the time she arrived here, she was sick and delirious. Still, she kept pleading with us to go get her daughter in Sudan."

"Can't you go to the camp and get the baby?"

Paul shook his head. "Not legally. You can't just walk in and take a child, and going through the proper channels is almost impossible. Red tape five miles long. Why, she'd be half grown if we went that route."

"What are you going to do?" asked Heather. "She needs surgery. I mean, my parents fix that kind of defect all the time."

Dr. Henry spoke up. "We can certainly repair her face back on the ship."

But Heather knew that the ship had sailed on by now and wouldn't return for another year. It was too long for the baby to wait. "Are you saying the baby's case is hopeless?" she asked.

"Not totally," Paul answered. "We have a friend, Dr. Ed Wilson. He's just come over as a volunteer to do medical service in the Sudanese camps. He's on the lookout for the baby."

"This kind of deformity makes it difficult for babies to suckle," Dr. Henry said. "And it's hard to say if someone is even going to the trouble of feeding her in the camps. Did the mother say anything about any other family members?"

Paul shook his head. "We surmise that hers was one of hundreds of small villages destroyed by the rebels. What's happening over there is pretty brutal stuff and not dinner conversation, but thousands have fled and are packed into these camps. Relief and health workers are overwhelmed by the sheer numbers of displaced survivors."

"How will you know if he finds her?" Ian asked.

"Ham radio," Paul said. "It's the only way we have to communicate around here. Our families in the U.S. have ham radios, and that's how we keep in touch. Ed is supposed to notify us if he turns up anything." Paul cut his eyes toward Kia, still crouched under the cot. "If she's still alive," he added in a lowered voice.

Heather felt such pity for Kia that tears welled in her eyes. "Doesn't she ever come out from under the cot?"

Jodene shook her head. "Hardly ever. She

runs outside to go to the bathroom. She eats when I put food beside the cot. She won't sleep on top of the cot, either. She sleeps under it, like a frightened animal. We tried to put her into one of the family units, but she ran away and came straight back here. Maybe because it was the place she last saw her mother alive."

Jodene chewed on her lip reflectively. "We'll never know what really happened to Kia and her family, but whatever happened totally traumatized her. And in all the time she's been here, she's never spoken a word. I know she understand us. Sometimes she sits and rocks and wails, so we know she can make sound, but she never speaks. Not one single word since her mother died. The only other person she has in the world is her baby sister. I would give *anything* if we could reunite them."

Once dinner was over, Ian and Heather went for a walk on the grounds, where the fronds of banana trees rustled, lending a kind of music to the night. Under the star-studded sky, the full moon floated above them like a ghost ship, adrift on an inky sea, and lit the landscape with a pale light.

"Thanks for inviting me tonight," she told

Ian. "Except for hearing about Kia, the evening was perfect."

"Yes, lass. It's a sad story. And there are so many sad stories. But the girl's with good people. Jodene and Paul will help her however they can. You know, I believe one by one a difference is made."

Heather held out her hand as if to catch the moonbeams. "If I could," she said, "I'd bring Kia these moonbeams. Maybe they would make her smile glow."

"Just the way yours glows," Ian said, looking at her and making her heart skip.

"It's only the moonlight."

"No, lass. It's *your* glow. It begins down deep in your heart and bubbles up till it spills out your eyes."

"If you want me to melt at your feet, keep it up."

He laughed, the sound rich and deep. "You make my days brighter, Heather. You make this place a better place for your being here. Sometimes, when I'm sitting with a patient I know will not live through the night, I think of you. I hold on to the patient, but my mind is all around you. It helps me let go of what I cannot change."

"It's the same for me, Ian." Her words came

out breathlessly. She found it difficult to give voice to the things she'd held silently in her heart for so long. "I can't picture my life without you in it."

"Careful. . . . I will not let you take back these words."

"I don't want to take them back. I can't help the way I feel."

"Feelings grow stronger in the moonlight. It's strange but true."

"I feel the same way in the clear light of day. I—I want to be with you."

He toyed with her hoop earring, saying nothing for such a long time that she was afraid she'd said far too much. She knew she was younger than he. She knew that he had plans and dreams that had never included her. But she also knew how she felt. She loved him. Although he'd never kissed her, never romanced her, never so much as hinted that she was anything more to him than a pretty girl on a mission trip, he had taken root inside her heart in such a way that she wasn't sure she could ever uproot him.

"This trip will end," he said finally. "You'll go back to your home; I'll return to mine. I have years to go before I finish my schooling. And you have college, too. You told me so. You'll want to go on with your life when you get home."

Her other life didn't seem important now. Here in the moonlight, under the stars of Africa, she wasn't sure she had another life. But *he* did. Was he telling her he had no room in it for her? "It's hard to think about that now," she said with a nervous laugh. "Must be moon madness."

"Yes," he whispered. "That's possible."

More than anything, she wanted to throw herself into his arms, have him smother her with kisses. More than anything, she wanted to say, "I love you," and hear him tell her the same. But he knew what he wanted for his future. She knew she shouldn't muddy his waters, cloud his dreams. It wouldn't be fair.

She stepped away and said in a forced, bright voice, "I promised Dr. Gallagher I'd come in early tomorrow, and if I don't get some sleep . . . well, I'll be dragging all day."

"I know. Me too."

They fell into step together beneath the moon and walked quickly back to the guest dormitory, touching shoulders but not speaking.

14

"I can't stop thinking about Kia." Heather was sitting on a bench with Ian outside the hospital.

"I know what you mean, lass. I think of her often myself."

It was a rare afternoon when they had both finished their day's work a bit early. Heather thought he looked exhausted, but she'd been wanting to talk to him about Kia for days. "I talked to Jodene with some ideas about getting Kia to open up," she said. "Back home, when I worked at the hospital as a volunteer for a summer, I helped with some autistic children."

"I don't think Kia is autistic."

"I agree. But I asked Jodene if I could try some of the things that worked with those kids."

Ian shut his Bible, which had been lying

open on his lap. Sun dappled his hair through the trees. "What things?"

"Well, every afternoon this past week, I've visited Jodene's and sat myself down on the floor next to the cot. I just sit there and hum to myself, paying no special attention to Kia, who stays hidden. I stay for about thirty minutes, and when I go, I leave a piece of candy. Jodene says Kia's been eating it."

"Yes, but she eats all food placed by the cot."

"I know, but I worked late on Friday, so I was late getting to the house. Jodene says Kia crawled out from under the cot and went to the window and looked out. She thinks Kia might have been looking for me."

"That's a good conclusion."

Encouraged by Ian's approval, Heather added, "I want her to trust me. She needs to trust someone again. She needs to come back into the real world."

"You're right, lass. She can't spend the rest of her life hiding under a cot."

"I feel so sorry for her. But I don't know if I'm the person to help her. I mean, I'll be leaving in another few weeks, and I can't take her with me. Maybe I should leave the job to someone more qualified."

Ian tilted his head, appraising her with his

intelligent blue eyes. "Have you ever read the Book of Esther?"

"Not for a long, long time. But what's that got to do with Kia?"

He opened his Bible, which was stuffed with notes on bits of paper. "It tells of how the Jewish people came to celebrate the festival of Purim, a celebration of their deliverance from annihilation at the hands of the Persians.

"At the time, the Jews were captives of King Xerxes, but they'd been living in Persia for so long that they had their own cities, homes, businesses, and normal, everyday lives. Anyway, the current queen fell from the king's favor, so he had all the young women of his kingdom brought in so that he could choose a new queen. He chose Esther, without ever knowing she was a Jew.

"The king had a wicked advisor, Haman, who hated the Jews, especially Mordecai, who, unknown to him, happened to be Esther's uncle. Haman plotted how he could destroy every Jew in his country, devised a plan, and even got the king to agree to it. So Mordecai sent Esther a message, asking her to plead with the king for mercy and spare their people." Ian opened his Bible and read, " 'For if you remain silent at this time, relief and deliverance for the Jews will arise from another place.' " Ian glanced up. "You see, Mordecai believed God *would* deliver them, one way or another, but he believed Esther was their best hope.

"Mordecai asked her, 'And who knows but that you have come to royal position for such a time as this?' " Ian turned to Heather. "But in those days, no one—not even the queen— could come into the king's presence unless the king summoned her. Queen Esther would be risking her life to go before the king without being invited. It would take phenomenal courage for her to leave her life of comfort and security in the king's court and face possible death.

"So Esther asked all her people to fast and pray for her, saying, 'When this is done, I will go to the king, even though it is against the law. And if I perish, I perish.' " Ian closed his Bible. "You know the rest of the story, don't you, lass?"

Heather, caught up in his telling of it, nodded but didn't speak.

Ian said, "Esther went to the king, and he received her. He heard her petition and granted it. In the end, Haman was hanged on the gallows he'd constructed for Mordecai, and Mordecai, the Jew, rose to a position of power and honor. Because of Esther's courage."

"Why are you telling me this, Ian?"

"Because we must always look at life in the grand scheme of God's sovereignty. Perhaps you have come to Uganda 'for such a time as this.' To help bring Kia back into life."

Tears misted Heather's eyes. "Maybe to balance out the baby I couldn't save," she whispered. "Maybe this one and not that one."

Ian's hand closed over hers. "God's given you a heart for caring, lass. I learned that almost from the first time we met. It's a wondrous gift, and I can't think of anyone I'd like to see use it more than you."

Their fingers intertwined, his flesh warm and firm in hers, and the moment seared itself into Heather's heart—the sunlight on the grass, the shadows flickering through the leaves, the soft breath of a lemon-scented breeze. All came together. She knew it would be a memory as vivid as any photograph. And one that she would hold in her heart forever.

For the next three weeks, Heather went to Jodene's every day after work, sat on the floor in front of the cot, and pretended to be interested in everything except Kia. She played board games with the three boys, bounced balls, played jacks and Pickup Sticks by herself. She sang and talked, and she laid a piece of wrapped hard candy under the cot when she left. Kia never ventured out.

"I'm running low on candy," Heather confided to Jodene one Sunday evening after the group dinner. "And I don't think I'm making any progress."

"I think you are. Kia crawled out yesterday and watched us eat dinner. She's never done that before."

Heather felt a spark of encouragement. "Did she do anything else?"

Jodene thought a moment. "She still peeks out the window if you're running late. And while she always goes outside to go to the bathroom, she's staying outdoors longer. She sits and plays with the dirt, lets it run through her fingers, like she's reconnecting with it somehow."

"That sounds good." Heather thought for a moment. "Listen, I have an idea. Tomorrow, instead of coming inside, I'm going to sit under the tree in your front yard. If she looks out the window, she'll see me. Maybe she'll come outside to be with me."

"It's worth a try."

Over the weeks, Heather had grown to admire and respect Jodene. She cooked her family's meals on a hot plate, or on open coals in the cooking hut outside her kitchen door. She washed dishes with rainwater under a hand pump mounted on her kitchen sink—which was a wooden counter with a large plastic bowl. She washed clothes, including Amie's diapers, by hand with the help of some of the older girls living on the premises. There was an endless line of laundry hanging out to dry.

"You need a washing machine," Heather told her.

"How would I plug it in?" Jodene answered with a grin. "Believe me, gas for the generator costs more than the energy to do it by hand."

Kevin and Dennis went to school with the Ugandan children, and after school they all played together, as carefree as colts romping in spring meadows. Heather compared them with herself as she was growing up. She'd had plenty to do—Montessori school, dance lessons, even two years of gymnastics for her and Amber—but she never recalled the sheer joy she saw reflected in the boys' faces.

In November, Jodene told all the Americans

in the compound to prepare to come to the house for Thanksgiving dinner. "It's when I miss home most of all," she told Heather. "I come from a big family, and every year we'd gather at my parents' home and have a feast fit for a Roman orgy."

Heather had all but forgotten Thanksgiving was approaching. At her house, the holiday meant going away on ski trips out West. She hadn't had a turkey dinner at home in six years. "I'll spread the word," she told Jodene. "But won't the others feel left out?"

"Thanksgiving is uniquely American, so no one cares about it but us. My mother sent me a care package with the missionary group that stopped by in October. So I have goodies to share."

Heather had learned that the missionary circle was small but well connected. No missionaries came through without goods from the States for those serving in Uganda. Whenever possible, reliable travelers hand-carried mail stateside for the missionary community. Nobody mailed packages in or out of the country because they never made it out of the airport, where local police, guards, and other officials helped themselves to whatever they wanted.

As for Heather, she had written several letters home, but mail pickup and delivery were sporadic. So she didn't hear from home often, and when she did, the news was weeks old. The last word she'd received had been all about October's homecoming and how Amber had been chosen for the court.

"I have something to bring for the feast too," Heather told Jodene.

"What?" Jodene's eyes lit up.

"I'll surprise you. In fact, I'll tell everybody to bring something to share."

No one was more ecstatic about the upcoming dinner than Boyce. "Hot dog," he drawled, "count me in. I'll find something to bring besides an appetite."

Thanksgiving. Now that she was so far from home, how special it seemed to Heather. She didn't care if they ate *matoke*, she just wanted to be with everybody for the holiday. It didn't even bother her that Ian would not be there. After all, he was Scottish, and the celebration meant nothing to him. "I'll work," he said. "You have your special day, lass, and enjoy it. Tell me all about it later."

Four days before the holiday, Heather went to Jodene's to help make table decorations: cutout paper turkeys, pilgrim hats, and cornucopias. They were working at the kitchen table by lamplight when Paul came out of his and Jodene's bedroom, looking excited.

"I've been on the ham radio," he said in a low voice as he leaned over the table. "I talked with Ed Wilson. He's located Kia's sister."

15

Heather's heart thudded expectantly. "He found her? How is she?"

Paul glanced toward the cot. "I'd rather not talk in here. Let's go outside, and Heather, can you find Ian and bring him to hear this? He wanted to know when the baby was found."

She wasted no time in locating Ian, who was having a Bible study with some of the older Ugandan teens living in the compound. By the time the two of them had returned to Paul and Jodene's, Paul had dragged four chairs into the front yard, and Jodene had put some candles on the windowsill. The flames flickered and danced, casting a pale yellow light into the circle of chairs.

"Heather says Kia's sister's been found," Ian said as he settled into a chair.

"It's true. I heard from Ed tonight."

"How is she?"

"Not good."

Heather's stomach tightened with the news.

Paul continued. "She's in the clinic at the camp, but conditions there are pretty grim. If not for the kindness of a nun, who's been feeding her with a special syringe several times a day, the baby would be dead already."

Heather recalled Dr. Henry's saying that babies with cleft palates didn't suckle well, so Kia's sister probably couldn't take a bottle. Heather realized that hand-feeding her had to be painstaking work, and she silently blessed the nun for taking on this labor of love.

"What about IV feeding?" Ian asked.

"Ed's got her on a drip now, but equipment and supplies are in high demand, and frankly, they're needed for more critical patients. He says the situation at the camp is chaotic. People line up under a tree for immunizations, and a few cases of cholera have broken out. Some nights they can hear rebel gunfire in the distance." Paul stopped talking, as if to let the bleakness of the situation sink in.

"Is there anything we can do to help?" Jodene asked. "It sounds as if, if we don't do something, she'll die."

Heather saw Paul and Ian exchange glances.

"We've been discussing it beforehand," Ian said. "Ever since I learned about Kia's sister."

Heather sat up straighter.

"I know that I have much to do here," Ian said, "but we all know that choosing to help this one is a special thing for all of us. So I'm going to fetch her. My mind's made up."

No one said anything.

"Isn't there anyone else who can go?" Heather finally ventured.

"I'm the best candidate. I have medical skills she'll need."

Paul nodded. "I agree."

"How will you get there?"

Paul said, "There's an air service—Mission Air—in Kampala that flies old DC-3s left over from World War Two into Sudan and Rwanda. They fly in most of our workers for the refugee camps, as well as World Health professionals and volunteers."

Heather knew that commercial airlines flew only into Entebbe; this was the first she'd heard of any other air service in the country. But World War II planes? They were ancient!

"The planes are old and without any refinements, but the pilots keep them in good mechanical condition," Paul explained, as if he'd read her mind. "Plus, they usually don't get any flak from authorities for doing humanitarian service. Of course, if there's shooting going on and a person absolutely must get in or out of either country, well, he can hire mercenary pilots. They fly small Cessnas under the radar. It's risky and expensive, but it's a way to get in and out."

Heather felt the blood leave her face. *Shooting? Mercenaries? Evading radar?* She didn't want Ian facing those kinds of dangers for any reason!

They talked some more, laying plans, but Heather could hardly bear to listen. And when Ian walked her back to her room, she told him how she felt.

"Please, don't concern yourself for me. Think about the look on Kia's face when she sees her sister. That's the prize for going."

They were almost to the room when they ran into Dr. Henry and Patrick coming from the village. Ian quickly filled them in on what was happening. It maddened Heather that neither of them spoke a single word of discouragement.

"I'll drive you into Kampala myself," Dr. Henry said. "When do you want to leave?"

"Paul says the planes only fly once a week, on Tuesday around noon."

"We'll leave on Monday, stay at the guest house."

"Why can't Patrick go?" Heather blurted out her question. "He's Ugandan and he's studying medicine. Why can't he go?"

The three men regarded her, but it was Patrick who spoke up. "I am Hutu, not Tutsi," he said, as if that explained everything. "Kia and her sister are Tutsi. The officials would not let a Hutu take a Tutsi child from the camp. Ian is white. And a doctor—or almost. People will look the other way."

"What are you talking about? What's a Hutu?"

"It is my tribe. In Africa, a person's tribe is most important, and the Hutu is one of the largest tribes. Most Ugandans are Hutu. The fighting in Sudan and Rwanda is due to militant Hutu rebels killing Tutsi."

Heather just stared at the three men. "They *kill* each other just because they're from different tribes? Why doesn't someone stop them?"

"No one can stop them," Patrick said.

"It's genocide. Ethnic cleansing," Dr. Henry added.

"But why do they do it?"

"It's about power," Patrick said. "Control of

the land. The Hutu rebels have killed thousands. Sudanese villagers have fled, looking for safety. Some get into neighboring countries. Most flee to the refuge camps, hoping to return to their villages . . . what's left of them. The world governments cannot police every country. They can protest and step in to help the victims, but Africa belongs to the Africans, the different tribes, and they must work things out among themselves."

Heather didn't know what to say. She had heard about the fighting in Africa, but she hadn't realized how much of it stemmed from tribal roots. "But you're different, Patrick. You're not that way. You're not going to kill anyone."

He gave her a kindly smile. "I am a Christian, Heather. When I became one, in my heart, I put away my tribal history and differences. But I cannot put away who I am to the Tutsi. They hate me on sight. In your War Between the States, brothers killed brothers. Our two countries are not so different."

She looked from one face to the other, seeing the big picture in ugly clarity. People in Africa were dying, murdered by their own. Kia's entire village had been destroyed simply because she belonged to the wrong tribe. Heather felt foolish—incredibly stupid. She had wanted to come to Africa to save starving children. Save them for what?

"It's getting late," Ian said.

Dr. Henry shook Ian's hand. "We'll talk more tomorrow."

Patrick bade them good evening and left.

When they were alone, Ian took her hands in his. "I will bring the baby here, lass. Don't be afraid for us."

She nodded, fighting tears. "You must go get her, Ian. Without you, she has no other hope."

Once word got around that Ian was heading off to rescue Kia's sister, friends came to wish him well. Boyce told him, "If you want company, I'll come along."

"I'll need to travel light," Ian said. "But thanks for the offer. And I'll need you to stay and keep a watch over everyone." He looked straight at Heather as he said it, and it made her heart beat faster.

On the Sunday before Thanksgiving, during church, prayers were said for Ian to have a successful mission. There was always a possibility that something would go wrong and he wouldn't be able to get the baby out of Sudan.

Her health was fragile, and that was also worrisome. What if she was too ill to travel?

Once evening had fallen and Heather found herself finally alone with Ian, she was hesitant to say good night.

Ian told her, "The plan is to fly in Tuesday and back to Kampala on Wednesday. Dr. Henry will stay in Kampala, pick us up as soon as we land, and we'll come here on Thursday. We'll be home before you finish with that holiday dinner Jodene has planned."

"You think so?" Having him back on Thursday would be the best Thanksgiving blessing of all.

"Yes." He smiled at her, his face bathed in moonlight. "And while I'm gone, you keep working with Kia. Her sister will need her eventually . . . once her palate is repaired. They can live here with one of the overseers and be a family again."

The image of Kia and her sister staying at the children's home, growing up safe and happy within a new family unit, made Heather feel better. They deserved the chance. "All right, I'll keep trying to reach Kia. And I'll count the minutes until you return."

Ian was gazing down at her, and she couldn't

control the beating of her heart. She rose on tiptoe and kissed his cheek. He caught her elbows and pulled her closer. "You know, lass," he said, his voice but a whisper in the night, "I would not forgive myself if I went so far away and didn't do what I have wanted to do since I met you."

"And what would that be?" Her words trembled with emotion.

"I would like to kiss you, lass. If I have your permission, that is."

"Not only my permission," she said, "but my blessing."

He held her face between the palms of his hands and lowered his mouth to hers. His lips were soft, his kiss breathtaking. Heather felt her knees go weak while pinpricks of light spun behind her closed eyes. She poured her soul into the kiss, hoping to tell him how much she loved him, how much he meant to her.

He pulled away, his breath ragged, and wrapped his arms around her. He held her against his chest, and she felt the thumping of his heart. She buried her face in his shirt, clinging to him like a flower needing rain. He smoothed her hair, kissed the top of her head. "I love you, Heather. I didn't want to speak of it, but I can't help myself. I love you, and when

I come back, we must speak of it together." He lifted her chin, and she saw that his expression was worried. "You don't mind that I kissed you?"

She smiled then, unable to contain her joy. "One question: What took you so long to get around to it?"

16

On Monday afternoon, Heather went straight from the hospital to Jodene's, where she sat down under a tree in clear view of the house. She placed a ring of candy in plain sight and opened a book. Time passed. From the corner of her eye, she saw Kia looking at her through the window. Heather waited expectantly, but Kia never came outside. When Heather finally gave up, she left a piece of candy on the ground for the child.

On Tuesday, the same thing happened. On Wednesday, she heard a movement in the bushes and looked to see Kia peeking at her from the foliage. Heather made eye contact, smiled and beckoned to the child to come. "I have candy," Heather said, holding open her hand. Kia lowered her gaze, then ran back inside the house.

Disappointed, Heather returned to her room, where Ingrid was grading papers.

"No luck?" Ingrid asked.

"She was off like a scared rabbit," Heather said, flopping onto the sofa. "I'm not reaching this child."

"Do not blame yourself. You have worked hard and tried your best."

"But time's running out. We're leaving in two weeks." She looked at the calendar Debbie had hung on the wall. The days were marked off in red, with the second Thursday in December circled and labeled *D-Day*. That was the day the minivans would come to pick them up for the drive to Entebbe airport. There they would board the British Airways plane that would take them to London, and from London they would each go their separate ways. At least Heather would be traveling on with the other Americans into Miami's airport—her final destination. All in all, the trip took two long, hard days.

Heather fluffed a pillow and stretched out. "Maybe when Kia sees her sister she'll begin to trust us. I keep telling myself how hard it must be for her. Ripped from her home and her family and plopped down with a bunch of strangers. And white strangers to boot."

Ingrid smiled. "*Ja*, we are a scary bunch."

Heather laughed. "I'll miss you, Ingrid."

"Same here."

"Will you come again?"

"I am not sure. My parents want me to finish at the university. I need to get my teaching license; then I can come as a real teacher. How about you?"

"I want to come back, and I don't want to wait until next summer."

"Could it be because of Ian?"

Heather sighed. "He's returning to school in Scotland."

"But you will write each other, *ja*?"

"I'll sure write to *him*. We've been together every day for almost six months. I can't imagine getting up every day and not seeing him."

"I will write to Boyce too. I have grown accustomed to him and the funny things he says. I will miss him, too."

Heather sat up, hugging the pillow to herself. "I didn't come over here to fall in love. It just sort of happened."

Ingrid nodded and grinned. "*Ja*. Love is like that—it just happens. I wish you and Ian much luck and happiness."

Heather knew she would need it. Miami was

an ocean away from Scotland and a lifetime away from Africa.

On Thanksgiving Day, six Americans showed up at the Warrings'—all except for Dr. Henry, who had remained in Kampala to await Ian's return. Paul said, "Before we eat, we're going into Lwereo to watch a soccer game. I mean, what's Thanksgiving without football?"

When they arrived, the stands were already packed with local fans, people who'd walked for miles through the surrounding countryside to get to the game. Heather and her friends squeezed into the pack and quickly chose their favorites.

"I've got to go with the guys in red and white," Boyce said. "Alabama's colors."

"Good choice," Paul said. "That's the local team, and if you cheered for the other side, you could cause a riot."

The playing field was rough and uneven, the goals' nets had large holes in them, and the players spanned a wide age range, but the crowd treated the team as though it were composed of superstars playing in the World Cup. Heather tried to get interested, but her thoughts kept returning to Ian. She was seated beside Jodene, and during the half, she asked, "Has it been hard to raise your kids so far from home? I see how hard you work."

Jodene pushed back her blond hair and smiled. "I came from a family of seven brothers and sisters, and my folks own a buffalo ranch. We always had a generator for electricity because the winters are pretty harsh and the ranch is miles from anywhere. My whole family's used to hard work, so coming to Africa hasn't been that big an adjustment for me. Except that it's a whole lot warmer here," she added with a laugh. "Paul was raised the same way. We met in high school, and I never really cared about any other guy."

"Sounds romantic."

"I love him and we both love doing the Lord's work. Neither of us care that our kids are missing TV and car pools."

"I watch them playing with their friends. They seem very happy."

"They *are* happy. We'll go home because we want them to be educated in the States, but once they're grown, Paul and I will return to Africa. We love it here."

"I love it here too. And I always thought I could 'rough it' and not mind. My sister,

Amber, well, she'd have a hard time over here. No malls."

Jodene laughed. "There are certainly things I miss. Like snow. And cooking on a real stove."

"I—I guess I'm wondering if I really could give up the things I'm used to in order to live over here. Maybe I like my life of comfort more than I suspected."

"You're smart to examine your values before making a commitment to serve over here." Jodene toyed with her wedding ring, a simple gold band that caught the sun. "I'm guessing all this introspection has something to do with your feelings for Ian."

There was no use in denying it, Heather thought. "I *am* attracted to him," she confessed.

"As he is to you."

"You can tell?"

"Only every time he looks at you."

Jodene's comment made Heather feel good, as if an all-over glow had settled on her. "Well, we'll be going our separate ways in a couple of weeks, so that'll be the test."

"People do it all the time. They get separated by going away to college, or by being in the military, or by jobs in separate cities. If you and Ian want to keep the flame alive, you can do it."

Jodene paused. "What you have to ask yourself, Heather, is whether you *want* to do it. You're correct when you say this life is hard; it isn't for everyone, but the rewards are worth the sacrifice. And I'm telling you, a man like Ian will need one hundred percent dedication from the woman he chooses to work by his side. Anything less will rob you both. And make you both miserable."

Heather believed Jodene, and she wanted to talk more about it, but the teams trotted back onto the field, signaling the end of halftime, and Heather's questions were drowned in a sea of cheers.

After the game and back at the house, they all squeezed around the table—Paul's family and Heather and her friends. Plump roasted pigeons commanded the center of the table. "In place of turkey," Paul explained. "They're good."

Jodene also served large bowls of mashed sweet potatoes and green beans, platters of tomatoes, cucumbers, and lettuce, all fresh from her garden. "I saved the best for last," she said, setting down a bowl of cranberry sauce. "All the way from North Dakota, compliments of my mother."

Everyone stared at it for a long reverent minute.

"Here's my contribution," Heather said. The plate she set on the table held the contents of a full jar of peanut butter, beautifully sculpted to resemble a turkey.

"Wow," Boyce said. "Can I have a leg?"

He stretched out his hand, but Heather swatted it away. "Not so fast, buster. Where's your contribution?"

He grinned, reached into a knapsack, and pulled out an unopened bag of Oreos.

Debbie draped her hand across her forehead dramatically and pretended to swoon. "Be still, my heart."

The three Warring boys squealed in delight.

"They've had Oreos once before," Jodene said. "They've never forgotten."

With a flourish, Bob Hoover set a large box of Fruit Loops cereal on the table. "Barbara gave it to me when I left the ship. Part of our private stock."

The whole table applauded his generosity.

One by one, the others laid their food gifts on the table. A bag of microwave popcorn made everyone burst out laughing. "What were you thinking?" Debbie asked.

Jason Walsh, who was on the construction team, was the donor. "Hey, my mom packed it in my gear," he said. "Who knew I'd be coming to a place that didn't have stoves, much less microwaves?"

Once the table was fully laden and the laughter had died down, Paul said, "Let's thank the Lord for this wonderful bounty."

They all clasped hands and bowed their heads, and as Paul asked the blessing, Heather's heart swelled. She'd never known a better Thanksgiving. All the ski lodges in the West, all the fancy restaurants and banquets, had never been as wonderful as the simple pleasures of this table. For this table held not just food, but gifts gathered and offered from the heart of a family born not of flesh and blood but of service and commitment.

Once the table was cleared and board games were set up, Heather made up a plate for Kia, who was tucked securely under her cot. Heather tried to lure the child with Oreos and candy corn. Kia refused to take anything from Heather's hand, but once Heather set the treats down and scooted away, Kia quickly dragged them into her hiding place.

"There's too much going on," Jodene said, in

an effort to make Heather feel better. "She's probably confused by all the noise."

"Probably," Heather said, but she was disappointed.

Outside, night had fallen. Still in a mood of celebration, Paul turned on the gas generator so that they could see to play by electric light. The guests cheered, then took up a collection among themselves for Paul to buy more gas.

Heather thought of her family, wondered if they had gone skiing this year or opted to stay in Miami. She wondered if Amber was still on the outs with their dad, wondered if any of her friends had come home for the holiday from college. She wished she could call home, but of course, she couldn't.

"Checkmate," Boyce called out from a corner where he was playing chess with Bob.

Heather halfheartedly joined three others in a game of Monopoly. Dr. Henry and Ian should be returning at any time, and she was a bundle of nerves. She couldn't wait to throw her arms around Ian and tell him how much she'd missed him. Neither could she wait to see the baby and to show her to Kia. Perhaps seeing her rescued baby sister would be the break-through they needed with the child.

"You landed on my property," Debbie said,

intruding on Heather's thoughts. "Let's see, you owe me two thousand dollars."

Heather was paying off her debt when she heard a knock on the door.

"Enter!" Paul shouted.

The door swung open and Dr. Henry came inside. Alone.

The second she saw him, Heather's heart began to thud with dread. Dr. Henry's face was the color of chalk. Everyone in the room froze. Something was terribly wrong.

"What's happened?" Paul crossed the room with giant steps.

Dr. Henry looked at the group mutely, his gaze darting from face to face, his eyes tearing up. "There was an accident," he said finally. "Ian's plane has gone down. There are no survivors."

17

G*rief.*
    Heather discovered that it had a taste: bitter. It had a feeling: cold. It had a color: gray. Grief was an abyss devoid of dimensions, and she was its prisoner, trapped within its life-crushing walls with no way out. Days later, she could not recall the sequence of events from Thanksgiving night. She remembered only images, snatches of questions and answers, sounds of crying. She remembered only pain.

Dr. Henry's story lay broken and fragmented in her mind. A Mission Air pilot, too sick to fly his regular route. Cancellation of the Tuesday flight. Ian, desperate to make it into Sudan and rescue the baby. A deal struck with a pilot of a two-seater plane.

Dr. Henry saying, "Perhaps it's best to wait until the DC-3 can go."

Ian answering, "Ed's expecting me. I need to get the baby out."

"I hear there's fighting. It may not be safe."

"It won't get any safer."

Ian's plane lifting off with an engine that sputtered. Dr. Henry watching until it disappeared into a cloud bank. Hours later, a mayday call from the pilot. Radio static. Radio silence.

Reconnaissance flights. A burned-out hole in a grassy field. Smoking rubble. No survivors. They'd never even made it out of Uganda.

For Heather, it was the end of a world of color and light. It was the beginning of her immersion in grief. Cold, bitter, gray, bottomless grief.

"Stay the night here," Jodene had urged. "You don't have to be alone."

"I'm not alone. I have my friends." Heather's teeth chattered, she was so cold.

Ingrid, Debbie, and Cynthia surrounded her all that night, and all the next day, too. They wept with her. And Boyce, Miguel, and Patrick came and took turns holding her, rocking her, weeping with her.

"He was my friend," Boyce said, his eyes red-rimmed. "I can't believe I'll never see him again."

"Not in this life," Patrick said. "In the next life."

Heather wanted to scream. She wanted Ian in *this* life. She wanted him now. She wanted to touch him, feel his skin on hers, hear him call her lass. It wasn't fair. *It wasn't fair.*

She knew that time passed because her friends told her when it was time to eat, covered her with a blanket, and told her when it was time to sleep. She did not go to the hospital to work. She could not be around death one more minute.

Dr. Gallagher came and talked to her, offered her some pills that made her sleep. He could give her nothing for the pain inside her soul. " 'The Lord gave, and the Lord has taken away,' " he quoted from the Book of Job. " 'May the name of the Lord be praised.' "

Heather tuned him out. God was cruel. He had no mercy. He had no pity. He had allowed Ian to vanish on a grassy African plain in a ball of fire. God could have prevented it but had not. Why?

One afternoon, she became aware that her roommates were packing. "We must go home on Thursday," Ingrid told Heather tenderly, as one might address a child. "We are packing up your things for you. We'll take care of every-thing. Do not concern yourself."

Inertia ruled her. Leaving seemed impossi-ble, requiring more energy than she possessed. How could she possibly make it across two continents and an ocean? Listlessly she walked to Jodene's. But once she arrived, she couldn't force herself to step inside the house where grief had first assaulted her. The house would be filled with the sounds of the Warring chil-dren. Their laughter. Sweet, adorable, innocent children. With hardly a clue of the cruel sor-rows life held.

She eased her back down the trunk of a tree, raised her knees, folded her arms, buried her face in her arms. Sobs racked her, heaving, gag-ging sobs that left her weak, as if she were be-ing turned inside out.

She heard a noise, a rustling. Choking back her tears, she looked up. Beside her, in the dry dirt, Kia sat, staring at her through large brown eyes. Too startled to move, Heather let out a long, shuddering breath, half gasp, half moan. She braced her back on the tree trunk and stretched out her cramped legs. Kia did not scamper away. Instead, she lifted her hand and, with a feathery touch, ran her fingers down Heather's damp cheek.

"He's gone, Kia," Heather whispered in a cracked, thick voice. "My Ian's gone." She knew the girl couldn't understand her words, but it didn't matter. She had to say them, taste the finality of them.

Kia crept forward. Wordlessly she curled into a tight ball, lay down on the earth, rested her head in Heather's lap. Heather stroked the child's head, the smooth, soft skin of her face, the tightly curled hair. "You know, don't you, little Kia? You know how bad it hurts."

The hot sun beat down from the blue sky, on ground tufted with patches of green, on two people from different universes. "We're connected now, aren't we, Kia?" Heather whispered. In a cruel and hateful twist of fate, with a bridge of tears, grief had bound them together. Here, in the heat of the day, they had been joined, not by overtures of friendship, not by bribes of candy, but by loss. The loss of Kia's mother, of home. The loss of Ian McCollum, of love.

Heather's sobs quieted as she continued to stroke the child's head. The air settled around them heavily, like a drugged sleep. And Kia's arms drifted around Heather's waist, holding on. Holding on.

* * *

"You can't be serious, Heather. I won't allow it." Dr. Henry's expression looked both alarmed and haggard.

Heather was standing in his room, where his gear lay stacked, ready for the pull out in the morning. "But I *am* serious," she said calmly. "I'm going to get Kia's sister."

"But there's no time left. We're leaving."

"The baby still needs rescuing. I'm not leaving until I finish the job Ian set out to do."

Dr. Henry raked his hand through his white hair. "No. No, you can't do this. It's noble of you, but—"

"I mean no disrespect, sir, but I'm eighteen. I'm an adult. I can do what I want."

"I'm responsible for you." He shook his head stubbornly. "Your family is expecting you to get off that plane in Miami. What am I supposed to say to them?"

"This won't take me but a few days. I can catch a plane in Entebbe next week, after I bring the baby back. Tell my parents I'll call them from London. My sister, too; Amber is my sister. They'll understand." She didn't know if that was true, and she didn't care. After days of despair, she'd discovered purpose. She wasn't going to let it evaporate. Ian had always told her to help one by one. This was now her mission.

"But you don't understand what it's like going into a camp." Dr. Henry's voice turned pleading. "The camps can be chaotic, perhaps even unsafe. I can't come with you. I'm responsible for the others."

"I'm not asking you to come with me. I'm going by myself." She'd never dream of taking him away from his duty to the rest of the team. Bob Hoover was already gone, on his way to reboard the Mercy Ship on the way to North Africa, to be with his family.

"Who will be there to protect you?"

"Dr. Wilson will be there. Paul talked to him on the radio last night. He said Kia's sister's still alive." Her heart was hammering now, her body running on pure adrenaline. She hadn't slept all night, not since she'd devised the plan.

"Someone else will go—"

"No." She interrupted him. "There's no one else. I'm going. Paul will drive me into Kampala on Tuesday. I'll catch the Mission Air flight. I'll go to the camp, pick up the baby, catch a flight back. Two days is all it will take."

"Heather, please, be reasonable. It isn't safe."

She shook her head, spilling her hair from its

clip. Tension filled the room. "I can do this, Dr. Henry. I *must* do it. For Kia. For Ian, too. Try and understand. . . . I'm not afraid."

"You should be afraid," he countered. "These are dangerous times."

Suddenly, the image of a long-dead Persian queen, the Jewish Queen Esther, who had spoken up for her people, rose like a specter in Heather's memory, and she recalled Ian's voice.

At the door, she turned and said, "Well, Dr. Henry, if I perish, I perish."

Dawn was breaking when Heather, Jodene, and Paul helped the group load up two minivans for the drive to Entebbe airport.

"I wish you were coming with us," Cynthia said, chewing on her lip.

"I won't be far behind you." Heather gave her friend a hug.

For the most part, the group had understood and supported her decision to stay behind and go after Kia's sister. But now, saying goodbye, Heather realized how much she was going to miss everybody.

"It won't be the same without you with us," Boyce told her.

"Just don't pig out on peanut butter when you reach civilization."

"Never happen."

Ingrid kissed both of Heather's cheeks. "Take care of yourself."

"I will."

Boyce reached into his backpack and hauled out a gray sweatshirt with the words *University of Alabama* written in crimson block letters. "Wear this." He draped it over her shoulders and tied the sleeves together. "So they'll know what tribe you're from."

Heather smiled, squeezed his arm. "You'd better write to me when we're both home."

She stepped back and watched as her friends climbed into the vans. Dr. Henry was the last one to board. "I—I'll pray for you," he said.

She stood on tiptoe and hugged him. "I'm going to be fine. You'll see."

The vans slowly backed up, made a wide turn in the open yard, and started toward the road. The sound of the engines broke the stillness, while beams from the headlights bounced up and down, shooting streams of light into the darkness. Heather watched until the taillights were swallowed up in the distance. She felt Jodene slip her arm around her shoulders.

"Come on," Jodene said. "Let's go get breakfast. We've got a lot to accomplish if you're to leave for the camp on Tuesday."

Heather nodded. She felt momentarily lost, a stranger in a strange land. But the feeling passed quickly, and she hurried into the house just as the sun flared over the tops of the trees.

18

"Things are heating up in Sudan again, but stay with the Mission Air people and you should be fine." Paul Warring stuffed clothes into a duffel bag while he talked to Heather. He was driving her to the airfield in Kampala in the morning. He'd wait until she returned from Sudan with the baby.

"The Mission Air pilots are usually retired military," Jodene added. "Many have been missionaries themselves, so they're sympathetic to our work."

"In the old days," Paul continued, "it was the only way they could get around Africa. You've seen the roads, so you know what I'm talking about. A family could get stuck in the bush for months, so men took flying lessons in order to move around more freely."

"What about a ticket?" Heather asked.

"You'll buy it tomorrow at the airstrip. And you can pay for it with your credit card."

Heather remembered being surprised at the large number of banks and ATM machines in Kampala. But with the number of international travelers coming through Africa, it made sense. The universal use of credit cards made purchasing things a snap for tourists.

"How much money should I take with me?" she asked.

Paul and Jodene exchanged looks. Jodene went to the closet, took down a pouch from the top shelf, and unzipped it. She reached in, pulled out several coins, and plopped them into Heather's hand. "Take these."

"I have money. I don't want to take yours."

"You don't have these," Jodene said.

Heather turned the shiny coins over in her hand. "What are they?"

"South African Krugerrands—coins made of gold bullion. We keep them on hand in case of emergencies. In case something terrible happens to Uganda currency, well . . . people will always take gold in payment."

"I have American dollars—" Heather began.

"If you run into any trouble, all paper currency may be useless. *Goldspeke* is the universal language, trust me. Use it if you need it. You can pay us back when you get to the States."

Heather took the gold, knowing its value. "If I use any, you'll get them back with interest."

"We can't put a price on the baby's life, now, can we?" Jodene said. "Keep them close to your body at all times. When I travel, I put the coins in a pouch pinned to the inside of my bra."

"And don't let go of your passport, either," Paul said. "Keep it with you at all times."

As the seriousness of her undertaking began to sink in, Heather felt growing apprehension. This would be the only attempt to bring Kia's sister out of Sudan. If Heather failed, the baby would surely die. Heather knew that even if her mission was successful, there were no guarantees. The baby's cleft palate must be repaired, and Heather didn't know whether Dr. Gallagher's team could perform the delicate surgery in their less-than-state-of-the-art hospital. Everything would have to go perfectly if the baby and Kia were to be reunited and live happily ever after, Heather told herself.

As for Kia, she still preferred the underside of her cot to the run of the house, but she did slip out more frequently. Especially when Heather showed up at the house. Kia took candy from

Heather's hand whenever it was offered and had taken to following Jodene around the yard as she hung out laundry. Kia had still not spoken.

Jodene said, "You'll be taking boxes of medical supplies on the plane with you. That will be your entry ticket into the country. At the airport, you'll hand over the supplies to Ed and he'll hand you the baby. Then get back on the plane. These pilots don't stay on the ground long. They load up and return ASAP."

Paul took hold of Heather's shoulders. "In and out, Heather. That's the plan. Hold your head up and act confident. You'll do fine."

Heather offered a weak smile. "That's my line, remember?"

The three of them laughed. Jodene sobered and looked Heather in the eye. "Listen . . . we'll be holding a prayer vigil for you. From the time you leave until the minute you return, someone here will be praying for you. We'll pray that God's angels go with you and bring you and Kia's sister back to us safely."

Angels. Heather would never have thought to enlist the aid of angels. She couldn't help wondering where they might have been when Ian made his journey, but she didn't say anything. It hurt too much to even think about

Ian. She turned to Jodene and smiled with as much confidence as she could muster. "Thank you. I appreciate all the help I can get."

Early Tuesday morning, with the Ugandan children from the home surrounding them in the front yard, Heather climbed into Paul's Jeep, which was piled with boxes full of supplies. She wore an armband with a bright red cross emblazoned on it, a plain black baseball cap, sunglasses on a cord around her neck, and a small knapsack that fastened around her waist. "Travel light," Paul had said.

Jodene leaned into the Jeep, kissed her husband, and squeezed Heather's hand. "Go with God."

Paul backed the Jeep and pulled onto the rutted road. Heather hunkered down, folded her arms, and pulled the cap low over her eyes. The noise of the wind made it impossible to talk, so they rode silently into Kampala. Every mile of the way, Heather looked for some sign that angels were following them, but she saw nothing except charcoal fires beside the road as people stirred to start another day of hunting up food to fill their empty stomachs.

The Mission Air airfield was simply a grassy expanse with a couple of low buildings and a single runway. By noon, the plane was ready to go. Paul hugged her. "I'll be here when you return."

"Well, at least you won't be hard to spot," she said, looking around the nearly empty room that served as the passenger terminal.

Heather walked out onto the field and up the steps into the belly of the propeller plane, which looked like something she'd seen in an old war movie. Seating consisted of two long metal benches bolted along the interior walls. Seat belts clamped on from the wall behind the benches, fastening over her shoulders and around her waist.

Her fellow passengers were men—two World Health Organization representatives from Great Britain and several Africans. The pilot came aboard and welcomed them, saying the flight time was approximately an hour and that they expected no turbulence. He and a copilot entered the cabin, and Heather glimpsed a maze of gauges and switches. With the cargo in the hold and the passengers loaded, the plane's engines roared to life. Heather twisted to see the spinning propellers through the porthole-sized window.

The plane began its slow roll down the landing strip, gathered speed, and lifted sharply, clearing the tops of the trees surrounding the field. Heather's heart pounded as she waited for the plane to level off. Commercial airplanes made it appear so effortless, but this plane seemed to groan and clank like a tired knight in rusty armor.

The engine noise filled the cabin with a dull roar. The air was warm and close. She was glad the flight wouldn't take too long. When finally the plane began to descend, she braced for the touchdown. She felt relief when the plane rolled to a stop and the door opened. She descended the stairs into blinding heat. She put on her sunglasses and walked into a small building, trying to act confident and self-assured.

Heather fell into a short line to clear customs, which consisted of two armed soldiers checking passports. They looked her over as they stamped her passport. The automatic weapons in their hands were black, with tubular steel stocks and barrels. Leather straps held the guns across their shoulders.

On the other side of customs, she went to where the cargo had been piled on the cement floor. Her boxes were clearly marked with bright red crosses, but when she approached, a soldier stepped in front of her. He held his rifle at his waist and gestured for her to stand aside. He said something to her, but she couldn't understand a word.

"Medicine," she said in English. "For doctors."

The soldier glared and his weapon came up. Heather thought she might pass out from sheer terror.

"Can I help here?" A man stepped between them. He said something to the soldier in Swahili, and the man lowered his gun and stepped away from Heather and the boxes. Heather stood frozen in place. Her rescuer was in his thirties. He held out his hand. "Ed Wilson," he said. "You must be Heather."

She nodded, not trusting her voice.

"Let's get you outside and into the Jeep. I'll send my driver, Barry, in to get the supplies." He spoke to the guard, took Heather's elbow, and walked her out of the building. A Jeep with a Sudanese driver waited at the roadside.

As she folded herself into the back of the vehicle, Ed said, "Sorry I wasn't here when the plane touched down. We left in plenty of time, but some farmer decided to herd his cows across the road and held us up for twenty minutes."

"It's all right." Heather found her voice. "I know all about those cows."

Barry was loading the boxes in the back. Ed said, "I'm really sorry about what happened to that Ian fellow. Did you know him?"

A sharp pain sliced through her heart. "Yes," she said. "I knew him well."

"Then I'm doubly sorry. Rescuing this baby—we've come to call her Alice—hasn't been easy."

Heather looked around the Jeep. "Speaking of the baby, where is she? Paul told me you'd have her with you and all I had to do was get back on board the plane with her."

"Well, it may not be that simple."

Heather's stomach did a flip-flop. "Why not?"

"The rebels have gotten aggressive again. They routed a village less than twenty-five kilometers east of here. The military is crawling all over the place, which means they've clamped down on travel."

"Are you saying I got in but maybe I can't get out?"

"Yes, *you* can leave. In fact, that plane's returning to Kampala in fifteen minutes. It might be best if you left with it."

"But what about the baby?"

"You can't take her with you."

Heather couldn't believe what she was hearing. She couldn't have come so far to fail! "I'm not leaving without her."

A soldier began walking toward them, waving them off with his rifle. Barry started the Jeep. Ed said, "Let's get out of here."

They drove off in a cloud of dust.

"Where are we going?" Heather asked.

"Into a town near here, to a hotel where most of us health workers and foreigners stay. If you're here more than a few weeks, it gets old living in tents at the camp, so the hotel becomes our permanent quarters. The baby's there with Sister Louise, the nun who's been taking care of her."

The Jeep bumped along a rutted road, swerving to miss a child playing in the middle. Heather swallowed hard against a rising tide of fear and watched as the airfield, and her means of escape, shrank in the distance behind her.

The town was a dusty collection of buildings—shops, a gas station, and the hotel. Men lounged lazily against walls and along the roadside. Chickens ran in circles, pecking at the hard-packed dirt.

The hotel rose only two stories and looked run-down. Chipped pink paint flaked off the walls. Intense sunlight gleamed off a roof made of tin. A courtyard held small tables and wooden chairs, where several people sat sipping coffee. Inside the lobby were a desk with a clerk sitting idly, a broken-down couch, and a TV. Ed nodded at the clerk, who waved. Ed told Heather, "My room's on the second floor."

They climbed a flight of stairs and went to a battered door. Ed knocked lightly, then opened it with a key. Across the small room, a nun sat by an open window, reading a book. She rose and smiled. "So glad you're here, Ed. Is this Heather?"

Heather greeted her and looked at the bed, where a baby slept on a folded blanket on a mattress that sagged in the center. The room felt stifling, and noise from the street drifted upward.

"Still sleeping?" Ed asked.

"Like an angel."

Heather tiptoed over and peered down. Alice lay on her back, her small fists tightly closed. Her dark face, marred by the birth defect, looked peaceful. Instantly tears welled in Heather's eyes. She thought of all the people who'd stepped in to try and save her. She thought of Kia. They were tiny, defenseless children, caught in a terrible drama of politics and death that was not of their making. All they had in the world was each other.

Just then Barry eased into the room. "He's downstairs," Barry told Ed.

"Heather, come with me. We're going to talk to a man about a plane."

Down in the courtyard, Barry, Ed, and Heather took seats at a table with a small, dark-skinned man whose gaze kept darting around the open spaces. Barry made introductions, calling the man Mr. Oundo, Odo for short. "Sometimes Odo flies cargo out of the area for us," Ed explained to Heather. "In spite of difficulties."

Odo sat stonily. Ed began to talk to him in Swahili, but Odo kept shaking his head.

A man brought them a tray with coffee cups and set it on the table. Heather's stomach churned.

More discussion, but still Odo remained adamant. "Too dangerous," he said in English, surprising Heather.

"Does he understand English?" she asked.

Odo's gaze darted to her face. "I speak English," he said with an odd accent. "The problem is, I do not wish to risk my plane at this time." He started to stand up.

Heather felt as if she was going to be sick. He couldn't just walk away and leave her and the baby stranded. He couldn't! "Wait! Just a minute. Please . . . I have something to say. Will you listen?"

19

Looking reluctant, Odo settled back into his chair. "I tell you, it is too dangerous to fly. We can be shot down . . . like birds by a hunter."

Silently Heather tuned her mind to the only ear she believed could hear her. She prayed, *"Dear God, help me."* Gathering her courage, she said to Odo, "I appreciate your caution, Mr. Odo, but I really need to return to Kampala. Will you consider this?" She reached inside her shirt and extracted a small cloth pouch. She opened it discreetly and poured five gold coins into her hand.

Odo's eyes widened, then narrowed.

"If you take me and the baby to Kampala today, I'll give you these." She placed three of the coins in a line on the table so that they could catch the sun. "And when you come back, Ed will give you these." She handed the other two to Ed. "Plus," she said, watching Odo lick his lips nervously, "once the baby and I are in Kampala safely, my friend at the airport will give you two more. That's seven gold Kruger-rands, Mr. Odo. Just for a short one-hour flight. What do you say?"

Heather's heart was thundering so hard in her chest, she was afraid everyone at the table could hear it. The air hung like a curtain, moved only by sounds from the street—the bleat of a goat, the *ding* of a bicycle bell moving past. Sweat trickled between her shoulder blades.

Odo reached out, but Heather covered the row of coins with her palm. "I'll give them to you tonight," she said. "After the baby and I are aboard the plane."

Time seemed to crawl as the man considered Heather's offer. An eternity later, he said, "I will take you." He turned to Ed, "Be at the field—you know which one I mean—at the hour of four in the morning. We must leave before the sun rises. If you are not there, I will not wait for you."

Heather watched Odo walk away, and she slumped in her chair.

"Let's go upstairs," Ed said. "Too many ears around here."

In the room, Alice still slept while Sister Louise watched over her. Ed studied Heather appreciatively, then shook his head. "That was beautiful, Heather. I was getting nowhere with all my pleas for humanitarian causes. He wasn't about to budge, either. Then you pulled the golden rabbit out of the hat and changed everything." A grin split his face. "Where'd you get the coins, anyway?"

Heather grinned ruefully. "An angel gave them to me."

He laughed out loud. "When I first saw you, I thought, 'What is Paul thinking, sending her? She's just a kid!' But you're no kid, Heather. You handled yourself like a real professional."

She felt as if he'd just held out a golden scepter to her. "I couldn't let our only chance for getting Alice out of here walk away. I knew I had to persuade him somehow. And my father always says money talks. So I thought I'd let it say a few things in Alice's favor." Heather sat cautiously on the bed, being careful not to wake the baby.

"Well, we're not out of the woods yet," Ed told her. "You'd best stretch out and catch some sleep. We'll have to leave around three A.M. in order to get to where Odo stashes his plane."

"All right," Heather said. She lay down

obediently, positive that she could never fall asleep, but within minutes, her eyes shut and sleep claimed her.

Heather woke to the sound of the baby's crying. Night had fallen, and a kerosene lamp lit the room. "What's wrong?" she asked groggily.

"Alice is hungry," Sister Louise said. "Come, watch how I prepare her food . . . in case you must do it."

Heather scooted off the bed. "Where are Ed and Barry?" The room was empty except for the three of them.

"Downstairs getting dinner. You should eat too."

"I'm not hungry. What time is it, anyway?"

"After nine," Sister Louise said. "Now, bring my little Alice over here."

Heather lifted the baby and walked to the dresser, where a small pan of water boiled atop a can of Sterno. "I'm saving the bottled water for you to take with you," Sister Louise said.

Heather watched as the nun poured a fine powder into the pan and stirred it until it cooled. "You want to keep it soupy," the nun said. "Like thin cream of wheat."

Next the nun picked up a large-gauge syringe from which the needle had been removed. She dipped the opening of the syringe into the gruel-like fluid, drew it into the barrel, and held it up to the baby's lips. Alice's oddly shaped little mouth grabbed the end greedily and sucked as Sister Louise eased down the plunger. "Now you try it." She handed the feeding syringe to Heather.

It took Heather a few tries, but she got the hang of it, and soon Alice had been fed. Heather held the baby on her shoulder and patted her back until she burped.

"Excellent," Sister Louise said. "We'll feed her again right before you leave."

The nun packed the small bag of powder in Heather's knapsack, along with a bottle of water.

Ed returned, bringing Heather a plate of *matoke* and rice. "It's all the kitchen had," he said apologetically.

"It's all right," Heather told him.

She ate. And then they waited.

Heather dozed, but at last Ed shook her shoulder and said, "Time to get going."

She gathered up her belongings while Sister Louise fed Alice again. Once she was finished, the nun held Alice close and said, "You be good for Heather." With tears in her eyes, she placed the baby in Heather's arms.

Wrapped tightly in a blanket, Alice seemed small and light to Heather, and she smelled of the protein powder she'd been eating. "She'd never have made it without you," Heather told the nun.

Sister Louise sniffed and stepped away.

"One more thing," Ed said. He took a small vial and a syringe from his pocket. "I'm going to sedate her. We want her to sleep for the trip."

Heather watched as he drew a few cc's of fluid into the syringe. He unwound the swaddled baby and stuck the needle into the fleshy part of her thigh. Alice wailed, but minutes later, her eyelids drooped and she slept.

Ed pressed the medication into Heather's hand. "In case she wakes."

Heather nodded, praying she wouldn't have to give Alice another shot, that they'd be back in Kampala before the sedative wore off—but also grateful for the weeks she'd worked at the Ugandan hospital, which had given her the skills to do it if she must.

"That's it," Ed said, glancing around the room. "Barry's waiting in the Jeep."

Holding Alice close against her chest, and without a backward glance, Heather followed Ed down the stairs and out into the darkness.

* * *

Without a moon, the night seemed impenetrable. The road was little more than a rutted trail, and Barry drove without headlights as much as possible. Although she'd wedged herself in the back of the Jeep, Heather bounced painfully. Her shoulders ached and her lower back screamed for relief. Sedating the baby had been a good idea. Alice slept peacefully, unmindful of the jarring.

"You okay back there?" Ed called to her from the passenger's seat.

Heather gritted her teeth. "Sure . . . but I'll probably need a kidney transplant when this ride's over."

"Not much farther," Ed told her.

The trail went up, then down. The Jeep slowed, then sped up. Heather completely lost any sense of direction. Eventually, Barry pulled into a stand of scrub trees and turned off the engine. Quiet descended. Slowly Heather's hearing adjusted to the hum of insects, then a faraway *pop, pop, pop.*

"Gunfire," Ed whispered. He stood up in the Jeep, peering off into the darkness. "Let's hope Mr. Odo's greed is greater than his fear."

Barry flashed the Jeep's headlights in three

short bursts. Heather's heart caught in her throat. What if the man didn't come? What if the rebels found them before they could leave?

From across the field came an answering burst of light.

"We're on," Ed said. He helped Heather from the Jeep, and while Barry stayed with the vehicle, the two of them ran, hunched over, across the field under the cover of night.

Mr. Odo, dressed in fatigues, waited for them. "Hurry," he said. He pulled branches off a large heap. Underneath was the smallest plane Heather had ever seen. He opened a door, helped her in with the baby, dropped a harness-style seat belt over her shoulders, and snapped it.

Ed reached in the window and took Heather's hand. "We'll pray for you and the little one."

"What about you and Barry? Will you be all right?"

"Don't worry about us. We're going away from the gunfire. We'll be in the camp reporting for duty at our regular time in the morning."

"Thank you, Ed, and tell Barry thanks too."

Ed moved back until Heather lost sight of him. Now she and Alice were together, but alone, with only a mercenary to shuttle them to freedom. She rotated her shoulders to ease her tension.

Odo settled in the pilot's seat and flipped switches, and the engine sputtered to life. To Heather it sounded like a broken lawn mower. "It can get off the ground, right?" she asked.

"Flies like a bird, lady."

She almost told him that penguins were birds too but couldn't fly two feet. Instead, she snuggled the sleeping baby closer and prayed.

Odo pulled on the throttle and the plane moved forward, bumping across the grassy field. It gathered speed; then just when Heather thought they'd crash into a clump of trees, the plane magically lifted. The darkness seemed to swallow them. She caught glimpses of the ground falling away behind them. "Pretty low, aren't we?"

"Have to fly beneath the radar," Odo said. "If the military sees us, they will shoot us down." He glanced over at her. "Don't worry, lady . . . we'll make it."

In the distance, she saw a reddish aura rising into the sky from the land. "What's that?"

"Another battle. A village burning."

Heather's stomach tightened, and she steeled

herself against images of screaming, dying people.

"Sit back," Odo said. "I'll radio Kampala soon to let the tower know we're coming in."

She reached into her pocket and removed the pouch. "Your money, Mr. Odo. I make good on my promises."

His fingers closed around the fabric, he jiggled it and, hearing the coins clink together, said, "You've paid much for so small a child, lady. And an ugly child, too. I do not know what makes her so valuable."

"I don't expect that you would, Mr. Odo. It's just that when I look at her, I don't see her body. I see her soul. And *that's* more valuable than all the gold in the world."

20

"It's sure taking us a long time to get to Kampala." Heather broke the silence between her and Odo. "The flight I took into Sudan only took an hour." It seemed to her that they were getting no closer to their destination, and the drone of the plane's engine was giving her a headache. The cockpit of the plane was so small, there was no place to rest her cramped arms. A few inches forward and she'd hit the instrument panel.

"Because we must fly lower, it takes longer to get where we're going. And my plane does not fly so fast. Don't worry, lady, Odo will get you where you want to go."

Heather gritted her teeth and tried to calm her nerves. Ever since she'd climbed aboard Odo's small plane, she'd been unable to forget Ian's fateful flight. It wasn't so much the radar and gunfire that frightened her as the memory of Ian and what had happened to him in a small aircraft such as this. Even the night at sea when the storm had raged had not seemed as long as this one. But that night Ian had been with her. She longed to have him with her now.

"Look," Odo said, pointing out the windshield.

To the east, the black layer of night was peeling back. The horizon resembled a cosmic sundae—a layer of pink, then one of gray, then a layer of blue black, and stars twinkling overhead like sugar sprinkles. "It's beautiful," she said.

For the first time Odo laughed. "Not at the sky, lady. Look at the ground." In the distance she saw flickering clusters of electric lights. "That is Kampala. Once again, Odo has cheated death." He sounded euphoric, making her realize how genuinely hazardous their trip had been. "I'll call the tower and get cleared for landing. What do you think of my little plane now?"

Relief flooded through Heather. "I think it's a wonderful little plane. The best."

"And Odo, your pilot?"

She sent him a sidelong glance. "The next

time I make a run for my life, I'll know who to call."

Still laughing, Odo picked up a hand mike and, in Swahili, requested permission to land.

True to his word, Paul was waiting for her at the terminal. "When you didn't get off that Mission Air return flight, I almost got physically sick," he told her after she'd cleared customs. "Then the news reports came about renewed fighting." He looked worried and haggard. "I knew you were with Ed and that helped calm my fears some, but, Heather, I've never been so glad to see anyone in my life."

"Same here. I would have called, but . . ." She shrugged.

"Yeah . . . no phones," Paul finished for her.

Heather turned the baby so Paul could see her. "Meet Alice."

"Hey, little girl," he said, taking the sleeping baby while Heather stretched her aching arms. "And this is my pilot, Mr. Oundo," she added. Odo had walked up after clearing customs.

Odo shook Paul's hand. "Thanks for getting them here," Paul said.

"We hid from the radar. It was a lucky trip."

Heather reached into her shirt pocket and pulled out another small pouch. "I believe I owe you this." Odo looked surprised. "Well, I couldn't give you *all* the money at once, now, could I?" she said.

He laughed heartily, as if she'd played some joke on him. "You are an okay person, lady. Very clever. Like a fox."

Once he'd walked away, Paul said. "I want to hear all about your journey, but first, are you hungry?"

"Famished. But is there anyplace where we can eat real food? I don't think I can manage one more plate of *matoke*."

He took her to a restaurant inside the Hilton Hotel in the heart of Kampala. Polished marble floors gleamed in the morning sunlight. Plush sofas and deep, cushy chairs graced the lobby. "I had no idea a place like this existed," Heather said, awestruck as she gazed around the lush atrium.

"You don't think wealthy tourists are going to stay at the Namirembe Guest House, do you?" Paul asked with a laugh. "I brought Jodene here for our anniversary. As missionaries, we're used to spartan lives, but every once in a while, we have to splurge."

The hotel was as opulent as any Heather had ever seen in the States, and she felt almost decadent sitting in such comfort, but after months of living in the bush, she couldn't get over how good it felt. She thought of the people she knew back home who honestly believed it was their lawful right to have running water and electricity. She hoped that when she did return to the States, she never took the blessings of her life for granted again.

"Let's eat," she said, picking up the menu and skimming it hungrily. Just then, Alice, who was lying on the seat of the booth beside Heather, began to stir and whimper. Heather lowered the menu and sighed. "After I feed Alice, that is."

It was midafternoon when they pulled through the gate of the children's home and into Paul's front yard. Jodene, the boys, and several of the older girls poured out of the house, everyone talking and laughing and raising their hands in gratitude. "When the two of you didn't get back last night, we feared the worst," Jodene said, hugging Heather. "Thank God you're all right. What happened?"

"I'll tell you everything, but I must do something first."

"Of course. You must be exhausted. Why not take a warm bath, grab a nap? We can talk at dinner tonight."

"That's not what I want to do first," Heather said. "Where's Kia?"

The little girl was staring from the window at the commotion in the yard. Heather lifted Alice off the Jeep's seat. The baby had slept off the sedative completely, and her dark eyes looked bright with curiosity.

Heather carried Alice into the house, and Jodene followed. Paul waited in the yard with the others. "Kia," Heather called softly. "I've brought you a present. Would you like to come see what it is?"

Heather crouched down, holding the bundled baby outstretched. Alice made a squeaking sound. Kia inched forward. "Come on," Heather said. "I've brought this present from far, far away . . . just for you." While she was certain Kia couldn't understand her words, Heather believed she could appreciate the softly urging, gentle tone.

Kia crept closer, until she was standing just out of arm's reach. She craned her neck to see inside the blanket.

"Just a little closer." Heather's heart hammered.

Kia dropped to her knees, leaned over the baby. She looked down. She looked up. Her eyes were round as saucers, and her mouth formed a perfect *o*. Then a smile, as bright as a thousand-watt bulb, spread across her face. She stretched out a finger and gently poked Alice's cheek, ran her fingertip across the baby's misshaped mouth.

"*Dada*," Kia said.

Goose bumps rose on Heather's arms. Kia had spoken.

" 'Sister,' " Jodene translated. "*Dada* is Swahili for 'sister.' "

"Yes . . . *dada*," Heather repeated, placing Alice in Kia's little arms. "Kia's *dada*. She's come back to you."

"We're going to miss you." Jodene came into the room where Heather was packing up the last of her things for her trip home.

It was days later, and Paul would be driving Heather first thing in the morning into Entebbe, where she'd catch the plane for London. "I'm going to miss everybody." She glanced around the room that had been her home for almost three months. While she missed her roommates, she'd been glad to have it to herself since returning from Sudan.

"Anytime you want to come back, you're welcome, you know."

"It may be sooner than you think. I talked to Dr. Gallagher and he's hesitant to attempt the surgery Alice needs. Says she really needs it done by a plastic surgeon with pediatric instruments." Heather flashed Jodene a smile. "I happen to know two very good plastic surgeons."

"Do you think your parents would come all this way to operate on one small baby?"

"We'll see." Heather was already plotting her strategy.

Jodene sat on the bed. "You know, there is one thing I want to talk to you about." She paused. "That's Ian."

The mention of his name raised the old, familiar hurt in Heather's heart. "What about him?"

"You haven't truly had time to mourn for him, you know. Once you're home, take time to grieve."

Tears misted Heather's eyes. "I'll always grieve for him. I still can't believe he's gone."

Jodene reached into the pocket of her skirt. "I have something for you." She handed Heather a book. "I found it in Ian's things when I bundled them up for Dr. Henry to give to Ian's father."

"What is it?"

"The journal Ian started for this trip. I

believe it belongs with you because your name is on almost every page. I only skimmed it, but when I realized what it was, well . . . I knew you should have it. Let's call it an early Christmas gift."

Heather ran her palm over the cool, smooth leather. "Thank you," she whispered.

"Read it when you have the strength. No hurry . . . you have a lifetime. He loved you, Heather. But he loved God, too."

Jodene left her, and Heather sat staring down at the book in her lap. *An early Christmas present.* Heather had forgotten about Christmas. At home, her family would be Christmas shopping. Familiar carols would be filling the air, and trees and houses would be decorated. On Christmas Eve she would go to the midnight candlelight service. And just before the congregation sang "Silent Night," the minister would read her favorite passage from Isaiah: "For to us a child is born, to us a son is given. . . . And he will be called Wonderful Counselor, Mighty God, Everlasting Father, Prince of Peace."

The miracle of Christmas was the gift of a child. The miracle of her time in Uganda was giving two children back to each other. Heather would remember forever the look of pure joy on Kia's face when she first saw her sister.

Had it been any different two thousand years earlier when shepherds, sent by a chorus of angels, came to gaze upon that other child? She didn't think so.

Heather wiped a trail of tears from her cheek and opened the book in her lap. On the first page, Ian had written:

The Journal of Ian Douglas McCollum

On page two, she read:

June
I met a girl today. She was looking out over the sea, tears clouding her blue eyes. She was the prettiest girl I've ever seen. And surely God has sent her, for her heart is kind and full of love. And together, we will sail to Africa. . . .

Angel of Hope

To my beloved Mother, who was
called home by the angels, and is now
reunited with my father forever.
See you both when I get there.

Bebe Gallagher
March 1, 1912–September 19, 1999

*"The LORD does not look at the things man looks
at. Man looks at the outward appearance, but the
LORD looks at the heart."*
1 Samuel 16:7
(NIV)

*"If only for this life we have hope in Christ, we are
to be pitied more than all men."*
1 Corinthians 15:19
(NIV)

1

January

Dear Heather,

I hope this letter finds you well rested after your big adventure here in Africa. I also hope you had a blessed Christmas and New Year's Day. We had an especially nice holiday. Visitors on safari, friends of Paul's parents in North Dakota, came through laden with two suitcases full of presents from home. Canned goods, flour, real chocolate chips, peanut butter . . . plus piles of gifts. The boys could hardly believe all their loot, but to their credit, they wrapped up many of the gifts and gave them to the kids here at the Children's Home. It warmed my heart to have them behave so generously. (All without me nagging them either!)

Paul whisked me away for New Year's Eve in Kampala at the Hilton. Decadent woman that I am, I soaked in a hot tub until I turned into a prune. Missionary life in the bush really makes a girl appreciate such goodies as perfumed soap and real shampoo!

I know you're anxious about word of Kia and Alice. Kia continues to blossom—thanks to you. As for baby Alice, well, she's won all our hearts. Both girls are living with us. Yes, it's crowded, but neither is ready to be assimilated into one of the family units yet.

The girls living in the family units are a big help to me with Alice. They take turns feeding her several times a day, plus give her plenty of hugs and cuddling. Unfortunately, Dr. Gallagher says he doesn't feel qualified to repair her palate. So I guess it's up to us and the Good Lord to keep her nourished and healthy until a qualified cranial-facial surgeon arrives from the Mercy Ship when it docks in Kenya this summer. I'm telling you this so that you won't be worried about her—I know how special she is to you.

We all miss you. You're one in a million, a bright and lovely young woman who deserves the best. I pray for you every day, that God will ease the ache in your heart and help you resume your life. Follow your dreams— whatever they may be now.

And give yourself permission to mourn for Ian for as long as you like. There is no time limit on grief, you know. None of us will ever forget you and the brave thing you did for Kia and Alice. Please write and keep us informed of your plans.

In His Love,
Jodene

P.S. Ed Wilson is mailing this for me when he returns to the U.S. He says "Hello" and that you're his hero (heroine) for all time!

Heather Barlow lay on her bed reading and rereading Jodene Warring's letter, memories of Uganda flashing through her mind like postcards. Some images were wonderful: the exotic beauty of the African landscape, the smiling faces of the children at the Kasana Children's Home and hospital, Paul, Jodene, their four children, Heather's friends from the Mercy Ship. Some pictures were frightening: the storm at sea, the sick and dying children in Kenya, her night flight to freedom with baby Alice. And over every picture in her mind's eye, she saw Ian. His smile. His deep blue eyes. She would never see his beloved face again. He would never hold her again and call her "lass" in his rich Scottish accent.

Sadness engulfed her, and she fumbled for his journal on her nightstand. *Thank you, Jodene, for giving this to me,* she thought. She ran her hand across the smooth leather surface. It was all she had of Ian now. All she would ever have. She wiped her teary eyes with the edge of her comforter.

She had spread photographs from her months in Africa on her desk, picking and choosing between the ones she would put on her bulletin board and in her scrapbook. Every face that smiled out at her made her long to turn back the clock and repeat every day of her trip. Against her parents' wishes, she had nixed enrolling at the University of Miami for the winter term. She didn't feel ready to jump back into her life stateside. And Jodene's letter had made her feel even less ready. She felt restless, at loose ends, unable to pick up her life where she'd left off before her mission trip.

A knock on her bedroom door startled her. "Yes?"

"It's me—Amber. Can I come in?"

Heather glanced at her clock radio. Four o'clock. Amber was home from high school, no doubt bursting with trivia she couldn't wait to dump on Heather. "Sure," Heather said, putting the journal aside.

Amber came to the bed and sat on the edge, careful not to disturb the rows of photos. "Still going to the movies with me tonight?"

Heather had totally forgotten her promise

to go out with her sister that evening. "Uh—sure." She held up the letter. "This came from Jodene today. She says Alice can't have her surgery until maybe this summer."

"That's not so far away."

"She needs the surgery now."

"It's not your problem, sis."

"How can you say that? What if everyone took that attitude? Who would take care of these orphans? Someone has to jump in and help, you know. Why not me?"

Amber leaned back and held up a hand. "Hey, I didn't mean to make you mad. I was just saying that she's there and you're here. She'll get the surgery eventually. What else can *you* do from three thousand miles away?"

Heather swung her legs over the side of the bed. "I wanted Mom or Dad to go over and lend a hand. I figured one of them would."

Heather had talked nonstop after returning home, certain she could infect her family with her enthusiasm for Uganda, positive that she could persuade one of her parents, both cranial-facial surgeons, to fly over and perform the necessary surgery on baby Alice. But although her parents had listened intently and praised her work, both had said they were overwhelmed with cases in their practice and couldn't possibly take a leave of absence. Plus, her father was training student doctors in the use of new laser technologies at Miami's medical school. Neither of them could possibly think about doing pro bono work overseas for a year or more.

Her mother had said, "You know your dad and I want to work in the developing world, Heather. My goodness, we spent years in the Peace Corps, so we know how great the need is for skilled volunteer help. And once we retire, we plan to help out plenty, but for now, we can't. We have hundreds of patients who depend on us. We can't just go off and leave them."

Now Amber was sounding as indifferent as their parents. "I don't think you can convince them to go right now," she said. "I think they'd really like to help you out, but they're not going to disrupt their lives just now. Or lose prospective patients."

"They make old people look young again," Heather fired back. "How noble is that? What does it matter if some rich woman gets her face redone when a baby like Alice needs reconstructive surgery to live a better life? And why are you defending Mom and Dad? You're the one who's usually at war with them."

"Well, excuse me if I see their side of the argument. For once I agree with them—you can't expect them to run off to Africa just because you think they should. You're not the only one in the family, you know."

"Well, thank you for your support. But what you're really saying is this is your senior year and you don't want anything to rock *your* boat. If Mom or Dad come to Africa with me, Amber just might be ignored."

"Whoa," Amber said, jumping to her feet. "You are majorly off base. School is perfectly boring and I'm forcing myself to even go to classes until June. This past year hasn't exactly been a picnic for me, you know. Dad's all over me about college in the fall." Amber did an imitation of her father's voice. " 'Have you filled out those admission forms yet, Amber?' 'Did you talk to your guidance counselor about the college that's right for you, Amber?' " She threw up her hands. "Has he ever asked once if I even want to go to college? Has he ever thought I might like to get a job and earn some bucks?"

"Get real. Of course you're going to college."

"You're not."

"But I will."

"When?"

"Trying to get rid of me?" Where did Amber get off, trying to make her feel guilty about taking some time to figure out what she wanted to do with the rest of her life? Amber had no idea what Heather had been through during the past six months. "What would you spend the money on, anyway? Your closet is already overflowing."

"Well, maybe everyone isn't cut out to save the world like you are. Maybe I'd like to have a good time before I grow old and die."

Exasperated with Amber's self-centered attitude, Heather said, "At least you have the opportunity to grow old. I met kids in Africa who'll never grow old. They'll be dead from AIDS or TB or malaria before they get out of their twenties."

"Then maybe I'll just sit around my room and feel sorry for myself like you do."

"Out," Heather said, pointing to the door. "This is my room and I don't need you sniping at me."

"I'm on my way. And forget about coming to the movies with me tonight. I'd hate to take you away from your pity party."

Heather slammed the bedroom door as soon

as Amber had walked out. Then she sat and seethed. What was the matter with her family? Didn't anyone understand what she was going through? Especially Amber. Her sister had always looked up to her, come to her for advice. Now they were at each other's throats. Why couldn't Amber understand how the past six months had affected Heather's life?

She threw herself across her bed, scattering the photographs across the floor. She didn't care. Amber was correct about one thing: Heather couldn't return to Africa and make everything right for Alice. At the moment she couldn't even make everything right for herself.

Her gaze fell on Ian's diary and her heart lurched. "Why, Ian? Why?" she asked aloud. What had it all been about? Why had she given everything in her heart to the missionary journey aboard the Mercy Ship and to Uganda, only to have it all snatched away? It made no sense. And she didn't have Ian to talk to about it either. She was going to have to go it alone.

Alone. The word sent a shiver down her spine.

Heather buried her face in her pillow and began to cry.

2

"Why are you acting antisocial today, Amber?"

Amber raised her eyes from the mush on her food tray and looked at Dylan Simms. "I'm in the dumps and didn't want to inflict myself on anybody else."

"I'm your guy, remember? You're supposed to tell me when you've got a problem." Dylan slid into the empty chair beside Amber at the table she'd chosen on the far side of the cafeteria. "So, did you and your old man go at it again?"

Amber stuck her fork upright into her mound of mashed potatoes. "Believe it or not, I got into it with Heather yesterday afternoon."

"Your sister? The Queen of Good-Deed-Doers?"

"Hey, show some respect."

Dylan held up his hands. "Sorry. It's just a surprise, that's all. You've only spoken of her in worshipful tones until now."

Amber made a face. "Do you want me to talk about it, or do you want me to dump my tray in your lap?"

"Talk. Please. I can't do this menu twice today." He rested his chin in his palm.

"We had a big fight, and she must have been really angry because she didn't come downstairs for dinner. She was asleep when I left for school, but I'm positive she's still mad at me."

"What happened?"

"You know how I've told you what a hard time she's having coming back to her real life from Africa." Dylan nodded. "Well, she had been doing better, but then yesterday she got this letter from the missionaries she lived with over there and it set her off again. She's totally fixated on that little baby she helped get out of Sudan. She acts as if unless she does something personally to help the baby, the baby will die. And if the baby dies, Heather's going to feel as if it's all her fault."

"And you said . . . ?"

"I told her to get over it. There was nothing more she could do. It was time for someone else to take over the project. She wants Mom or Dad to drop everything and zip over to Africa and operate on the baby—which neither one can do. Heather's sore at me because I actually see their side. I know she thinks I'm insensitive. I'm not, but there's only so much one person can do. She's got to realize that she can't fix everything that's wrong."

"You've always told me the two of you were different."

"I don't want to go out and save the world like she does. I know my limits."

"Her thing isn't your thing. And that's why I love you—you're fun. We have fun together. Blow off your funk, girl. I'll take you out tonight. That'll make you feel better."

"You know Dad won't let me date on a school night."

"So sneak out. You have before."

Amber sent him a sideways glance. She could tell by his expression that he had lost interest in her problems. "I don't want to sneak out. I want to get things right with my sister."

She watched Dylan's gaze drift toward a group of his baseball buddies coming through the door. He waved them over.

"I'm talking here," Amber said irritably,

wishing he'd be more sensitive to her feelings. "Can you give me a few minutes?"

"Yeah, sorry. So you want to meet me someplace tonight?"

"Didn't you hear me the first time? No, I don't."

Dylan patted her hand. "Look, Amber, from what you've told me about your sister, all you have to do is say you're sorry. She's probably dying to forgive you."

Dylan's friends stopped at the table, and Dylan stood and started talking to them. Amber suddenly felt like excess baggage. It was usually that way when Dylan's friends came around. She had once accused him of wanting to be with them more than he wanted to be with her, which he'd denied. She sighed. There would be no getting his attention back. She knew too well what would happen next— the guys would talk, Dylan would make an excuse to leave, and they'd wander off in a herd.

Minutes later he asked her, "Mind if I bug out?"

"Be my guest. I was alone before you came over here, remember?"

She watched him saunter off and wondered what good it was to have a boyfriend if he wasn't around when she needed him. His juvenile buddy bonding was frustrating enough, but he'd practically ignored her concerns about Heather. Amber's already crummy day had turned crummier. In truth, Heather's time in Africa had changed her *and* her relationship with Amber. There was a wall between them that Amber didn't know how to scale, and although Heather had shared her adventures with her family, Amber got the impression that there was much she hadn't shared.

For starters, Ian McCollum, the medical missionary Heather had cared deeply about and lost so horribly, was rarely discussed. Just the mention of his name brought tears to Heather's eyes, as did the photographs of the two of them together. Heather practically slept with his journal under her pillow, reading and rereading it. Growing up, Amber and Heather had shared everything, but not this. Amber felt shut out and cut off.

She came home to the aroma of freshly baked chocolate chip cookies. She called out for the housekeeper, then remembered it was Dolores's day off. Walking into the kitchen, Amber found Heather removing a cookie sheet from the oven. "What's this? You baking?" she asked, genuinely surprised. Most afternoons Heather was hidden away in her room.

"Peace offering," Heather said with a quick smile. She set the cookie sheet on the marble-topped island in the center of the kitchen. "I was rude and nasty to you yesterday, so I thought I'd bake my way back into your good graces."

Amber fished a piping hot cookie from the sheet and blew on it. "Good choice. You know I can't resist anything chocolate." She bit into the cookie, savoring the rich, buttery taste as much as Heather's apology. "But you didn't have to bake me cookies. Although I'm glad you did. I was all set to tell you I was sorry too. And I am, Heather. I didn't mean to sound like I don't care about baby Alice. I do care. But mostly because you care about her. Understand?"

"Perfectly." Heather pulled off her oven mitt and gave Amber a hug. She stepped back to the counter and began moving the warm cookies to a plate. "It's a little like looking at those magazine ads with pictures of hungry children. Sure the photo tugs at your heart, but it's easy to close a magazine and forget the picture. But when you actually see the baby, when you hold her in your arms, you've got a memory. Whenever I shut my eyes, the memory comes calling. Do you know, I can still feel the weight of little Alice just like I was holding her? I can still remember how she looked when she smiled up at me. Her little eyes lit up, and in spite of her birth defect, I knew she was happy. Of course I saw hundreds of needy children, but I truly made a difference for Alice and her sister. I know how important being close to a sister is."

Amber nodded, feeling a mixture of sympathy for the baby and shame that she hadn't grasped the true depth of Heather's feelings toward her. "I guess I expected you to be the same sister I remembered growing up with instead of the one who came back from Africa."

"Well, I'm not the same sister. I'm the one who watched babies die just because they couldn't get to a doctor in time. I'm the one who saw mothers abandon their children because they couldn't take care of them. Many people in our country take life for granted. No, worse . . . they think life is a guaranteed right.

Of course we have poverty here, but not as overwhelming and widespread."

Amber listened, unsure of how she was supposed to respond. She hadn't experienced what her sister had, but Heather had gone through what Amber now was going through— a dull senior year of high school and apprehension about her future. Amber kept hoping that Heather would remember that she herself had been feeling much the same way this time last year before she took off to Africa. Still, she thought it best not to bring that up now. "I'm glad you're home," she ventured. "I missed you. And I'll try to be more sensitive to the new Heather."

"I missed you, too. And I don't mean to act so serious all the time. Besides, I had a pretty good day. A friend called me, Boyce Callahan. We were on the mission trip together."

"You wrote about him in your e-mails. You said he had a thing for your Swedish roommate, Ingrid."

"That's history," Heather said with a wave of the spatula. "Ingrid is dating her old boyfriend again, and Boyce is back in class at the University of Alabama. Talking to him today brought back good memories. He was always cracking jokes and making us laugh. And he was nuts about peanut butter. Did I ever tell you that?" Amber shook her head. "He feels a lot like I do—life is tame and dull by comparison after Uganda."

"I guess Miami and your old life can never compete again," Amber mused, feeling a pang of jealously.

"Probably not."

Heather had no idea how much her answer stabbed at Amber's heart. Amber knew she should feel glad because Heather had found such dedication and zeal in her life, but right now she felt only envy because Heather's world was so much bigger than hers. And yet there was no way Amber was ever going to sail off to Africa to capture the dreams that had given her sister such a sense of purpose.

Amber held out a cookie. "I'm hogging these. Don't you want some? I'll pour us both some milk."

"No, thanks." Heather wrinkled her nose. "My stomach's been bothering me."

"Too bad. More for me." Amber scooped up two more cookies and headed to the refrigerator for milk.

"Plus I'm too excited to eat," Heather added.

Amber paused and turned. "What?"

"Boyce is studying engineering at 'Bama, and he told me he can shave off a semester of school if he participates in a work program. He says he's already talked to the head of the department and the professor has agreed to endorse Boyce's plan to the dean."

Great . . . one more person with a life, Amber thought. "And the plan is . . . ?"

"He's returning to Uganda in March."

"Good for Boyce. What's that got to do with you?" Amber asked, suddenly suspicious of Heather's smug smile.

"One way or another, I'm going with him."

3

"Heather, you can't be serious!" Dr. Ted Barlow exclaimed at the dinner table that night after Heather had revealed her plan.

Dr. Janet Barlow set her fork down on the plate with a clink. "You're supposed to be choosing a college, not talking about running off to Africa again. It's time to get on with your life, honey."

Amber sat silent, in total agreement with their parents. She'd been in shock ever since Heather had told her about her plan to return to Uganda. She didn't want Heather to go so far away again. Amber wanted her sister close by, to talk to, to help with her own problems.

Heather considered her parents thought-fully. "No disrespect, but I'll be nineteen in April. Of course I can return if I want to. I know Jodene and Paul will give me a place to stay. And Dr. Gallagher will be ecstatic to have an extra pair of hands helping in the hospital."

"That's what you want to do with your future?" Janet asked. "Work in a Third World hospital? If it's hospital work you want, your father and I can get you any number of jobs right here in Miami while you attend college."

"It's not about working in a hospital. It's about working in *that* hospital—the one in Uganda. This isn't about me, Mom. It's about them—the kids in Uganda. Boyce is designing and building an irrigation system on the property belonging to the Children's Home. Getting water to the back acreage will allow the kids of the village to expand their living quarters fivefold. That means the home can open itself up to even more orphans. They'll learn to farm and sell their crops and support themselves. I can help with setting up a small clinic for the girls, screen them for serious illness, give immunizations. It's a wonderful plan, and I want to be a part of it. The sooner I get there, the more I can help."

Her parents exchanged glances.

"Honey," her mother began, her tone sympathetic, "I know how difficult it is to come down from the high of the kind of adventure you had in Africa. When I first returned from the Peace Corps, the last thing I wanted to do was begin medical school. But your grandfather insisted, and I'm glad he did. I might never have gotten my medical degree if I hadn't begun classes when I did."

"We enrolled in med school together. It offered us another kind of adventure," her father added with a wink at his wife. "Heather, listen to us. You're intelligent, and you have so much potential. You can do anything you set your mind to. Don't waste the opportunities we can give you. Go to college, get a degree. Then, if you still want to return to Africa, go with our blessings."

"But I want to go now," Heather said, shoving her plate to one side, the food hardly touched. "You always told Amber and me that the years you spent in Central America were life-changing. You told us that one day you'd go back and use your surgical skills to help the poor. Well, here it is, years later, and you've never gone."

"First we wanted to get you girls raised," her mother said. "We wanted the two of you to have a normal life—go to college, get a leg up in the world—before we ventured off."

"Do you know what I think?" Heather didn't wait for an answer. "I think you've gotten too comfortable. You've forgotten your dreams, your ideals. You've sold out."

"That's uncalled for," Ted said, tossing his napkin on the table. "We've worked hard to build our reputations in this community with both our peers and our patients. It's our hard work that enabled you to run off to Africa in the first place. Remember, you had to raise all your own funds to secure a place on that Mercy Ship. If I recall, I simply wrote a check for your portion. So don't act as if we've somehow abandoned the world's underprivileged simply because we aren't packing our bags and heading off to do charity work."

"I've never acted ungrateful for all that the two of you have done for me," Heather said quietly. "And I'm not trying to put a guilt trip on either of you. I'm simply reminding you that the two of you are the reason I wanted to go on the trip in the first place. Your stories about your days in the Peace Corps have inspired me all my life. I thought you'd be pleased that I want to follow in your footsteps."

Janet reached across the table for Heather's hand. "Of course we're pleased, honey. To have a child who's acting as socially responsible as you do is a point of real pride for your father and me. It's just that we're confused about why you don't enroll at the university as you once talked about doing. One trip to Africa shouldn't change goals you've had all your life."

Amber bit her tongue to keep from jumping into the argument. While she didn't want Heather to wander off to Africa, her sister did have a point. It was her life and she should be able to do what she wanted with it. Amber was almost ready to say something in Heather's defense when Heather spoke.

"The trip wasn't at all what I expected. The things that happened to me last summer changed me and my goals. I met missionaries who were interested in the condition of people's souls, not just in their physical well-being. They're giving people a stake in eternity, a hope beyond this life. Maybe I'm not explaining it very well, but I know I'm different than when I left. I see a bigger picture now. A higher good. And that's the thing I want to reconnect with in Uganda. That's the main reason I want to go back."

"You had a religious experience?" Her father looked incredulous. "Is that what you're saying? You want to put your life on hold because you felt something spiritual?"

"Why is that so weird?" Amber could no longer keep quiet. "Maybe Heather's right. Maybe there's more to life than making money and telling your kids what they should do with their lives."

All eyes turned her way. She squared her jaw.

"I don't see you doing anything especially productive, young lady," her father said. "You're graduating in June and you haven't filled out a single college application. Do you think some college is going to take you simply because you wear good clothes? Which, by the way, you spend plenty of my money on."

"Heather's right," Amber shot back. "You two have sold out. What's important to you isn't important to us."

"Well, this is just great." Ted threw up his hands. "Neither one of our daughters wants to take advantage of the things we've worked for all our lives to give to them."

"Now, Ted, no one said that," Janet said.

"*I* said it." He shoved his chair away from the table, stood, and looked hard at Heather and Amber. "Tell you what—the two of you come up with a game plan and start paying for it yourselves. Heather, a plane ticket to Africa should cost in the neighborhood of a thousand dollars. Amber, when you graduate, get a job. Since the two of you are so intent on making your own choices for your lives, you can pay your own way." He walked out of the room.

Janet sighed and looked at both girls. "Listen, your father's upset. I'll talk to him."

Heather leaned toward her mother. "You understand, don't you, Mom? You heard what I was trying to say, didn't you?"

"Yes. But I'm not sure I agree. You aren't qualified in medicine. You aren't qualified in theology. If feeding people body and soul interests you, go to school and get some training in both fields. Then you'll be able to contribute something worthwhile."

"What about on-the-job training?" Amber interjected. "Isn't that valuable too?"

"Amber, your experiences in life don't weigh nearly as much in my book as your sister's, so your future plans consist of attending college in the fall. Get used to it. Go to your school counselor and start filling out applications tomorrow." Janet turned back to Heather. "Your heart's in the right place. It always has been, but you must honestly evaluate the best way to follow your heart. Your father and I are asking you to explore all your options before making a commitment. That's all."

"I have a better idea, Mom." Heather leaned forward eagerly. "Come with me. Just for a few months. See for yourself. Chase your dream again—the one that inspired you in the Peace Corps. After we've worked in Uganda side by side, if you still can't see the value in what I want to do, I'll come home and enroll at the University of Miami. That's a promise." She settled back in her chair, her hands held out beseechingly. "What do you say? Will you come with me?"

"Well, tonight went over like a lead balloon." It was later in the evening, and Amber was sulking in Heather's room, still angry about the way her mother had ordered her around. Didn't she have any say-so in her own life?

"Dad *was* pretty mad," Heather said. Their father had gotten a call from the hospital and had hurried off to stitch up the face of a car accident victim. "I wish I could make him understand my point of view."

"How about Mom? She gets it, but she treats

both of us like we're still babies. She'll never go to Africa. You're wasting your breath."

"She didn't say no." Heather lay on her bed, staring up at the ceiling. "All I want her to do is seriously think about coming with me."

"You mean you're still planning to go?"

"Yes."

"What about the money? You know when Dad says something, he means it."

"I have a savings account. This trip will clean it out, but so what? That's what a savings account is for."

Amber had no extra money, having recently bought a new stereo system for her car. Now she wished she hadn't. "I'm broke, so I guess I really will have to go to work," she said glumly.

"The other day you told me you might get a job when you graduated instead of going to college. Now you sound as if it's a prison sentence. What changed?"

"A job became Dad's idea," Amber confessed.

Heather giggled. "Fickle girl. Listen to your big sister. Go to college. You've got no good reason not to. Plus, Dad will pay for it."

"It's not that I don't want to go, it's just that I'm burned out with school, and the thought of facing four more years of studying books gives me a headache."

"Lots of frat parties," Heather teased.

"Don't you know? My life's one big party," Amber said glumly. "I feel like I'm standing on the outside looking in on other people's lives. Like I'm watching a movie where everyone's busy and having fun except me. All my friends have plans for their lives. I don't know what I want."

"You could come meet me in Africa when school's out. There's plenty for you to do over there."

"First Mom, then me. Soon you'll persuade Dad to go and we'll *all* be over there building huts and nursing sick kids."

"There are worse things than doing good for others, sis. I'm going, and if anyone wants to go with me, they'll be welcome." Heather stretched as she lay on the bed. "But right now I'm throwing you out of my room and crashing. My stomach's killing me and I'm tired to the bone."

Amber rose to leave. From the bed Heather added, "But think about what I said about coming to Africa with me. You just might begin the adventure of your life."

4

Saturday night Amber went to a party with Dylan at the home of one of his friends. The luxurious houses faced an inland waterway that cut through sections of Miami Beach. Expensive late-model cars spilled out of the driveway, across the lawn, and down the street. Music roared from poolside speakers, although no one was swimming on the chilly February night, and inside the house cigarette smoke hung like a pale curtain. With his arm possessively around Amber's waist, Dylan dragged her from group to group of their high-school friends. After an hour she disengaged herself and said she was going to the bathroom. Instead, she went out onto the patio and breathed deeply. The fresh, cool air helped clear her head. She wished she'd never come to the party.

She couldn't think about having a good time after the bombshell her mother had dropped that morning. Janet had strolled into the kitchen, where Amber and Heather were having breakfast, and said, "Heather, I'm going to Africa with you."

Heather, who was toying with her food, jumped up. "You are? Honest? Why did you change your mind?"

"Your father and I talked well into the night when he returned from the hospital, and we agreed that anything that was this important to you should be important to us, too. Most people your age are trying to get away from their parents, but you want me with you. I should be flattered instead of telling you no."

Heather flew across the kitchen and threw her arms around her mother. "But your practice—you said—"

"I know what I told you at Christmas, but I've made some arrangements over the past few days. Your father will take over some of my cases, and Dr. Liberman will handle the others. None of my patients will lack care. And besides, I won't get rusty. I intend to perform surgeries while I'm in Uganda. I'll begin with fixing that little baby's cleft palate."

Heather started crying. Amber sat in stunned silence, feeling as if a door had been slammed in her face and she'd been left standing out in the cold.

"Mom, this is—is wonderful," Heather stammered. "I—I'm overwhelmed."

"I talked to Ned Chase—you may remember him, he's a colleague. Anyway, he and his wife, Britta, donate six weeks every year to an organization called FACES. It's a network of cranial-facial surgeons who donate their time and talents to helping in developing nations. Ned practically burst with enthusiasm when I told him what you wanted me to do. He's also connected me with the organization, which will help clear away red tape. You know, I can't simply waltz into Uganda and start operating without special sanction. The FACES group will handle the details for me."

"That's fabulous! Can we get it all done by March first?"

Janet smiled. "Probably not that soon. I have some loose ends I can't tie up before then." When Heather looked crestfallen, her mother added quickly, "But certainly we'll leave by April first."

"I'll write Jodene and tell her the good news.

She'll be really happy to know that Alice is going to get the best surgeon in the world."

Janet laughed. "I'm not the best in the world, but I will do my best."

"You're the best to me," Heather said. She gave her mother another hug and hurried out of the kitchen.

Amber sat in stonelike silence.

"You don't seem overjoyed," Janet said. "Do you have a problem with our plans?"

Amber shrugged, not trusting her voice.

"I'll only have a six-week visa, Amber. I think you and your father can tough it out for six weeks, if that's what's bothering you."

Amber said, "I could care less," pushed aside her unfinished breakfast, and left the room.

Now, recalling the morning in vivid detail, she wished she'd said all that had been on her mind when she'd had the chance. She felt like an afterthought instead of a real member of the family. Heather's needs, Heather's wishes, always came before Amber's. Not that she wanted to go down the same road as Heather, but she did want—had always wanted—the respect for her own thoughts and plans that Heather received for hers. Her parents treated her like a baby, and she hated it.

"There you are." Dylan's arrival on the porch broke Amber's reverie. "Why'd you run off?"

"I didn't run off. I wanted some fresh air."

"I've been looking all over the place for you." He sounded irritated.

"What? I have to check in with you when I want to escape the smog in there?"

"No, but you could have mentioned you were going outside."

"Would you have even heard me?" She didn't wait for his answer. "Listen, Dylan, I don't need a lecture from you about reporting in on my whereabouts. My father gives them to me often enough."

"Well, excuse me for caring."

"About me?" She scoffed. "What you care about is not losing face in front of your buddies. Wouldn't want them to think you don't have control of your woman."

"Hey, knock it off." His face reddened. "Look, lately you've been a real b—"

"Don't say it," Amber warned.

"You haven't been one bit of fun ever since your sister got home from Africa. You're all uptight. And mad at the world. Maybe it would have been better if she'd never come home."

Amber balled her fists and stepped towards

him. "Don't you dare say anything bad about Heather. I missed her like crazy and I'm glad she's home. She could have died over there, you know."

"Yeah, well, she didn't. But you're acting like *somebody* died."

"Kids die over there every day. As if you care."

"And you do?"

He'd hit a sore spot, and she resented it. "Heather does," she said. "That's good enough for me."

Dylan looked confused. "What are we arguing about here? I'm trying to be sympathetic toward your crummy moods, and you're cutting me off at every turn. Are you—you know—having that PMS thing?"

She rolled her eyes. "Oh, grow up." Earlier she'd thought she would tell him about her morning and the shock she'd felt at her mother and Heather's decision to take off to Africa together. But now she didn't want to tell him anything. She crossed her arms. "Let's just forget the whole thing. There's no way I can explain it all to you, and besides, we came here to party, not stand around on the porch talking."

"Hey, that's more like it. That's the Amber I

remember . . . my party girl." He put his arm around her.

"That's me," she said, forcing a smile and allowing him to lead her inside. Dylan stayed next to her the rest of the evening, refusing to run off with his friends to buy more beer when they asked. Yet despite Dylan's presence, despite all the noise, music, and laughter, Amber felt as alone as if she were stranded on the moon—far away and looking down on a scene that she didn't want to be a part of, in a crowd she felt would never understand her. How could they? She couldn't understand herself. All she knew was that there was a void widening every day, setting her apart from them and the world of high-school popularity she'd once coveted.

"I don't know what's wrong with me," Amber told Heather days later. She had decided to try to explain her inner turmoil to her sister. She'd missed their long heart-to-heart talks, and if Heather was heading to Africa, Amber might not be able to talk to her face to face for months. "I mean, I have everything I ever thought I wanted. I have tons of friends, a boyfriend—Dylan's one of the most popular guys in school. I have a car, clothes coming out the wazoo—Dad's right about that much. But some days I hate getting up and going to school and pretending life is fabulous when it isn't."

The afternoon had turned warm, and they were out by the pool, dangling their legs in the bright turquoise water. Heather stared into the water, making lazy circles beneath the surface with her toe. "You've got a lot going on deep down," she said. "You have it all, but you're mixed up, unhappy, feeling like no one understands you, no one *wants* to understand you, and yet you're supposed to make life-altering decisions while you're in this state of turmoil. Is that about it?"

"That's exactly it. I know I'm supposed to be grateful—and I am," Amber added hastily. "But, jeez, is this all there is?"

"If you could do anything in the world, have anything in the world, what would you want?"

"You mean besides fame and fortune without having to put myself out for it?" Amber sobered and stared hard at the cool water. "I don't know, sis. I just don't know."

"Do you want to marry Dylan?"

"Yuck! No way."

Heather laughed. "He doesn't seem so horrible."

"He's all right. But he acts like a jerk sometimes. He throws temper tantrums if everything doesn't go exactly his way, or if I don't want to tag along with him and the gang to some mindless party. And sometimes I don't want to."

Heather continued to make circles in the water with her foot. "How about a job? Maybe if you worked for a while it would help you zero in on something else."

"And what kind of a job can I get just out of high school? I sure don't want to lean out a window and ask, 'Do you want fries with that burger?' a million times a day."

Heather punched Amber playfully. "There's always retail. You love clothes. Maybe you can get a job in a store selling clothes."

Amber rolled her eyes. "Oh, sure. And see every fashion mistake in the city walk in and out the door. How could I tell some girl that a dress looks fabulous on her when it doesn't?"

"Mom and Dad have tons of friends. You could get an office job."

"Doing what? Sorting mail? Making the lunch runs for the other workers?"

"There's the hospital."

"Eek! I pass out at the sight of blood."

"You do have a problem, sis."

"You think I'm useless too, don't you?" Amber's gloom deepened.

"No. I think you just haven't discovered your passion yet. I was lucky. I've known ever since the fifth grade what I want to do."

"You want to save the world," Amber said, feeling envious because Heather's dreams were happening. And Heather's dreams won a high approval rating from all who heard them. Helping sick and hungry children was noble.

"I learned that I can't save the whole world," Heather confessed, her expression enigmatic. "Still, I want to do whatever I can to help. That's why I'm going back. I can help these orphans."

"I'd give anything if I felt that way."

"Sometimes you have to do it before you feel it."

Amber sighed. "Maybe you're right. Maybe I should go to Africa with you."

"You could, you know."

Amber studied Heather's face. "You're serious, aren't you?"

"Very serious."

"I can't see that happening. Dad would pitch a fit."

"And there is the problem of your final

couple of months of classes. You are going to graduate, aren't you?"

"Of course. It's just so boring, I can barely stay awake. One of my teachers calls it senioritis."

"I had it too," Heather admitted. "Every senior gets it. This time last year, all I could think of was my upcoming trip on the Mercy Ship. It pulled me through my slump."

"If only I had something to look forward to like that."

Heather patted Amber's hand sympathetically. "I've invited you to Africa. It beats passing out burgers and fries."

"And don't think I'm not worried about it. Dad may have let you back into his good graces, but I'm still in the doghouse."

"He'll ease up on you once we're gone."

Amber wanted to beg Heather not to go, but just then the phone rang. She hurried to answer it, making wet footprints on the stone patio.

"Kelly here," her friend's voice announced.

"What's up?"

"Bad news, I'm afraid. Dylan asked Jeannie Hightower out and she said yes. I thought you should know."

5

Amber felt herself go hot and cold. "So?" she asked, keeping her voice controlled.

"Well, everybody knows you and Dylan have been together for months. And now all of a sudden he asks Jeannie out. What's going on? Did you two break up?"

Amber heard Kelly pause, no doubt waiting for an explosive reaction. Refusing to give her one, Amber said, "Maybe it's a study date. They're in the same calculus class."

"Some study date. Jeannie told Brooke that Dylan's taking her to a movie."

"And you believe Brooke? You know she just talks to hear her own voice."

"I checked it out with Liz. She said it was true."

Liz was Dylan's freshman sister, so the story probably was true. "It's a free country," Amber

said. "I guess he can date whomever he wants."
She was reeling on the inside, but she was determined not to let Kelly know. If she fell apart over the news, the gossip mill would have a field day.

"Did something happen between you two?" Kelly tried again to pry information from Amber.

"Nothing that I recall."

"How about at the party Saturday night? You were outside talking for a long time—"

"Look, Kelly, nothing happened. And I really could care less what Dylan does and who he does it with. I have more important things on my mind." By now Amber's hand ached from gripping the receiver so tightly. "But thanks for the update. Where else could I have heard such news except from a friend?"

The subtle insult passed unnoticed. Kelly said, "Um—well, okay. Just so long as you aren't hurt, I guess it's no big deal."

Amber's only satisfaction was hearing the disappointment in Kelly's voice over her non-reaction. "It's no big deal," she echoed, and hung up.

She stood shaking with anger, holding the receiver, for a long time. Dylan was dumping her. And he didn't even have the guts to tell her to her face. "So what!" she said aloud. "I was bored with him anyway." She stalked off, making it to her room before she started to cry.

Amber didn't want to return to school the next day but knew she had to in order to save face. As long as she pretended not to care, the gossip mill wouldn't have as much to talk about. One crack in her facade would ruin everything. She felt the gaze of her classmates on her as she walked down the hall or entered a classroom. And when she saw Dylan and Jeannie huddled in a corner of the cafeteria, she almost caved. All she wanted to do was deposit her food tray on their heads.

A pop quiz in chemistry added to her misery. By the time she arrived home, she had a headache and a need to punch something. She went to the gym room at home and worked out with a kickboxing tape. The wall of mirrors told her she wasn't very good at it, but after forty-five minutes of kicking and thrusting, she felt better.

She was running on the treadmill when Heather found her. "I wondered where you were. Everything okay?"

"No." Amber turned off the machine and sank to the floor, her back braced against a wall. "It's been a crummy day." She told Heather what had happened, all the emotion gone out of her.

"You told me Dylan wasn't that important to you. Was that the truth?"

"He wasn't. It's just that I've always been the dumper, not the dumpee."

"So your pride's hurt. Is that it?"

Heather had settled next to her on the floor, and Amber looked sidelong at her. "It's just one more thing to add to my list. You see, that's the problem—no one thing is huge, but added all together, my life is nowhere."

"You're positive you're not really broken up about Dylan. You've dated him a long time. You used to tell me about how much fun you two had together."

"That was a lifetime ago."

"You never loved him?"

"I don't love him. Why the third degree?"

Heather picked at a thread on the carpet. "Did you ever . . . ? Well, have you and Dylan ever . . . ?" She left the questions hanging.

Amber wiped perspiration on a towel. "Did I ever go all the way with him? Is that what you want to know?"

Heather's face turned red. "It's none of my business. I shouldn't have asked."

"The answer is no. I could have. He asked me plenty of times, but I never did."

"That's good."

"I sure think so now. How about you?" Heather shook her head. "Not even with Ian?"

Tears filled Heather's eyes, and Amber regretted prying. Still, Heather chose to answer. "The first time I kissed him was also the last time I kissed him. We stood in the moonlight together under the skies of Africa. He held me and he kissed me. He told me he loved me. I was too overwhelmed to say 'I love you' back to him. I thought I'd have all the time in the world to tell him how much I loved him. I thought I'd kiss him a hundred more times. But I didn't.

"I've never been sorrier about anything in my life. I should have told him how I felt when I had the chance. I had one chance, and one chance only. Then it was gone. Then *he* was gone." Heather took a deep, shuddering breath. "That's why I asked you about Dylan. If you really care for him, fight for him. Don't let your pride stand in the way of telling someone you love him and want him back."

Tears welled in Amber's eyes as she felt the depth of Heather's pain and loss. They made her own problems suddenly seem petty. Many times she had wished that Heather would talk to her about Ian. Now that she had and Amber saw how raw and open the wound was on her sister's heart, she realized that to have discussed Ian carelessly would have lessened what he and Heather had shared. Amber clasped Heather's hand. "I've never felt that way about Dylan. I've never felt that way about anyone. I wish I could have met Ian. He must have been very special to have snagged my sister's heart so completely."

Heather wiped her eyes and gave a self-conscious laugh. "I didn't mean to get carried away. You were talking about your problems and I butted right in with mine. Sorry. I remember how stupid high school can be at times. But by June it will be behind you. You'll have something else going on and high school will be a memory."

"And by June you and Mom should be heading back from Africa," Amber said, attempting to brighten the mood. "Just in time for my graduation."

"Well, at least Mom will."

"What about you?"

"You may as well know this. I'm going to find a way to stay. I belong there. And Amber, this time I'm not coming back."

Ted Barlow came into Heather's room waving a packet. "Guess what I picked up from our travel agent today."

"Our tickets? Oh, Dad, let me see." Heather snatched the packet from his hand and opened it. "Yes!" she said. "Here they are." She waved the tickets high in the air, then hugged her father.

Amber watched from her perch atop the desk chair in Heather's room, her heart sinking. It was really going to happen. Heather and their mother were going off to Africa in a week. Amber and their dad would remain behind.

"You'll land at Gatwick in London, spend the day sightseeing, then board a British Air flight for Entebbe," he said. "The trip takes two full nights of flying. I hope you're up to it."

"I did it at Christmas, remember?"

"Then I hope Janet's up to it." He appraised Heather through narrowed eyes. "You look a bit thin to me. You eating right?"

"I'm not very hungry these days—too excited." Heather stuffed the tickets back into the packet and plopped it beside Amber on the desk. "See—I'm packing."

A large suitcase lay open in one corner. Casual clothing, shoes, and other personal items lay in neat, organized rows across the floor.

"You've been packing for days," Amber grumbled. "How long can it take?"

"Don't you have homework?" Ted asked.

Amber bristled. "No."

"Did you finish the application forms for the University of Miami you brought home last week?"

"Almost."

"How long can it take to fill out a simple form? Amber, please get serious about this. The freshman class will close out and you won't get in."

"Wouldn't that be a tragedy?" she muttered.

Heather stepped between them. "You two have got to learn to get along better. Neither Mom nor I will be here to referee."

"Referee what?" Janet stepped into Heather's room. She kissed her husband and he slid his arm around her.

"The dynamic duo." Heather inclined her head toward Amber and their father.

"We're going to be fine," Ted said, leveling a look at Amber that dared her to disagree.

"I hope so," Janet said. "I received my itinerary from the FACES organization today, and I've got quite a surgical schedule facing me. First we go to the hospital in Lwereo for two weeks."

"Alice will be Mom's first patient," Heather said, waving a letter. "Paul and Jodene are thrilled. You're going to love them, Mom."

"I'm sure. But afterward I head to Kampala, where I'll have four weeks straight of nonstop surgery. Not only will I have local residents, but they're bussing in refugees from Rwanda and Sudan as well. Lots of children with deformities, but also plenty with war injuries. I hope I'm up to the task."

Ted gave her shoulders a squeeze. "You're up to it."

"I wish you were going with me."

"Next time."

Amber's stomach tightened. Not once had anyone in her family glanced her way as they made their plans. She was invisible.

"I'm staying with Paul and Jodene the whole time," Heather said.

"I'd rather we weren't separated," Janet said, "but you really are better off at the Children's Home. By the end of each day I'll be ready to drop, so I really won't be fit company for you."

"I'll have plenty to do in Lwereo, believe me. Boyce will keep me company."

Amber listened to Heather and her mother make plans, heard her father interject a comment now and again. They never once looked at her, never once asked her a question. She was Amber, the Nonexistent One. Without a word she slipped from the room, and no one seemed to notice.

An unfamiliar sound awakened Amber in the middle of the night. She pulled her pillow over her head, but the noise intruded. She sat up, listened. It sounded as if someone was being sick in the bathroom. From beneath the bathroom door that adjoined her and Heather's bedrooms, Amber saw a fine line of light breaking the darkness in her room. She threw off her covers and padded to the door.

She knocked softly. "Sis? Is that you?"

No answer, only the sound of retching.

Amber knocked a second time. "Heather, are you okay?"

The sound stopped, but the quiet sent an ominous chill up Amber's spine. She twisted the doorknob and eased the door open. She blinked in the glaring light and stifled a scream. On the floor, Heather lay unconscious, her blood staining the toilet bowl and the pristine white tiles like a ring of bright red fire.

6

Amber had been around hospitals all her life, but she had never been so unprepared as she was in the emergency room that night waiting to hear word of her sister. Hours before, when she'd discovered Heather on the bathroom floor, she'd run yelling into their parents' room. She'd awakened them, followed them back down the hall, listened to them as they worked on Heather, bouncing between the roles of terrified parents and seasoned medical professionals. An ambulance had been called, and Heather, still unconscious, had been whisked away.

"Stay here!" Ted Barlow had barked as he and Janet climbed into the ambulance with Heather and the paramedics.

"No way," Amber had muttered beneath her

breath as the ambulance screeched out of the circular driveway. She had hopped into her car and followed the screaming ambulance through the late-night streets to the sprawling Jackson Memorial Hospital complex, where she now paced, frightened and trembling, across the floor of the emergency room waiting area.

The wall clock told her it was three A.M., but based on the number of people waiting to be treated, it could have been the middle of the afternoon. Old people, young people, sick people, and some who looked perfectly well sat in rows of chairs, talking, crying, drinking endless cups of coffee bought from a vending machine. The admittance desk had a line of people waiting to be processed. At the end of the hall stood the doors to the triage area, which had swallowed up Amber's family hours before.

Amber had begged a busy nurse to tell her parents she was in the waiting room, but she had no way of knowing if they'd gotten the message. She figured her father would be angry with her for coming, but she didn't care. Surely he must realize that Amber couldn't have sat at home waiting for the phone to ring. Surely her mom had to know how scared Amber must be. Once again she felt invisible, as if her feelings and concerns didn't count for anything with her parents.

She had almost screwed up her courage to barge through the triage doors when she saw her father coming toward her, looking worried and exhausted. She rushed to meet him. "How's Heather? What happened to her?"

"We got the bleeding stopped, but we still don't know what's caused it. She's going upstairs into Internal Medicine's ICU, and we'll begin more extensive tests tomorrow."

"Sh-She's not coming home?"

"She's taken a unit of whole blood since we've been here. She can't go home until we get to the bottom of this."

"Where's Mom?"

"Upstairs with Heather."

"Can I see Heather?"

Ted raked a hand through his already disheveled hair. "I came to take you to her."

They hurried to the elevator and rode up in silence. Amber shivered, more from tension and fear than from cold. "Are you mad at me for coming?" she asked.

He shook his head. "I know you're worried too."

"I am, Daddy. I really am. Th-There was so much blood. . . ." Her voice broke and she began to cry.

Her father put his arms around her and held her. "I'm mad at myself," he said against her hair. "I should have had her in for a thorough physical exam when she returned from Africa."

Amber lifted her head. "You think going to Africa made her sick?"

"I don't know. It's possible, though."

Amber's mind spun at the implication. Heather had lived half her life with the dream of going to Africa. How cruel it would be if the fulfillment of her dream was the source of her illness. "Maybe it's just the flu or something," she mumbled.

The elevator stopped and the doors slid open.

"Maybe," her father echoed.

They walked down the dimly lit hall hand in hand, his grip telling Amber that he didn't believe for a minute that Heather had a complicated case of the flu. Amber didn't believe it either, but it was the only straw of hope she had to grasp at.

*   *   *

Three days later, after a battery of tests and no definitive answers, Heather was released from the hospital and sent home. She was restricted to bed rest and a bland diet, neither of which she welcomed. "I don't feel like staying in bed," she told her mother. "And I don't want anything to eat."

"Since when are your doctor's orders up for debate?" Janet asked, fluffing the bed pillows.

"But I feel fine."

Amber, who was busy sorting through a stack of videos she'd rented for Heather to watch, listened but kept her opinions to herself. Heather's mysterious malady had given all of them a real scare, and to Amber's way of thinking, it seemed as if Heather's doctors had let them down by not discovering the source of her abdominal pain and bleeding. Their parents were frustrated and baffled as well, but without a diagnosis, they could do nothing more than keep a close watch on Heather. Amber knew that Heather still had pain because she sometimes saw Heather grimace. And despite Dolores's secret recipe for delicious chicken soup, Heather still wasn't eating properly.

Janet put her hands on her hips and in a no-nonsense voice said, "You will stay in bed, young lady, until you return for a checkup at the end of the week. *If* your doctor gives you permission to resume regular activities at that time, *then* you may. End of discussion. Now, I've got to return to my office; I have a consultation at five. If you need anything, ring for Dolores. Or ask Amber. Once school's out for the day, she'll be your personal slave. Right, Amber?"

Amber curtsied. "Just snap your fingers and I'll do your bidding, Cinderella."

Heather made a face. "I don't want to be waited on. I've still got things to do before we leave next week."

Janet's eyes narrowed. "You're not going anywhere."

"But the trip—"

"Is out. Don't argue," Janet added firmly when Heather opened her mouth. "Even if you were well, which you aren't, your immune system is weakened. Africa is no place for someone who isn't one hundred percent physically healthy. I shouldn't have to tell you that."

Amber came over to the bed, reading the shock and disappointment in Heather's face. "How about you, Mom? Will you go?"

"I've got a call in to the FACES headquarters to explain that I'm dropping out. They'll understand."

"But people are counting on you!" Heather cried. "You can't cancel. Don't you understand? You're the hope for a normal life for Alice, for lots of children over there. You have to go!"

"I have to stay home and take care of my daughter," Janet answered calmly.

"But I have doctors to take care of me. Isn't that so?" Heather protested. "And Dad will be here. He won't let anything happen to me. Please go."

"I don't want to go alone. I only agreed to go in the first place because you wanted it so much. I was going because of you, Heather. And because I could do some good, but *you* were the impetus to get me to Uganda."

"But you gave your word. Jodene and Paul are expecting us."

Heather began to cry, and Amber shot their mother an anguished look.

"No one expects a mother to go off and leave her sick child," Janet said, attempting to soothe Heather. "Others will go. Someone will fill in for me. You'll see."

"But we already have our airplane tickets—expensive tickets. Are you going to just throw them away?"

"The money is the least of my concerns. I don't like backing out either, honey, but you are my first priority. What kind of a help would I be if I was thinking about you day and night? Listen, I'll make a deal with you. You get well and get your doctor's okay, and we'll go later."

"But Alice can't wait. She needs her surgery now—before she learns to talk. You know kids with cleft palates have serious speech problems. You're sentencing her to a lifetime of ridicule."

"That's not fair, Heather. Don't lay a guilt trip on me because I'm choosing you over a needy baby."

"I'll go in Heather's place." Heather and Janet swiveled toward Amber. She lifted her chin and repeated her statement.

"That's impossible." Janet waved her hand in dismissal.

"Wait," Heather said, leaning forward. "Hear her out, Mom."

Amber took a breath. "I know what you're going to say, Mom. 'You have school.' Well, I only have about six weeks of classes left, and everyone knows we seniors are just marking time in our final days. As for my grades, they're passable. B's in everything except chemistry, and that's a high C. What if I talk to each of my teachers and get their permission to take my finals early? If they say yes, that should take care of your and Dad's objection about school, shouldn't it?"

"Amber, it's your senior year. You're getting ready to graduate. You'll miss out on all the fun."

"What fun? Toilet-papering the campus for our senior prank? Having the principal threatening to hold back our diplomas until the culprits confess? I don't mind missing that."

"Your offer's generous," Janet said with a shake of her head. "But I still can't go halfway around the world while Heather's in a medical crisis."

"I accept Amber's offer," Heather blurted out. "It's the next best thing to going myself. And I'll be a lot more agreeable, a lot more cooperative, if I know the two of you are going ahead with our plans."

"I don't know. . . . Your father—"

"Think about it," Heather urged. "Send Dad to talk to me. He'll agree."

Amber stepped back, her heart hammering. Heather was doing the job of persuasion without her help, and she thought it best to leave it that way. Her offer had been genuine, and while she wasn't all that crazy about hanging out in Africa for six weeks, she'd do anything to help her sister. She was finished with high school anyway. Just that morning she'd learned that Dylan had asked Jeannie to the prom. Not that Amber had wanted to go with him after the way he'd been treating her. However, she knew that going to Africa would not only make Heather happy, it would also release her from the social shame of being unceremoniously dumped by her longtime boyfriend. Amber gave her sister an encouraging smile, knowing that while she might not be able to save the world, at least, for the time being, she could save herself.

It was Ted Barlow who came up with the solution for his wife to be in constant communication with him and Heather. "A special technically advanced satellite system phone," he said at the next evening's family meeting, held in Heather's room. "How do you think journalists and disaster relief workers communicate when they disappear into parts of the world without normal means of communication? International wireless cell phones use low-Earth-orbit satellites to send and receive signals. We'll get one for you, honey. No need for you to be cut off from us. You can call anytime to check on Heather, plus we can call you, too."

"But what if I'm in surgery when you call and I don't hear the phone ring?"

"We can get you an international pager if that will make you feel more comfortable. I'll leave you a voice mail, and you can pick it up whenever you're back to the phone."

"Mom, it sounds like the answer to my prayers," Heather said. "You can keep your word to FACES *and* stay in touch. We can talk every night if you want. I mean, after you take into account the seven-hour time difference."

"The FACES organization did sound disappointed when I called them," Janet said. "They said the hospitals where I was being sent were already taking applications for surgeries. Plus other doctors were coming to observe."

"Doesn't sound as if backing out is going to be easy," Ted said.

"Don't let them down, Mom," Heather pleaded. "I'll be the best patient in the world while you're gone. And I'll get well, too. I promise."

Amber sensed that her mother was wavering, so she cleared her throat and stepped forward. "I got a verbal okay from every one of my teachers." She didn't mention that her chemistry teacher had insisted she turn in a theory paper before she left. Or that her English teacher had demanded a ten-page report on Chaucer.

"Now, hold on," her father said. "I'm not in favor of *you* going. But there's no reason for your mother to back out. We both know the difficulties in picking up a qualified surgeon at the last minute. So, with her commitment made and the phone problem covered, I believe she should go. As for you—"

"But I want to go," Amber said, knowing that this had to be the most persuasive speech she had ever made. "I can help do the work Heather had agreed to do. And I can keep Mom company." She looked her father in the eye. "I could tell you that it's a great educational opportunity for me, but you probably wouldn't buy it. I could promise that I'll be perfect and not cause any problems, but you wouldn't believe that, either. But, Dad, Mom, I want this more than anything I've wanted in a long, long time. I want to go with Mom to Uganda. Say yes, Dad. I'm begging you—will you *please* let me go in Heather's place?"

7

It wasn't until Amber was well over the Atlantic Ocean ten days later that she could take a deep breath and relax. She considered all that she'd had to accomplish to accompany her mother to Uganda. In school she'd finished two papers and six exams in five days and three all-nighters. She'd passed everything, not much caring about the grades, only wanting to leave the high-school scene far behind.

She'd gotten the immunizations necessary for travel to Africa, told her friends she'd see them at graduation, and pointedly ignored Dylan. She'd heard through the grapevine that he and Jeannie had been at each other's throats and that he was avoiding the girl. Amber couldn't say she was sorry to hear the news.

With school behind her, she'd spent two

days shopping, then packing under Heather's watchful and often teary gaze.

"I'd give anything in the world to be going," Heather had said.

"You just concentrate on getting well. Who knows? If your checkup goes okay, maybe you can talk Dad into flying you over to join us."

"Maybe."

But Amber didn't believe that would happen. Heather still had terrible abdominal cramps, and although her doctor had switched her medication twice, she had difficulty keeping food down.

Amber had listened to everything her sister told her about Africa—which was plenty. She learned names and faces from photographs of the people Heather cared about, the kinds of food to avoid, the way Africans kept time ("They don't. They just show up whenever they feel like it.") and, by poring over a map, learned the various regions Heather thought she might enjoy visiting. Amber had taken notes and made silent promises to herself never to venture any farther than she had to. She wasn't the least bit excited about facing outdoor bathrooms and rainwater showers, but she'd never let on to her sister.

"I'll be your eyes and ears," she'd promised the night before leaving.

"Better yet, be my heart," Heather had told her.

Amber and her mother had boarded a five P.M. flight to London, settled into their first-class seats, and buckled their seat belts. Amber's last image of home had been the city of Miami spread out like colorful confetti along a shoreline of glittering green water as the plane soared toward the clouds. Her last image of Heather had been of her holding their father's hand, sobbing and throwing them kisses from the gangway.

"I hope we're doing the right thing," Janet said now, half to herself, as the plane leveled off above the clouds.

"It's what Heather wants," Amber reminded her.

"You too, evidently. I've never seen you apply yourself with such determination in your life."

"I did it for Heather," Amber said. "Africa would never be my first choice for a vacation spot."

They landed in London, where the weather was cold and rainy, and spent an exhausting day sightseeing. Amber had toured the city with her parents the previous summer when they'd left Heather aboard the Mercy Ship. Then Amber had been terminally bored. Now the city seemed regal to her, like a stately old woman. Dark cabs and bright double-decker buses sputtered in jammed traffic. Busy Londoners huddled under their umbrellas as they hurried down streets lined with towering old houses. Gardens were just beginning to bloom, and trees wore the bright, lacy green of new spring.

They returned to the airport that night and caught the ten o'clock flight to Entebbe. After a second restless night of sleeping in their airline seats, they landed at eight the following morning on the runway of the only Ugandan airport large enough to accommodate a big jet. By then Amber's eyes felt gritty and her mind foggy. After clearing customs and exchanging currency, Janet negotiated a cab ride in a mini-van into Kampala.

"The Hilton," she told the driver.

The air was warm but lacked Miami's soggy humidity. The sky was a vivid blue, the earth red and brown, spattered with bursts of green foliage. Cattle were being herded alongside the busy roadway by Ugandan women wearing colorful native dresses and balancing jugs of water and bundles of sticks on their heads. Their children tagged behind them like ducklings.

The smell of burning charcoal from cooking fires set up at endless small campsites saturated the air. Young girls held babies on their hips; small boys swatted flies with sticks and poked grazing cows into obedient circles. Groups of people walked briskly toward the city of Kampala, their bare feet sending up clouds of dust. Amber stared wide-eyed out the minivan's window, feeling more like a foreigner than she ever had in London. Now she was visiting a colorful and exotic world that she found fascinating.

This is the country my sister loves, she told herself. *I don't think I can.* She was greatly relieved to see the oasis surrounding the Hilton Hotel rise out of the heart of the city, an island of calm, quiet green. They exited the minivan, only to be accosted by a cluster of children asking for money. "Street trash! Go—leave these nice ladies alone!" the doorman barked, but before he could shoo them away, Janet gave each child an Ugandan dollar.

Inside, the hotel of stucco and glass was as modern as any in the United States, and Amber and her mother's spacious suite was cooled by welcome air-conditioning. Amber flopped across the bed and stretched luxuriously while Janet ordered room service.

"First I want a hot shower," Janet said. "Then we'll call home and let your father and Heather know we're here. Then we'll both take a nap. Paul Warring is meeting us in the lobby tomorrow morning at nine. Enjoy this bit of civilization, Amber, while you can. It's the last we'll see of it for a while."

Amber nodded and yawned. Her mother went into the bathroom, and soon Amber heard the shower. A kaleidoscope of images of home flashed in Amber's mind's eye, and suddenly she was engulfed by a wave of homesickness. She was halfway around the world, thousands of miles from all she had ever known. And she realized she was ill prepared.

Her skills—driving a car, navigating the mall, shopping for fashionable clothing, hanging out with her friends at the beach—counted for little in this exotic land where people set up housekeeping alongside the road, where cattle roamed the streets like privileged citizens and children darted from stranger to stranger begging for enough money to feed themselves.

Amber's mother woke her at seven the next morning. "Let's get a move on," Janet said. Amber moaned but obeyed. By nine they had their gear packed and were in the lobby, where a brown-haired man in his early thirties introduced himself as Paul Warring.

"You look like your sister," he told Amber. "Jodene and I are sorry Heather couldn't come. She's an extraordinary young woman."

As they chatted, Paul loaded their things into a minivan. An Ugandan driver, introduced as Patrick, smiled his welcome. "I met your sister on the ship," Patrick said. "She is a one-and-only person."

"Heather told me about you," Amber replied. "She said you and Ian were good friends."

"Yes. . . . So sad about Ian. But he is with God now. A better place to be, I think."

Amber refrained from saying that Ian's leaving had brought Heather immeasurable heartache and that she personally wished God had not taken Ian away.

"Patrick's studying for the pastorate," Paul said. "Ugandan ministers are in great demand within the country."

"And when you write your sister, please tell her that I have found the girl of my dreams and that I'm engaged. Tell her I plan to be the husband of only one wife for all my life," Patrick said with a laugh.

Heather had told Amber about the Ugandan custom of polygamy. It had spread the AIDS epidemic through the population as well as causing many other problems. "I'll tell Heather. She'll be very happy for you both."

"She is invited to the wedding in September. Perhaps her illness will have passed by then."

"Hope so," Amber said, wondering again if Heather's health problem had been caused by something she'd picked up in Africa.

Paul and Janet spoke about Alice, and Amber listened, all the while watching the countryside bump past. The road was poor, covered with potholes that often forced the van to a crawl. They stopped once to buy the finger-sized bananas Heather had called "delectable." The vendor's small wooden cart stood at the side of the road next to a sign declaring that the area was on the equator. Paul snapped a photo of Amber and Janet beside the sign.

Hours later they entered the compound of the Kasana Children's Home, where Paul's family emerged from a brick house. After introductions, Jodene showed them to the small guest house. Amber chose the same room and bed where Heather had told her she'd stayed. She imagined Heather in every corner of the room. And while Amber didn't share Heather's attraction to Africa, she found it oddly comforting and less lonely to be in the same space that her sister had occupied.

Janet dumped her luggage and insisted on going straight to the hospital to check out the facility where she would operate on Alice. "I'd like you to bring Alice over this afternoon," she told Jodene. "I want to give her a thorough physical exam so that I can map out a surgical strategy."

With her mother gone, Amber was left to explore the grounds. She freshened up and set off, looking for the spots Heather had described so vividly. She found the pavilion where church suppers were held, and the outdoor kitchen, whose oven was being tended by several kids baking bread. They smiled and waved. She found the tree where Heather used to sit and wait for Kia. She turned when she heard the front door of the house slam. A little girl ran toward her, her face lit with a smile. She skidded to a stop in front of Amber, her smile exchanged for a look of puzzlement.

Amber bent and extended her hand. "I'll bet you're Kia."

The child nodded.

"Did you think I was Heather?"

Another nod.

"I'm Amber; Heather's my sister. You know, my *dada*." Amber used the Swahili word for "sister," which Heather had taught her. "Heather couldn't come, so I came for her. She gave me this to give to you." Amber reached into the pocket of her pink shorts and pulled out a piece of hard candy.

Shyly Kia took the candy and unwrapped it. "Thank you, Amber."

The girl's sweet smile touched Amber, and she understood how Heather had fallen in love with her. "Heather told me a lot about you. I hope we can be friends too."

The soft air hung around them like folds of a blanket.

"Heather!" a male voice shouted.

Amber turned to see a guy trotting toward her. He wore khaki shorts and construction boots and was bare from the waist up. His body was streaked with dirt and sweat. A red bandanna held reddish brown hair off his forehead. His smile reminded her of the sunlight. He was, in her quick evaluation, the best-looking creature she'd ever laid eyes on.

8

Amber straightened. The bare-chested young man skidded to a stop in front of her, a look of confusion clouding his face. "I'm sorry—I thought you were someone else," he said with a heavy Southern accent.

She grinned. "I'm Amber. I'll bet you're Boyce Callahan."

"Guilty. How'd you know?"

"Heather showed me pictures."

"I knew you'd be coming in her place, but when I saw you from a distance—well, you looked so much like her that I thought somehow she was well and had come instead."

He looked disappointed, and Amber felt a twinge of jealousy. No guy had ever seemed as eager to see Amber, and Boyce and Heather were just friends. At least, that was what Amber had thought. "No, she's still under her doctor's care. And we really don't look that much alike . . . do we?"

He grinned, and his green eyes crinkled at the corners. "It's sort of like looking at two roses. Same flower, just different styles."

Flattered, not knowing how to respond, she looked down at Kia. "I—um—was just getting to know Kia. My mom went to the hospital to take a look around. I'm sure you know she's going to—" Amber interrupted herself, afraid to say too much in front of the little girl. "Well, you know," she finished lamely.

Boyce crouched and gave Kia a grin. "What've you got there?"

Kia held out the candy, now grown sticky in her hand. "From Heather," she said with an adoring look at Boyce. "Heather's *dada*," she added, pointing at Amber.

"Heather sent you a present too," Amber told Boyce.

He stood. "She did?"

He looked like an eager puppy. "It's back in my quarters," Amber said with a laugh.

"I'm taking a lunch break. Could I get it now?"

"What do you say, Kia? Should we go get his present?"

Kia slipped her hand into Boyce's, and the three of them returned to the guest house. Inside, Amber rooted through her duffel bag and pulled out a jar of peanut butter.

"All right!" Boyce said.

"She told me how much you liked the stuff."

"Good timing. My supply's getting low." He opened the top and scooped a large dollop onto his finger. It was halfway to his mouth when he stopped himself. "Oh, sorry. Want some?" He tipped the open jar toward her.

"I'll pass this time."

He sucked the goo off his finger and replaced the lid. "Nectar of the gods," he said. "Thanks for hauling it all the way from the States. You made my day."

"Gee, it took so little. What do you do around here for fun?"

"Why don't I come by later and take you around and *show* you what we do for fun?"

Her heart skipped a beat. "It just so happens that my evening is free."

He set a time, then took Kia's hand again. Amber stood on the porch, watching them walk away, and told herself that so far Africa was turning out to be a really interesting place. She'd not been in the country two days and already she had a date with a gorgeous guy. "Not bad," she said under her breath. "Not bad at all."

She and her mother went to dinner that evening at Jodene and Paul's, where the table was filled with platters of vegetables fresh from the garden, home-baked bread, and a roasted chicken. Amber thought about Heather back home, unable to eat.

"What's your opinion of Alice?" Paul asked Amber's mother. "What are her chances for a successful surgery?"

"I assessed her thoroughly today. Sometimes there's a host of other problems that go along with the clefting. Fortunately, Alice's case isn't the worst type of this defect. It's operable. The actual surgery is done in two steps. I'll fix the palate first. That takes around an hour, with a five-day recovery time. Then the lip will be repaired next week and her nostrils brought into a more normal alignment. Dr. Gallagher and I both think she's an ideal candidate for the surgery."

"Will she have a scar?" Jodene asked.

"Yes, until she's a bit older; eventually it will begin to fade. More surgery when she's older will enhance her face cosmetically, but that will have to be evaluated by another surgeon. She's been well cared for, thanks to you two, and that's in her favor also."

"Believe me, it was a group effort," Jodene said. "I couldn't have done it without the help of all the young women who live on the premises. Everyone pitched in. We want her to have as normal a life as possible, and her physical appearance is an important part of the quality of her life. Thank you for taking time out of your busy life to come all the way to help Alice and kids like her."

"Heather sent me," Janet said with a smile. "She can be very persuasive."

"We know that," Paul said with a laugh. "But regardless, we're grateful."

"When will you operate?" Jodene asked. "I want to prepare Kia for the separation from Alice."

"Tomorrow. Once I'm certain there aren't any complications, I'll head back to Kampala." Janet looked directly at Amber. "And my thanks to you for letting Amber stay with you while I work in the city. I'm taking her to the hospital tomorrow, and Dr. Gallagher will assign her some work. If there's anything you need her to be doing, just let her know."

"We're delighted to have her," Jodene said smoothly. "Any sister of Heather's is welcome."

They laughed, but Amber was steamed. Her mother made it sound as if Amber couldn't be trusted to be productive on her own.

After dinner Boyce stopped by the house, met Janet, and invited Amber for a walk around the compound. Once outside, Amber blew out a sigh of relief. "Thanks for the rescue," she said. "My mom and I've spent entirely too much time together these past few days."

"That's me—Sir Boyce the Lionhearted." Dusk was falling, and the sky's brilliant shade of red orange had faded to a dusky purple. "Come take a look-see at the irrigation project while there's still enough light." Boyce took her hand and started up a trail through the bush.

They emerged into a clearing where trenches were being dug in a pattern. "Irrigation canals," Boyce explained. "My idea is to shuttle water down them to the sides of fields where crops can be planted. The water will come from this concrete reservoir—it'll collect rainwater. We're also digging a well to an underground lake. In a year or two this whole area will be green and fertile."

Amber gazed out over the parched ground, cracked from the blazing sun. "It's hard to imagine," she said. "But I believe you'll do it."

"It'll take most of three months to get it going. Paul will take over when I have to leave. If I don't finish up at Alabama by the end of next year, my daddy's going to write me off."

"How could he? You're doing so much good."

"Dad wants me working in his engineering firm. Personally, I'd rather put in a few years over here before settling down stateside. Africa gets in a person's blood, you know."

"Yes, it happened to Heather."

"But not to you?"

She didn't want to tell him how much the lifestyle *didn't* appeal to her, so she just shrugged and said, "I've only been here two days. Maybe in time."

"And here I am dragging you around when you'd probably rather be catching some Z's."

"I can sleep in tomorrow," she said. "Show me more."

The moon began to rise over a clump of trees and cast the land in a cool, pale light. Amber wished she was with Boyce back in Miami, where she knew of many places they could go to be together. She'd love showing him off to her friends. To Dylan, too.

Boyce took her to an area on the grounds with large thatched-roof buildings of cinder block. "These are the family units. I'll take you to Patrick's."

They found Patrick leading his group in a Bible study. "Come in! Come in," he told Boyce and Amber. "We are almost finished."

The main room held a mixture of hand-carved and secondhand furniture. Short hallways branched out from the larger room, separating the boys' and girls' sleeping quarters. The concrete floor was covered with a woven grass rug. Shields and masks hung on one wall; a painting of Jesus praying in the Garden of Gethsemane hung on another. When Patrick saw Amber staring at the shields, he said, "This reminds us of our heritage." He nodded toward the painting. "This reminds us of our hope. 'He who lives by the sword, dies by the sword,' " he quoted. " 'But the Word of the Lord stands forever.' "

Unable to think of anything to say, Amber smiled politely.

"Be right back," Boyce said. "I need to talk to one of my foremen."

Amber stood, feeling self-conscious and out of place. The group of Africans stared at her, some smiling, some whispering. "Meet my fiancée," Patrick said. "This is Ruth Musembe, soon to be Mrs. Patrick Sugabi."

Ruth, a diminutive young woman with a pleasant smile and wide-set features, didn't look much older than Amber. "Congratulations," Amber told her.

"I remember your sister," Ruth said. "She was so very brave to bring Alice out of Sudan. A dangerous place for both of them."

"That's my sister. Trying to save the world."

Patrick went to talk to Boyce, and Amber found herself alone with Ruth, forced to make small talk. "So where's your family?"

"In Rwanda. My parents are missionaries serving in my uncle's village, doing the work of the Lord."

"I'll bet they're looking forward to your wedding."

"Yes. It is an honor for me to marry Patrick." Ruth cut her eyes toward her fiancé, and her expression turned wistful, almost sad. "I pray each day to the Lord Jesus that I will be a good wife."

"I'm sure you will be." Amber thought Ruth far too serious for one who was soon to become a bride. She wore no engagement ring. Neither had she talked about a honeymoon, or buying things for herself or a new house. "Will you live here?"

"For a time, yes. Then we will become missionaries and move out into the bush to spread the Gospel."

Amber realized she didn't have much in common with this girl. Becoming an itinerant preacher's wife before she was twenty and living off the land didn't sound very appealing to her, but she hoped she seemed more enthusiastic about it than she felt. She didn't want to hurt Ruth's feelings.

When it was time for Amber and Boyce to leave, Ruth said, "It is pleasant to know you. You are like your sister in some ways, but you are yourself, too."

On the walk to the guest house in the moonlight, Amber asked, "Everybody loved Heather, didn't they?"

"Yes," Boyce said.

"You too?"

"She's my sister in the Lord. I love her like a sister. Believe me, Amber, a lot of workers come through the Mercy Ship program, and most are dedicated. But few have the intensity, the heart, the sheer love for mankind that Heather has. God used her in a mighty way while she was here. Perhaps he will use her again. I don't know. I do know that I count it a privilege to know her." He stopped at the doorway of the guest house. "You've come as her emissary, and I think that's admirable too."

Her heartbeat quickened. "We're different," she said. She didn't want him to think she was her sister's clone. "We don't exactly think the same way."

"Maybe not as different as you think. Wait until you've been challenged. Then you'll see what I mean."

He told her good night, and she went inside. Her mother was asleep, so she got ready for bed quietly and slipped under the clean sheets. She lay in bed, staring at the moon through the screen of the bedroom window, her mind jumbled with thoughts.

It dawned on Amber that Heather had truly achieved a kind of cult status at the compound. Amber's motives for coming hadn't been pure—she had wanted a change of scenery, a way to perk up her boring life. Coming to Africa on Heather's behalf seemed logical and altruistic. But it had also been self-serving. She felt like a fish out of water among these gentle people dedicated to serving God. How long before one of them discovered that she was a fraud?

9

Amber's plan to sleep in changed quickly when her mother routed her out of bed early the next morning. "We have to be at the hospital in an hour," Janet said. "This isn't a vacation, you know."

Although her mother's bossiness irritated Amber, she refrained from complaining. After all, Heather had kept such a schedule, and so could she.

At the hospital her mother went off to perform surgical duties, and Dr. Gallagher assigned Amber to the Women's Clinic, an outpatient operation that handled routine immunizations, performed TB testing, and dispensed information about birth control and HIV. Local women were lined up with their children from the minute the doors opened. An Ugandan nurse named Grace explained the counseling process to Amber, and to Amber's great surprise, she was left on her own to counsel native women about the various forms of birth control.

She felt overwhelmed at first, and embarrassed to be talking about such things with strangers. The women seemed incredibly young, and most had two or three children clustered around their chairs. But they looked eager to learn what she had to say, and before she knew it the morning had flown and Grace was excusing her to go to lunch. She stepped out the door and ran into Ruth.

"I didn't know you worked here," Amber said, pleased to see a familiar face.

"I do counseling in another room."

"What do you tell the women? Saying the same things about birth control all day long sure gets old. Maybe you can help me do a better job. Maybe we should work together. That would be good, don't you think?"

"I counsel women with other problems." Ruth looked uneasy, as if Amber's suggestion had upset her.

An awkward moment of silence passed. Finally, noticing that Ruth's hair was covered by a white cloth and her dress by a white apron, Amber asked, "Are you a nurse? You look so professional."

"I am an apprentice. When Patrick and I are serving in the bush, I will have to care for villagers. I am learning how."

"Can we eat lunch together?" Amber changed the subject when her stomach rumbled.

"Thank you, but I do not have time."

"So where's the cafeteria?"

Ruth gave Amber a blank stare.

"You know, the place where the staff go to eat their meals."

Ruth shook her head. "You must bring food with you. Only the patients are fed at the hospital."

Embarrassed by her *faux pas*, Amber shrugged. "Silly me. I forgot to bring anything. Oh, well . . . I'll skip lunch. Besides, it's almost time for Alice's surgery, and I'd planned to hang around until it's over. Can you please tell Grace what's going on? Tell her I'll be here in the morning, though. I don't want her to think I've deserted her." She realized she was babbling. "Got to run. Catch you later."

Amber took off toward the surgical wing, made a wrong turn, and found herself in an unfamiliar ward filled with male patients.

Every bed was occupied, and more patients had been placed on mats lining the floor. A man in a makeshift traction device consisting of wooden rods, pulleys, and rope, called out to her in Swahili. *"Maji. Tafadhali, maji."*

"I—I don't understand."

The man in the bed next to him said, "He wants water, please."

"I—I'll get a nurse." Amber looked around for someone—anyone. The room held only the sick and hurt. There were no nurses or orderlies.

"You are a nurse," the man said.

"No. I—I'm only a helper."

"Maji, maji," another called.

All at once other patients began to cry out to her, some in pain, some in anger. One man on the floor grabbed for her foot, making her squeal. Panicked, she said, "I'll send someone." She backed out of the ward, turned, and ran toward an outside door with the men's cries chasing her.

"Mom, I'm not cut out for this."

An hour later Amber stood in the area directly outside the operating room with her mother, sniffling back tears and telling her mother what had happened. Janet was dressed in pale green scrubs, preparing for Alice's surgery.

Janet shook her head. "Listen to me, Amber, you can't fall apart. I don't have time for it. I know things are hectic—"

"Things are *bizarre*," Amber corrected. "Sick people are lying on floors, the equipment is dilapidated, there's not enough of anything to go around—"

Janet took hold of Amber's shoulders. "Stop it. I know conditions are primitive by our standards, but this place is first-class compared to others I've seen. Now I have to go in there and operate on that baby. I have to concentrate and can't be worrying about you. So pull yourself together and wait for me. Jodene is coming over with Kia. Neither of them needs to see you in shambles." Janet let go of her daughter's arms. "You will be all right."

Chastised, Amber hung her head. "I—I'm sorry."

The operating room door opened and a nurse said, "We are ready, Dr. Barlow."

Janet tied her surgical mask over her mouth. "I've got to scrub. Can you manage?"

"I'm fine."

Her mother stepped inside the operating room. Amber glanced out the window and saw Jodene and Kia coming across the hospital's neatly trimmed grass. "How did you do this, Heather?" she asked under her breath. When Jodene and the child walked into the area, Amber put on a smile and announced, "You're just in time. Alice just went into surgery."

Jodene told Kia, "We'll visit Alice when the doctor is finished. Now we must wait."

"Does she understand what's happening?" Amber asked.

"I told her that Dr. Janet, the Mother Doctor of sisters Heather and Amber, is going to make Alice's face look like Kia's face. I think she gets it."

They sat on a hard wooden bench along the wall to wait. Unexpectedly, Kia handed Amber a small package wrapped in a banana leaf.

"What's this?" Amber took the green leaf and opened it. Inside lay two pieces of home-made bread.

"It's a peanut butter and honey sandwich," Jodene said. "Boyce and I thought you might be hungry. You know, it's not everyone he shares his peanut butter with," she added with a chuckle. "You must really be special."

The unexpected gesture of kindness touched Amber. "Thank you," she said to Kia. "I forgot to pack a lunch, and I'm really hungry."

The child's wide, trusting eyes tangled with Amber's gaze. "Mother Doctor will make my *dada* so that she can smile very pretty."

Emotion closed Amber's throat. "Yes," she said, suddenly proud of her mother's skills. She smoothed Kia's hair. "My mother can do that. She will make Alice's smile very pretty. Just like yours."

The surgery took an hour. Alice went to the recovery room, and Janet bent the rules and carried Kia there to see her sister. Jodene and Amber waited in the hall while Amber wondered if the sight of the surgical dressing would scare the child. But Kia returned looking satisfied, not frightened.

"I'm going to stay around for a while," Janet told Amber. "Why don't you go back to the house?"

"You're both having dinner with us," Jodene interjected. "Come straight over when you're finished."

"We've got to learn to fend for ourselves,"

Janet said. "You can't be feeding us every night."

"Nonsense. We like your company. And when you head off to Kampala at the end of next week, we expect Amber to eat all her meals with us."

For that Amber was grateful. Heather had had friends to eat with every night, but Amber would have no one once her mother left.

"Thanks," Janet said to Jodene. To Amber she said, "We'll call home tonight. I know your sister's sitting by the phone waiting for a full report."

Amber was certain her mother was correct.

After dinner Amber helped Jodene do dishes at a sink with a hand pump connected to an underground well, and Janet returned to the cottage to place the phone call. "Give me about twenty minutes to talk, then come," she told Amber.

Amber waited the allotted time, then hurried to the house to take her turn on the phone. "Hi, sis."

"Hi yourself. Mom says you've pitched right in at the hospital. It's different from medical care over here, isn't it?"

"I'll say. I feel sorry for the people. I'm counseling women about birth control," Amber added quickly. "Who'd have thought it?" Hurrying on, she said, "Patrick has a fiancée—Ruth."

"Patrick's engaged? That's wonderful! What's she like?"

"Sort of quiet. She and I don't have a lot in common, so it's not easy to have conversations with her. She's worrying about being a good missionary wife. She seems really nervous about it."

"Well, I'm sure if Patrick picked her out, she must be special. How's Boyce?"

"You didn't tell me he was so totally hunky."

"You saw photos of him."

"Grainy little snapshots," Amber corrected. "Up close and personal, he's pretty awesome."

"I'll write and tell him you said so."

"Don't you dare!" Amber squealed. "I'll never speak to you again if you do."

Heather laughed. "All right, I'll keep quiet. Now, tell me about everybody else. I want to hear what you think about everything."

Amber launched into a monologue about Alice and Kia, Jodene and Paul—anything she thought Heather might want to hear. Once she'd finished, she asked, "And how about you, sis? How are you doing?"

"I'm still having problems. The doctors are baffled, and Dad's on their backs all the time. I'm seeing another specialist on Friday. He's from Atlanta's CDC—Centers for Disease Control and Prevention."

"They think you're contagious?"

"No—but since they can't figure out what's wrong, they're trying everything. Maybe I did pick up something while I was in Africa." A chill went through Amber, but she didn't say anything. "I told Dad that hundreds of people travel to Africa and never catch anything, so if you're worried about it, stop worrying."

Amber blushed. Her sister knew her too well. "I'm not worried."

"I'm doing exactly what I'm told," Heather added. "Staying in bed, taking my medicine . . . Truth is, I don't feel much like doing anything else."

"Then do nothing! You can always shop QVC."

Heather laughed. "You nut! How's that shopping gene helping you in Uganda?"

"Give me time. I've only been here a few days."

"I miss you, Amber."

"I miss you, too." Amber swallowed the lump of emotion sticking in her throat and saw her mother signal her from the bedroom doorway. She told Heather, "Mom's giving me the evil eye. I'd better hang up."

"She said she'd call again after Alice's second surgery. Take care," Heather said, sounding teary. "And go easy on Boyce. He's already had his heart broken by Ingrid."

Amber hung up, thinking about everything Heather had said to her. She took the phone to her mother in the living room, asking, "What's your opinion of Heather's being seen by someone from CDC? What do you think he's looking for?"

"Your father's worried that she might have a mutant strain of the hepatitis virus."

"That's bad?"

"Yes," Janet said in her gravest tone. "That could be very bad indeed."

10

"I'm telling you, Boyce, it could be serious." Amber had sought out Boyce the next evening as soon as both had completed their work for the day. They had met under the pavilion because the sky was threatening rain.

"What exactly did your mother tell you?" Boyce asked. He was freshly showered, his hair still damp.

"She had some medical mumbo jumbo about the different strains of the hepatitis virus. It seems like science is constantly discovering some new strain of it—A, B, C . . . all the way up to G. The worst is C because it destroys a person's liver." Amber paced as she talked.

"Can't doctors give you an immunization shot against it? I got an armful of shots before I came here."

"Sure, for hepatitis A and B. But not C. And

according to Mom, there's no known treatment for it. What if Heather has hepatitis C? What if she begins to lose her liver function? A person can't live without a liver, Boyce."

Boyce took Amber's hand. "Slow down, girl. You're jumping to conclusions. What exactly did your mother tell you?"

"She said that a small percentage of the people who have it die from it."

"A *small percentage*," Boyce emphasized. "Besides, you don't know for sure that Heather even has the virus."

"That's why the doctor from CDC is coming to examine her. According to Mom, he's an old friend, someone they knew years ago when they were in the Peace Corps. He's some kind of specialist in infectious diseases. Not that Heather's contagious or anything. But what if she picked up this virus?"

"Then this guy will figure it out."

"Mom's going to call again before she heads off to Kampala. But she's taking the phone with her, so how will I find out anything?"

"If it's serious, she can reach Paul on his ham radio unit."

Amber chewed her bottom lip. "I'm worried

about her. Really worried. I don't want anything to happen to her."

"Heather's in good hands, and I'm sure her doctors will get to the bottom of her problem soon," Boyce said soothingly.

"I feel helpless. I wish there was something I could do for her."

"You can pray. Patrick and I meet every night for prayer. We'll put Heather at the top of our prayer list."

Amber didn't have as much confidence in prayer as Boyce did. "Do you really think God listens?"

"Yes. And because you come from a family of doctors, you should know that plenty of doctors also believe in the power of prayer. I read some studies scientists have done on the subject, and it's documented that people who pray, people who believe in God, recover more quickly and with a lot less stress. Even people who are prayed for without knowing that they're being prayed for recover faster."

"Really?" That sounded hopeful to Amber. If such a scientific study had been done, there had to be some truth to it. "I don't mean to sound skeptical," she said. "I—I just don't feel the same way about things that you do. About God and all."

Boyce looked her in the eye. "Faith is a gift from God, Amber. No one's born with it."

"I've never heard that before."

"Think about it. Our brains want everything spelled out for us. We want proof of something before we believe in it. Faith is trusting in what we can't see or touch. It's being changed from a person who must have things proved to a person who accepts the unprovable as true and real. That's a big leap for a lot of people. And one that only God can accomplish by faith."

Amber considered his explanation. Her sister had always been a person who wanted to help others. When the two of them were growing up, Heather had been the one who raised money for charity and organized food drives. But when she'd come home from Africa, she'd been different.

"Coming here, meeting up with you, Ian, Jodene, and Paul, changed Heather," Amber told Boyce. "Losing Ian was part of it; she was sad and she kept to herself more. But she was also more . . . focused. Quieter. It's hard to describe."

"She encountered a different world over

here. I know, because so have I. Being here changes your perspective on *our* world. Our American, sanitized, white-bread world," he elaborated. "Being changed isn't necessarily a bad thing, you know."

"Maybe, but to be honest, her change has bothered me. I've felt cut off from her. We're in the same house, but not in the same place. You know what I mean?"

"I think so."

"She said something happened to her spiritually. She and Dad had a discussion about it. I don't think any of us understand it, but it's real to Heather. She still wants to help people and all, but she wants to help them in a deeper way."

"Before God got to me, I was pretty wild," Boyce said. "In trouble at school, driving my parents crazy. But once God changed me, I felt like some fire was living inside me. I wanted to do something good with my life, something for others. Trouble was, no one believed I had changed. Coming to Africa was part of proving it. While I was on the Mercy Ship, I met a whole lot of people who felt the same way. Building something over here has made me feel useful. Like my life was counting for something. Not just for the sake of the orphans living here, but for God, too. Not that God needs any help from me," Boyce added with a laugh, "but it feels good to do something for him when he's done so much for me."

Rain had begun to fall, and the drops on the thatched roof made a muffled patter. Amber felt wrapped in a cocoon of softness and cut off from the march of time. "You sound like Heather," she said.

"I can't change who I am, Amber. I'm a man who loves God."

No guy had ever talked to Amber with such sincere, open honesty. It moved her. And it made her feel inadequate, as if she was missing a piece of something bigger. Back home, with her friends, with Dylan, she'd been able to feel as if she fit, as if pleasure and enjoyment were central to the scheme of life.

From Boyce and her work at the hospital she was discovering something outside herself, something independent and unimpressed by her presence. She stood at a doorway, but a doorway into *what* she did not know. Still, she had sense enough to realize that if she went through the door, she too would be changed.

And that was what made her feel uneasy. Once through it, there would be no turning back.

"I admire you for knowing who you are," she said above the patter of the rain. "I don't know that much about myself, although I wish I did. But I trust you. And if you're praying for Heather, I hope it will help her."

"Prayer is a way for us to talk to God, to ask him for something we want. Heather's in his hands. He'll watch over her."

And so was Ian, Amber thought, though she didn't say it. All the prayer in the world hadn't made a difference for him.

Alice's second surgery at the beginning of the next week went well, and once the dressings came off, everyone could see the dramatic improvement in her appearance. With Jodene and Kia, Amber visited the ward where Alice lay recovering. "It's the repair on the inside of her mouth and nasal cavity that's going to make the most difference in her life," Janet said when Jodene raved about her surgical skills. "Now she'll be able to learn to eat and talk properly."

"But it's the outside that people see," Jodene

reminded them. "Looking normal will really improve the quality of her life. You've worked wonders for her."

Janet waved aside the woman's praise. "By the time she's a toddler, the scar will be as thin as a pencil line." She smiled and smoothed the baby's hair. "Amber, take a few photos to mail off to your sister."

"I'll send along pictures as she improves," Jodene promised. "I know how much this little girl means to Heather."

"I'm turning her over to the nursing staff," Janet said, "and packing up for Kampala."

"Paul will take you whenever you're ready."

Once her mother left, Amber would be on her own, and although her work was going smoothly and she'd forged friendships with Jodene, Boyce, and a few others, this would be the first time in her life that she would be totally out of touch with her family. She thought back to the many times she'd wished they'd get out of her face—just disappear. Now that it was about to happen, she had mixed feelings.

Two days later, in the early hours of the morning, Janet prepared to leave. A call stateside the day before had revealed that the CDC specialist had been delayed in his trip to Miami, so nothing new had happened for Heather. "Don't work too hard," Heather had said cheerfully. But to Amber, her sister's voice didn't sound strong.

Paul loaded Janet's belongings, and Janet hugged Amber goodbye. "You going to be all right?"

"Jeez, Mom, I'm seventeen. I think I can handle a few weeks away from my mommy."

Janet sighed. "I was just asking."

Amber held herself rigid. "I'll be fine. When you talk to Heather, tell her I miss her. And Mom, if you find out anything about her health—"

"I'll get word to you," Janet said. She stepped into the van and leaned out the window. "Be good, okay?"

Amber rolled her eyes dramatically. "As if I could even find trouble around here."

"You have a knack, honey. . . ."

Paul started the engine and, as Janet waved to the small group gathered in the yard, pulled out. As the taillights disappeared, tears spilled from Amber's eyes. "I'm fine. I'm fine," she said, holding up her hand to ward off sympathy.

Boyce slung his arm over her shoulders. "Hey, it's Saturday. What would you say to taking the day off with me? We'll borrow the Jeep and I'll take you to one of the most beautiful places on planet Earth."

Boyce drove to the town of Kabale, in Uganda's mountainous region. "Lake Bunyoni, a crater lake six thousand miles above sea level," he told her as they took a winding, rough road cut through a thick jungle of towering trees and fallen branches. As the Jeep chugged upward, the air turned cooler, less humid and smothering. At the crest of the slope, the ground flattened and Amber looked out onto a breathtaking view of lush acres of mountain forests surrounding calm blue water. In the center of the lake she saw an island, and on it, a building that resembled a fortress. "What's that?"

"It's a school now, but once it was a leper colony built by the Dutch."

"Lepers! Like in the Bible?"

"We have a few cases in our hospital. The patients are housed in the back buildings, along with the AIDS and TB patients. But leprosy is treatable, even curable with modern drugs. We can paddle out to the island by canoe later if you want."

"I'll think about it," Amber said, shivering at the vision of people with open sores and rotting skin.

There was an inn at the top of the hill, accessible by steps carved out of the ground. A patio faced the lake. Boyce took Amber's hand. "Come on. I'll buy you lunch." They settled into chairs facing the lake, and Boyce ordered strong Ugandan coffee. Happy to get her mind off disease and sickness, Amber took a lungful of rain-scented air and listened to the exotic calls of wild birds and monkeys.

"This rain forest is the home of the only mountain gorillas in the world," Boyce told her. "They're shy animals that keep to themselves, and tourists come from all over the world on photo safaris to Bwindi National Park. Rangers protect the animals, but poachers still kill them."

"That's terrible."

"Sure is, especially when you consider there're only about six or seven hundred left."

"People certainly mess up the planet, don't they?" Amber sighed. "I'm glad you brought me here. It's really beautiful."

"I hoped you'd like it. When I'm up here, I feel like I'm on top of the world. Hard to believe that Rwanda is less than fifty kilometers away."

"Isn't that where some of Ruth's family is living?" Amber craned her neck in the direction Boyce pointed in, but all she could see were vast forests of trees.

"Yes. She once lived there too. Never again."

"What's wrong with Rwanda?"

"Civil war broke out in '90, and Ruth's village was burned to the ground."

"That's terrible. Was she hurt?"

Boyce furrowed his brow. "You mean you don't know?"

"Know what?"

"Her parents were away doing missionary work the night the rebels came and looted and burned her village. She was twelve years old and they dragged her off into the underbrush, raped her, and left her for dead."

11

Amber felt as if she'd been kicked in the stomach. "I—I didn't know. She's never said a word."

"That's why she counsels rape victims at the hospital. She knows what they're going through. She knows how violated they feel."

Amber had assumed that Ruth did the same type of counseling she did. Not counseling for rape victims. "Twelve . . . she was just a child."

"Right. But they didn't care. They were animals."

Amber shuddered. "She could have told me."

"I guess it's not something she talks about except to other rape victims. Besides, I think she's slightly in awe of you."

"Of me? Why?"

"You're Heather's sister. You're an American, and wealthy, and confident. Ruth's not had much contact with Westerners. She admires you."

Amber felt her cheeks color. "I'm the one who admires her. Especially now. I thought she didn't like me." All her life Amber had been shielded and protected, given good things and plenty of opportunities. In the light of Ruth's horrible trauma, Amber's life was a fairy tale. "Why did the rebels do such a terrible thing? Why destroy Ruth's village?"

"Because she was from the wrong tribe," Boyce explained. "Civil war is a fact of life in Africa. So is political unrest."

"Why didn't her parents leave Rwanda? I would think they'd never want to live there again."

"Staying took courage, all right. Plus, they're missionaries. It spoke volumes about forgiveness to villagers who had been attacked by the rebels. If Ruth's family had been home that night, they would have been murdered. But they weren't home. They believe God spared them to do good works, to spread the Gospel of love, not hate."

"How about Ruth? Why didn't God save *her*?"

"What makes you think God didn't save her?"

"But she was raped, and you said they were trying to kill her! What was she saved from?"

"What those men meant for Ruth's destruction, God used for her good. What happened to her was terrible, but it also sent her into Uganda. It put her with the Children's Home. It led her to Patrick and to their engagement."

"Well, I would think God might have figured out some other way to accomplish the same thing," Amber said indignantly.

Boyce toyed with the handle of his coffee cup. "God permits evil to exist, and he often uses evil to accomplish his purposes. God doesn't micromanage the universe, Amber. People have free will, and just because we don't get it doesn't mean it's not part of a bigger plan we can't see when we're going through something bad."

Boyce's notion that life worked out for the best regardless of the circumstances irritated Amber. "I still don't think it's fair. Ruth didn't deserve to have that happen to her."

"I agree. But it did happen to her. And because it happened, she's able to help others who've gone through the same thing. And don't you know? Life isn't fair." He tipped his head to one side and flashed her a mischievous smile. "If life *was* fair, I'd be able to get a stack of peanut butter and jelly sandwiches for lunch."

"Are you changing the subject?"

"Yes. But only because I brought you here to have a good time, not to make you mad at me."

"Fair enough," she said with a toss of her hair. She didn't like arguing with Boyce and didn't want their relationship to turn adversarial. "I'm hungry too. Maybe I'll be less crabby after lunch."

"You're not crabby," he said, signaling for the waiter. "You're curious. That's allowed. Ask questions whenever you want."

The waiter, a boy of about thirteen, hustled over and Boyce asked, "What's to eat?"

"Crayfish from the lake. Or chicken. Very good food. Very fresh." A grin split the boy's face.

Boyce opted for the crayfish; Amber chose the chicken.

"Below is the village," the boy said, pointing to a cluster of huts along the side of the lake. "I will gather a cook."

"It could be a long wait for lunch," Amber said, dismayed.

"Here, have some of these." Boyce opened a small backpack he'd laid by his feet and doled out two finger bananas and a pile of peanuts.

"I thought Uganda didn't have peanuts."

"They call them groundnuts." Boyce popped a handful into his mouth. "What they don't have is peanut *butter.* Instead they turn the nuts into a sauce to pour over meat. They also don't have bread, so I guess there's no reason for peanut butter to exist, is there?"

"Well, I've eaten *matoke*—Uganda's excuse for bread. It tastes like library paste."

"What's wrong with library paste? I ate a steady diet of it in second grade."

"I'll bet if we flavored it with peanut butter, you'd still eat it."

"Got any?"

Amber poked him in the side. "Don't make me slap you around," she joked.

They sat together in a long, comfortable silence, watching a woman walk up the hill. The boy who'd gone to get her was already back and stealthily tiptoeing up to a clump of bushes not far from the patio. He crouched and clucked softly. All at once a large rooster squawked and darted out from under a bush with the boy in hot pursuit. Amber began to laugh but stopped as the truth dawned on her. She grabbed Boyce's arm and straightened in her chair. "Uh—do you suppose that's my lunch?"

Boyce studied the drama unfolding below. "Probably."

"Yikes! Tell him to stop! I can't eat that poor thing!"

"Why? Where did you think they were going to find your chicken?"

"In a refrigerator."

Boyce laughed heartily. "There's no refrigeration up here. No stores, either. If you're hungry you pick it or catch it, then cook it and eat it."

Amber's stomach churned. "I think I'm going to be sick. Make him stop, Boyce. Tell him I've changed my mind."

Still laughing, Boyce called out to the boy in Swahili. The kid looked up, gave Amber a curious look, then shrugged and hiked up to the patio. The rooster stopped flapping and settled down to peck at bugs on the ground. "What would the lady like for lunch?" the boy asked. "The cook is waiting for the chicken."

By now the woman from the village was inside the building behind them, and Amber smelled the aroma of sautéing onions and tomatoes. Normally her mouth would have been watering in anticipation, but her appetite had fled. "Vegetables would be good," she said. "Just a plateful of cooked vegetables, please."

The boy exchanged looks with Boyce, who shrugged. "I still want the crayfish," he said. He handed the boy a few Ugandan dollars. "More coffee. I think the lady needs it."

She needed it, all right. She also needed a constant reminder of where she was: She was in a place where chicken didn't come in tidy little cellophane-wrapped packages. And wicked men thought nothing of taking a young girl by force simply because she belonged to a particular tribe. Simply because she was in the wrong place at the wrong time, with the wrong ancestors.

It was well past dark when Boyce and Amber returned to the mission compound. Jodene met them in the yard with an oil lamp. "The lake is beautiful, isn't it?" Jodene asked as Amber exited the Jeep.

"Gorgeous," Amber said. "But I think we hit every pothole in the road home. I wish I could soak in a hot bath."

"I know how you feel," Jodene said. "When we first arrived, we stayed with another missionary couple. They had a huge old Victorian tub—perfect for soaking. In fact, in the cities, many Ugandan homes have tubs left from the time the British ruled the country. Trouble is, the tubs have no plugs. The Ugandans threw them all away."

"How do they take a bath without a plug to stop up the drain?"

"No African would ever sit in dirty bathwater. They were appalled at the British custom. Instead, they fill a container with water, sit in an empty tub, and pour the water over themselves. All the dirty water goes down the open drain." Jodene shook her head, bemused. "Besides, water is precious during certain times of the year, and for one person to fill a tub and bathe when the same amount could water a field of crops, or some cattle . . . well, you can see how it appears wasteful to them."

Amber understood, but she still yearned for

a tub of hot water and scented bubbles. "I guess," she said with a sigh.

Boyce excused himself. "Church tomorrow," he said. "I'm speaking, and I want to see Patrick tonight."

"Speaking of Patrick, there's been some excitement," Jodene said. "Ruth received a message from her parents that her cousin Ann is also getting married. In fact, her father suggested that Ruth and Patrick come to Rwanda, to her uncle's village, and get married at the same time."

"Rwanda!" Boyce said.

After their conversation at the lake, Amber understood his alarm.

"Is she going?" he asked.

"They were waiting to talk to you. Ruth's scared, but she really wants to go. If you'd go with them, they might do it."

Boyce hurried off to Patrick's hut, Amber right on his heels. At Patrick's living quarters oil lamps burned, and they found Patrick, Ruth, and their family of orphans sitting in a circle on the floor, praying. "Come," Patrick said, taking hold of Boyce's elbow. "We've been waiting for you."

Amber inched inside behind Boyce, hanging

back, trying not to be in the way. Boyce went to Ruth, crouched in front of her, and caught her hands. "Jodene told me. She said you wanted me to go with you and Patrick."

Ruth's large brown eyes looked serious. "I love my cousin. I would love to share this time with her. And I want to marry Patrick without waiting until September. Yet I am afraid." A wry smile crossed her face. "It seems as if God is calling me home to face my demons, doesn't it?"

Amber realized the difficulty of Ruth's choice. Returning to the place where her life had been so cruelly changed would take great courage.

Patrick said, "I told her we will do whatever she wishes. I only want her to be happy. If you come, Boyce, we can go together as health care workers. Therefore, the visas into Rwanda will be easier to acquire. There is no danger in going there now, but it will take away your time from the irrigation project. We would be gone at least seven days. Four days for traveling, three at the village."

Boyce looked at his foreman. "The project is in good hands. I could spare a week." He turned back to Ruth. "The decision is yours. We'll both do whatever you want."

Tears made Ruth's eyes shimmer in the light. "In my heart, I want to go. It is foolish for me to be afraid of what happened years ago. I have not seen my family in a long time. There would be such a time of rejoicing for us to be together again . . . and for such a happy event as a double wedding." She slid her hand into Patrick's. "And once we are married, we can begin God's work in earnest. Yes," she whispered. "If you will come, Boyce, I will go."

"We'll go to Kampala and get our visas this week. The sooner the better."

An excited buzz circulated through the group, and laughter leaped from person to person as plans solidified. Amber stepped out of the shadows and cleared her throat. "Um— excuse me." All eyes turned toward her. She took a deep breath. "I—I'd like to come with you. Can I come to your wedding? Please?"

12

"Are you sure your mother approves of this trip, Amber?" Jodene stood at the foot of Amber's bed while Amber stuffed clothing into a duffel bag.

"I talked to her when we were in Kampala getting our visas. She was perfectly all right about my visiting Rwanda for a few days." Amber had played down the excursion to her mother, saying that it was a wedding party with a group going to a nearby African village. Was it Amber's fault that her mother automatically assumed Jodene was also going? "Ruth needs company on the trip," Amber told Jodene. "She shouldn't go alone with Patrick and Boyce. Besides, I'd love to take pictures of the wedding for Heather."

"Any word on your sister?"

"Not yet."

"I worried about Heather when she took off to Sudan to rescue Alice," Jodene said with a sigh. "Now I guess I'll have to worry about you, too."

"But things are different for me. There was shooting going on in Sudan."

"Don't ever assume Africa will remain peaceful. You never know when trouble will boil over—"

"No gloom and doom, please," Amber insisted with a radiant smile. "We're going to a wedding. Ruth's wearing a traditional Ugandan dress, but she's asking me for details about weddings in the States. Don't you see, Jodene? At last I have something to share with people. I mean, if Amber Barlow doesn't know fashion and trends, who does?"

Jodene laughed. "You are irrepressible. Very different from your sister."

"Is that a bad thing?"

Jodene considered Amber thoughtfully. "No. Heather was very dedicated, but also very idealistic. Maybe too idealistic for this kind of life. You're more practical, which will serve you better in the long run, I think."

Amber felt flattered. She hadn't wanted to be compared to Heather and found wanting.

"Well, life around here is different, all right, and personally, I don't know how you do it. My father always told me that I'd better marry a rich man because I have such expensive tastes."

"First you have to fall in love with a rich man, don't you?"

"A small detail." No matter how much she loved a guy, Amber realized she couldn't make the kind of sacrifice it took to live in a foreign country without the comforts and modern conveniences she'd enjoyed all her life.

"Well, there are few rich men in the mission field," Jodene added. "At least, they're not rich in the conventional sense."

"No problem," Amber said, wondering if Jodene's comment was her way of warning her not to fall for Boyce. "I'm sticking to my game plan. A long and happy life in close vicinity to a mall."

Jodene cocked her head. "We'll see," she said breezily. "Sometimes God has a way of changing our plans whether we're willing or not."

The next morning Boyce and Patrick packed the Jeep. Amber sat up front with Boyce while

Patrick and Ruth wedged into the back with baggage and sleeping bags, content to snuggle for the two-day ride to the Rwandan village of Ruth's uncle. They spent the first night in a small hotel in Kabale that had a long balcony stretching around the second floor, overlooking the street. Amber and Ruth settled into their room, then met Patrick and Boyce on the balcony, where they sipped colas and watched the sun set over the mountains.

The rich green rain forest hugged rising peaks covered with misty clouds, and the voices of rain frogs and crickets sang a song of welcome to the approaching night. As twilight deepened, the street filled with people, and small charcoal fires flared to life. Grilled food perfumed the air with savory scents.

Boyce dug out a map and flattened it on the table. "The village should be about here," he said, making a circle with his finger.

"Don't you know for sure?" Amber asked. The map was blank in that space.

"Old map," Patrick said. "As we get closer, people along the way will tell us. All we need do is ask for the house of Edward Kaumahome. He is the wealthiest man in the area, with the best farmland and the most cows. Three cows will be given as part of Ann's dowry. It will be a good start for her and her husband."

Heather had told Amber that Ugandans in the bush measured wealth by the number of cows they owned, but still it was odd to hear Patrick say it.

"You do not give cows away at weddings in America?" Ruth asked.

"If someone says the word *cow* at a wedding in our country, it's usually to describe an oversized bridesmaid," Amber joked.

Boyce chuckled, but Patrick and Ruth gave her blank stares.

"You do not own a cow, Amber?" Ruth asked.

"No way. We have city ordinances against keeping livestock in our garages."

Ruth's incredulous expression turned to one of bewilderment. "But—But how can this be? You are a rich American. Where do you get your milk?"

It occurred to Amber suddenly that Ruth had asked her questions in complete innocence—she had absolutely no knowledge of dairy farms, grocery stores, refrigerated trains and trucks, or interstate highways. Amber cleared her throat and answered thoughtfully and gently, "Back home, milk comes in big plastic jugs. And the jugs are kept in special stores. I don't own a cow, Ruth, but I own a car that I drive to the store to buy the milk."

Ruth's eyes grew wide, and a lovely smile broke over her face. "Ahh! A car . . . you are a very rich American indeed."

With a lump in her throat, Amber said, "Yes, Ruth, I guess I am."

When Boyce and Patrick said good night, Amber and Ruth went to their room, a small cubicle with unpainted walls and two beds. The mattresses sagged pitifully, but the sheets were clean and smelled like sunshine. A wooden nightstand held a beat-up metal pitcher and bowl, which Ruth filled with water from the communal bathroom at the end of the hall. Amber remembered the bathroom at home that she shared with Heather—luxurious as a queen's by comparison. She washed her face, brushed her teeth with bottled water, and crept cautiously between the sheets.

Ruth clicked off the light, a bare bulb hanging from the center of the ceiling. Moonlight poured through the lone window, bathing the room in silver. The air felt warm, but not sticky or humid, and the scent of lemongrass drifted on every faint breeze.

"Are you excited about getting married?" Amber asked. They were to be in the Jeep by six in the morning, but she wasn't the least bit sleepy.

"I am anxious," Ruth said, her voice sounding hesitant in the dark. "I know there is much more to being a wife than the wedding ceremony."

"Boyce told me what happened to you when you were twelve. I—I'm very sorry."

"I have talked to many women who have been defiled by rape. I know all the things to say, to help victims with their pain." Ruth took a ragged breath. "But still, I wonder if I can be a proper wife to Patrick. He tells me he will be gentle with me. That he loves me. But still, sometimes in my bad dreams, I remember. In the dark places of my soul, I feel those men's hands. I remember how they held me down, tore my clothes. I remember how they hurt me." Her voice broke. "I cried for my mama. . . ."

Amber slipped out of bed and sat on the edge of Ruth's mattress. She took Ruth's hand clumsily, at a loss for words, not knowing how to help Ruth deal with her grief. Her experience extended only as far as listening to a girlfriend weep when some boyfriend had dumped her. Amber's response had consisted of trashing the guy and telling her friend she was truly cool and that the breakup had been the guy's loss.

Her only experience with real grief had come in fifth grade. A girl named Lisa had lost her mother in a car wreck. Amber recalled wanting to stay clear of her, as if Lisa's tragedy might somehow rub off on her if she got too close. As if Lisa's sadness might suck the class members under, like the vortex of water that gobbles a sinking ship. And so, with Amber's help, Lisa had been carefully ostracized, cut out of the circle of normal girls by the fear of contamination, until she had gone away. Now Amber was ashamed of the way she had acted. Ashamed and sad. She wanted so much to soothe Ruth, to protect the terrified child Ruth had been that night from the terrible thing that had happened to her. Yet it was as if she'd been struck dumb.

"It hurts my heart," Ruth whispered. "They took from me the treasure I wished to save for my husband. I know I must forgive them for what they did to me. There is no other way to leave the memories behind. And yet, tonight, I am sad inside. I am sorry for what was taken from me. What have I to give my husband now?"

Forgiveness? Amber could hardly comprehend it. Those men didn't deserve forgiveness. They deserved to die! "You have plenty to give him." Amber found her voice. "You have your heart to give him. You have your love, only for him. Those men stole your virginity, but not your love. That has always been yours to give away. Now you've given it to Patrick. And"— she paused, sensing that Ruth was listening— "you'll give him babies, too. A boy. A girl. Much better than many cows."

Ruth let out a tiny laugh. "We shall have cows, for we have no magic jugs filled with milk, only the udders of the cows to feed us."

"Just remember," Amber said, "Patrick loves you. Isn't that why you're going to your uncle's village? To pledge your love to each other forever?"

"Yes. Before my countrymen. Before God."

"You'll be a good wife, Ruth. You and Patrick will be happy. I know this because . . . well . . . just because I know these things."

The room fell silent. Amber watched the

moonlight move across the floor until it became a pale white sliver. Thoughts swirled in her head . . . thoughts of her parents, working side by side all their lives to build a place of safety and comfort for their daughters. Of Dylan, whom she'd liked but never truly loved. She was glad she'd always told him no when he'd pressured her for sex. And she thought of Boyce, too. Wondered if he thought her the silliest and most frivolous of girls. She had all but invited herself on this trip. Perhaps he thought her pushy. She'd hate having him think that.

"Thank you for listening to my heart's worries, Amber. It has helped to say them aloud," Ruth said, breaking the stillness. "I—I was afraid to say anything."

"Why?"

"You have no reason to listen to the thoughts of a girl such as I."

"I sure do! We're girlfriends," Amber insisted fiercely. "Girlfriends can say anything to each other. Repeat after me: 'Hey, girlfriend.'"

Ruth imitated Amber's intonation, then giggled. "*Rafiki*, that is 'friend' in Swahili."

"*Rafiki*," Amber repeated. "I'll remember it."

Darkness closed around the room as the moon slipped away from the window. Amber listened to the serenade of night creatures, felt her eyelids growing heavy.

"Goodnight, girlfriend," Ruth whispered.

"Goodnight, *rafiki*," Amber whispered back.

She returned to her bed and fell asleep to dream of a great white ship drifting on a bright blue sea, and of a man standing on the deck, shielded by shadows. She strained to see his face but couldn't. And no matter how hard she tried, no matter how close she came, his face would not come into focus.

13

Early the next morning, Amber and her friends drove off in a ground fog that rapidly dissipated as the sun rose over the African bush country. Midmorning, their Jeep was stopped at the Rwandan border for a check of their visas by an intimidating trio of border police wearing dark blue uniforms. Pistols hung from belts around their waists, and they balanced Uzi automatic weapons expertly in their hands.

Patrick spoke to them amiably in Swahili, offering permits and documents, making a great show of the Red Cross armbands the four of them had put on that morning. The police insisted on taking a look at Amber's passport, which Amber wore in a pouch around her neck, and Boyce's too. Finally the police returned all the documents, had a few more words with Patrick, and waved them through.

"Not a very friendly group," Amber said once they were well on their way.

"They are keeping out undesirables," Patrick said.

"And that's us?" She was insulted.

"It is their job to be suspicious."

"What did they say at the last?" Boyce asked, his face set like stone. "I caught some of it, but not all."

"They said to be careful. Bandits and marauders have been in the area. They reminded us that only a year ago, a group of French and British tourists were attacked and two were killed."

Amber felt a sick sensation. She turned, and the look on Ruth's face was one of fear. Amber's heart went out to her.

The roads in Rwanda weren't any better than the roads in Uganda and worsened when Boyce turned onto a dirt trail that zigzagged through the countryside. Amber had tucked her hair under a safari hat, wrapped a wet neckerchief around her throat, and slathered herself with sunscreen, but there was no protection from the dust. She took small, frequent sips from her water bottle; the inside of her mouth felt gritty.

She was surprised at the number of huts she saw as the Jeep bounced over the hard ground. The dwellings showed no sense of order, no sense of community, sitting alone on the plain as if dropped at random. Women tilled parched gardens, babies strapped to their waists. Children wearing frayed shorts and torn T-shirts herded clusters of goats under trees and fanned flies off grazing cattle. The few men Amber saw sat under trees, smoking and talking together. "Don't the men help out?" Amber asked.

"No, farming is women's work," Patrick explained.

"So what do the men do?"

"They marry," he said with a laugh. But Amber didn't think it was funny. She'd met too many women at the hospital clinic who were exhausted and worn out from hard work and childbearing before they were thirty.

Boyce stopped around noon, and the four of them ate a lunch of fruit and cold boiled rice. "There'll be a feast in the village after the wedding," Boyce assured Amber.

"Chicken?" she asked with a sinking sensation.

"Probably roasted goat," Patrick said. "Very delicious."

"Yum," Amber said while her stomach rebelled.

In the afternoon Boyce turned north and the scenery became greener, the land more hilly. About three o'clock Boyce pointed to a cluster of thatched-roof huts in the distance.

"My uncle's village!" Ruth cried. She stood, held on to the roll bar, and began to wave.

The Jeep halted in the center of the village amid a cloud of dust. People poured out of huts, smiling, chattering, surrounding the Jeep. Ruth leaped down and ran to a man and a woman who enveloped her with welcoming hugs. Amber found herself caught up in the joy of the moment, even though she couldn't understand a word that was being said. "They're glad to see us," Boyce told her with a broad smile.

Ruth introduced her parents and the members of her extended family. Amber's head swam with a deluge of names she would never remember.

"You are just in time for afternoon tea," Ruth's mother, Winnie, said in perfect English. "And we will discuss all the plans for the wedding."

She led them into the largest hut in the village, where a small table was set with a beautiful porcelain tea service. Amber found the contrast between the delicate cups, saucers, and teapot and the rough mud walls and packed earthen floor poignant—the old British custom seemingly archaic and quaint so far from its moorings of polite English society. Ruth and her cousin Ann held hands, and talk of the wedding bounced between two languages. Amber picked up only fragments of the conversation.

Finally she and Ruth were shown to their quarters, a hut divided into two areas by a colorful bolt of cloth hanging from a wooden beam that supported the thatched roof. Shoes were left by the front door. Woven straw mats and rugs covered the earth floor. On the other side of the curtain lay straw pallets. Amber dropped her backpack with a thud. "Our beds?" All at once she wished for the sagging, lumpy mattresses from the hotel.

"Yes," Ruth said. "The village is honored to have Americans for visitors, so a family has moved out in order for us to have their home during our visit."

"You grew up in a village like this?" Amber glanced around. One small window cut out of the hardened clayey mud allowed light and air into the room. The only other furniture consisted of a single chair and a small wooden table.

"Not one nearly so large and fine. Our home was much smaller, but I was happy there. Until the rebels came." Water had been placed in a basin, and Ruth indicated that Amber should wash her hands. As Amber knelt over the basin, Ruth said, "My uncle's village is successful because it has a steady supply of fresh water. In the bush, water is a most precious asset. That is why Boyce's work in irrigation is so important. Better access to water means not having to move away when the supply runs out."

Amber understood. Without water to nourish the people, crops, and animals, there would be no farming. "Uganda's greener," she said.

"Yes. In Uganda, water is more plentiful—" A giggle sounded behind them, interrupting Ruth. Amber turned to see a small girl balancing on crutches. "Rosemary?" Ruth said, her smile lighting up. "Is that you, cousin?"

The child hobbled forward, and Amber saw

that her back was severely twisted, her head permanently tilted to one side. Ruth knelt to hug her, then introduced her to Amber. "Pleased to meet you, Amber," the girl said with perfect diction and a radiant smile. "I have a new dress for the wedding. It is green with white flowers, and my mama bought it for me in Kigali at the big store. And I have shiny black shoes and new socks, too."

"I—I can't wait to see you all dressed up," Amber said, charmed by the child, shocked by her physical condition.

"I will come to your hut later and we will have a long visit," Ruth told the girl. "But now Amber and I must rest."

"Have a pleasant rest," Rosemary said, offering another heart-melting smile, and hobbled out on her crutches.

"How old is she? What happened to her?" Amber asked as soon as the child was out of earshot.

"She's seven, and she contracted TB when she was a baby. It affected her spine. Rosemary is one of the reasons I want to learn about medicine. Many problems can be prevented with the correct medicine given to the very young."

Amber knew that TB had been all but eliminated in the United States for years. Ruth's choice to devote herself to learning about medicine and helping not only relatives but strangers made perfect sense. Amber thought of her own sister. Suddenly Heather's feelings for baby Alice made perfect sense too. Saving one child in the midst of all these bleak problems seemed like a small thing, but surely it made a difference. And enough small differences could have a real impact. Amber felt proud of her sister. And her pride gave her courage. She looked back at Rosemary.

"She's adorable," Amber said, still shaken by the child's deformity. "There's absolutely nothing to be done to help her?"

"No. It is too late for Rosemary. She had no medicine when she needed it." Ruth sighed, then brightened. "I have chosen her to be the one who holds our wedding rings during the ceremony. She is excited."

Tears misted Amber's eyes. The difficulty of the trip; the simplicity of the village; the splendidness of the tea service; Ruth's kindness; the knowledge that she, Amber, as an honored guest, had been given the best the villagers had to offer; the sheer beauty of Rosemary's smile suddenly overwhelmed her and left her feeling humbled. "You've chosen well, Ruth, *rafiki*," Amber said. "She's the perfect ringbearer . . . the perfect choice. And I can't wait until tomorrow to attend the wedding of the year."

Both brides wore traditional Ugandan marriage dresses for the double cermony, which was held near the village in a small cinderblock church, where Ruth's father was the minister. People dressed in their best finery sandwiched themselves into the pews, stood along the inside walls, spilled out the doors, and clustered outside in the hot sun. To Amber it looked as if the entire countryside had turned out for the event. Amber and Boyce had seats in the same row as Ruth's family. When the pianist began playing "Jesu, Joy of Man's Desiring," on an old upright, all eyes turned to watch the bridal procession.

That morning, as Amber had watched a nervous Ruth dress, she'd said, "You're going to be fine. Just remember to keep smiling."

"Is this how brides in your country feel on their wedding day? All shaky on the inside?"

"Nerves are natural. Back home I get twitchy every time I have to dress up in a formal. I think it's a side effect of putting on panty hose. Anyway, I calm right down when my date hands me a present. Here. Wear this. It'll help *you* stay calm." Amber slipped a gold chain with a heart-shaped sapphire pendant from her neck and fastened it around Ruth's.

"It is beautiful!"

"Keep it. It's yours."

Ruth's eyes widened as she admired the necklace in a small hand mirror propped on the table. "I cannot take such a gift."

"But it's perfect on you. And it's the way we do things in America. On her wedding day the bride carries four things: something old, something new, something borrowed, and something blue. Now, your dress was your mother's, so it's borrowed, and your Bible is new. The necklace is old *and* blue, so there's both things in one."

"And this is your custom?"

"Absolutely."

Now, as Amber watched Ruth come down the aisle, she was certain she'd done the right thing. Never mind that she'd begged her parents last Christmas for the expensive necklace. It looked perfect on Ruth. She only wished Heather could be there to see the service.

After the ceremony, while the pianist played, the congregation sang songs and danced in the aisles. Finally the group broke up and returned to the village, where Ruth and Mary's families threw a giant party. On the outskirts of the village a great pit had been dug, and a glowing charcoal fire roasted several goats on a spit. Amber watched their charred carcasses being turned by several small boys, wishing she could sit down in a restaurant and order something off a menu.

"They *are* pretty tasty, you know," Boyce assured her. He offered her a warm soda from a nearby plastic bucket. "Barbecue's a Southern tradition. Even you folks in Miami must have cookouts in the summer."

"Hello—in Miami the meat is in cute little patty form, not on the hoof."

He laughed. "Well, they're going to slide a slab onto your plate, so tell them thanks. It would be a great insult if you didn't take any."

"Swell. What if I throw up? Will that be insulting too?"

"Bring it to me and I'll eat it for you."

"You must have an iron stomach."

"I'm from Alabama, where scorched meat is a way of life." He draped his arm casually over her shoulder. "By the way, I noticed you gave Ruth your necklace. That was nice of you."

"I couldn't let her only wedding present be some cows, could I?"

"Don't worry, they'll have plenty of gifts. When we get back, Jodene will throw a bodacious party for them. Paul's making them a wedding bed. He's carving the headboard himself."

"Ruth's nervous about that part. You know . . . the sleeping together. The sex."

"So is Patrick."

"Really?" Somehow the news relieved her. She didn't want Ruth to have a bad experience with the man she loved and wanted to be with until death parted them.

"Patrick loves her. He knows she'll have trouble getting over what happened. He won't hurry things. Plus, they have a lifetime to work it out. The right girl's worth waiting for," Boyce added.

Boyce's eyes were bright green, set off by a tan gained from hours of hard work under the African sun. She saw the outline of rock-hard muscle through his shirt, the golden hair of his forearms glinting in the light. His hands were work-worn and rough, his mouth dangerously close to hers. Her pulse pounded.

"How do you know when the right one comes along?"

"They say you just know."

"Do you believe that?"

A smile turned up the corner of his mouth. "With all my heart."

Amber woke with a start in the inky darkness of her room. After the banquet and party, each newly married couple had been loaned a special hut, where they were to celebrate their wedding night, and Amber had returned alone to the hut she'd shared with Ruth. She heard the noise of someone moving in her room, and suddenly, knowing she was no longer by herself, she was wide awake. Terrified, she opened her mouth to scream.

A large hand clamped down on her face. Boyce's voice whispered urgently, "Don't be afraid. It's just me. Get your things together quickly. We've got to get out of here."

14

"Do you understand what I'm telling you?" Boyce asked in the darkness.

Amber moved her head up and down, and Boyce slid his hand off her mouth. Her heart thudded crazily, and adrenaline flooded her body.

"I'm sorry to wake you up this way, but I couldn't risk you screaming."

"Wh-What's wrong?"

"A runner came—a friend of Ruth's family. He said some bad men, some very bad men," Boyce said with emphasis, "are headed this way. They heard about the wedding and figured there would be things for the taking. The villagers will try to protect themselves, but if they fail . . ." Boyce paused. "Well, let's just say it would be terrible if we Americans fell into their hands."

Amber trembled from sheer terror. "What are we going to do?"

"We're going to make a run for it. You and me and Patrick and Ruth."

"What do you want me to do?"

"Get your backpack, take only the essentials—one change of clothes, extra socks—and meet me outside the hut. And hurry."

He was gone. Amber scrambled to her feet, dressed in the dark, found her flashlight, and, keeping the light aimed at the floor, stuffed her backpack as he'd instructed. Her fingers felt cold and stiff, though perspiration poured off her face. She grabbed her passport and visa, insect repellant, sunscreen, a few T-shirts, socks, and her hat. She never thought once of what she was leaving behind. Outside, Boyce took her hand while the villagers scurried in the dark to take up defensive positions.

He led her to Ruth's parents' hut, where Ruth and Patrick waited. An oil lamp burned dimly, and one look at Ruth's face revealed that she was in worse shape than Amber. "We won't let anything happen to you," Amber said, putting her arms around her friend.

Boyce and Patrick crammed each backpack with bottles of boiled water and emergency rations. Amber recalled asking Jodene why they had to take so much extra stuff when they would be gone only a week, and Jodene had answered, "Always be prepared. What if the Jeep breaks down?"

"Is the Jeep ready?" Amber asked, longing to put distance between them and the village as quickly as possible.

Boyce never looked up. "I've disabled the Jeep. We'd be sitting ducks in it. We're going out on foot."

"But—But how will we know the way?"

He glanced up. "We have a compass."

Terror choked her. Winnie pulled Amber and Ruth into her arms. "God will protect you. He will watch over you."

"What of you all?" Amber asked.

"He will be with us, too."

A man entered the hut, carrying Rosemary. The little girl was crying. "The children have scattered into the bush to hide. She cannot go," he said, setting her down. "She will have to stay in the village."

Ruth knelt and smoothed Rosemary's tangled hair and looked around the room.

"We'll take her." Amber hadn't realized the words had come out of her. The others stared at her. With a decisive movement, she picked up the child. Rosemary seemed weightless.

"She will impede you," Winnie said. "We will try to protect her here."

"If she's captured, you know what will happen to her," Ruth said woodenly.

"It will happen to all of us," Winnie answered.

Amber interjected, "I won't let it." She gave Boyce and Patrick a pleading look. "Please. We must make a difference even for one child."

Boyce stood and hoisted two backpacks. "We'll take turns," he said. "I'll take your pack for now."

A man stuck his head in the doorway. "Hurry! They are coming through the bush. They have guns." The *pop, pop, pop* of gunfire sounded in the distance.

One more quick round of hugs; then Amber settled Rosemary on her hip and followed Boyce into the night. Shouting, running people almost collided with them. Several of the huts had been set on fire. "Diversion," Boyce shouted.

Crouching low, the five of them ran into the night, like leaves blown by a cruel wind.

Amber had no idea how long they darted through the bush, but soon her lungs felt on fire, her arms and legs screamed from exertion, and Rosemary felt like a lead weight. "I—I can't keep up . . . ," she gasped.

Boyce stopped, relieved her of the child, and helped her slip a backpack onto her shoulders. "We've got to keep moving," he said. "Stay low."

Ruth stooped over, panting hard, and Patrick adjusted her backpack. "I will carry it for you."

"No," Ruth said. "I can do it."

Amber heard the sound of more gunfire, and the sky behind them wore a halo of eerie red orange. Tears welled in her eyes. "Will they be all right?"

Boyce took long deep breaths. "Ruth's uncle has firepower too. He'll fight."

"Can we wait it out?" Amber asked. "Go back when the fight's over?"

"Can't take a chance," Boyce said. "We've got to keep going."

"Which way?" Amber asked. With only the light of the stars to see by, she had lost all sense of direction.

"North," Boyce said, hoisting Rosemary higher on his hip. He pointed toward a star, brighter than the others. "To Uganda."

* * *

Amber passed the point of exhaustion some-where in the long night. She was disoriented and scared, and the backpack felt heavy as a boulder. Her shoulders and back begged for mercy, but she knew she didn't dare complain. This was a race for their lives. If the rebels caught up with them . . . *Pick up foot, put it down* became her mantra. The others were tired too, but to stop might be suicide. The village was far behind them by now, but in the dark they had the best chance of escaping detection.

She struggled over the rocky ground, stum-bled, and fell with a cry. Boyce and the others huddled around her. She began to cry. "I—I'm bleeding." She was wearing a skort and strong hiking boots, but the sharp edge of a rock had sliced open her knee. "Maybe you had better go on without me. I'm just holding you up."

"No!" Boyce said. "No one gets left behind." He pointed toward the horizon on their left. The sky was turning gray and the stars were fading. "Dawn's coming. We'll need to find a spot to sleep."

With Ruth on one side of her and Patrick on the other, Amber hobbled after Boyce, who led the way to an outcropping of rocks shielded by another hill. They fell into an exhausted heap and struggled to catch their breath. As the light of day broke, Ruth leaned over to check Amber's knee. "The cut is not deep," she said. She unpacked a small first-aid kit, smeared the cut with ointment, and dressed it with a bandage. Amber felt nothing. She was beyond pain.

Beside her, Rosemary patted her cheek, making Amber feel like a baby. The child was comforting her instead of the other way around. Amber offered the little girl a brave smile. "It's much better now."

Boyce passed around a bottle of water. "Two swallows," he said.

Amber longed to gulp the entire bottle but passed it quickly to Ruth to keep temptation at bay.

"Do you think we got away?" Ruth asked.

"From the rebels, yes," Patrick answered. "Now we must get away from the sun."

"We'll only travel at night," Boyce said. "It'll be harder, but cooler. There could be other groups of bad guys out here. Remember what the border police told us."

"How far are we from the border?" Amber asked, her voice trembling.

"Maybe sixty, seventy miles. With God's help, we can do it."

Amber almost gagged. The distance on foot across rugged terrain seemed insurmountable. "Now what?" she asked faintly.

"First we sleep. Then we count up our rations and see how long we can go without hunting food and water. We don't have enough of either with us."

"I'm not hungry," Amber said.

"You will be," Ruth said, her gaze fastened on the unfriendly, scruffy landscape. "We'll *all* be very hungry before this is over."

Amber remembered stretching out and resting her head on the backpack, then nothing until Boyce shook her shoulder. "Time to eat," he said.

She climbed out of a stuporous sleep, disoriented and groggy. Every muscle in her body hurt. "Eat without me. I'll eat later." She turned over, seeking the warm embrace of oblivion.

"Come on, Amber. In another hour we're going to have to start moving again."

"I don't think I can."

"Please, Amber. Come with us." Rosemary's teary plea snapped Amber fully awake.

She groaned and sat upright. Ruth sat hugging her knees, and Patrick was sharpening a knife on a stone. "Look, I'm up," Amber told Rosemary.

Boyce passed around the water bottle, again restricting them to a couple of sips apiece. "Now," he said, "here's what we have to eat."

On the ground he spread out eight cans of potted meat, a crushed box of granola bars, ten packages of peanut butter crackers, and an assortment of dried fruit packets. They stared at the pitiful selection, which would have to sustain five people over however many days it would take to reach safety. "What? No goat?" Amber asked, which made the others laugh.

Boyce picked up a can of meat and pried open the lid with its tab key. He passed it to Rosemary, Ruth, and Patrick, who each picked out a chunk. It came to Amber, who fished out an unappetizing lump and handed it back to Boyce. He took what was left and bowed his head. "We need to thank the Lord."

For what? Amber wondered, then felt ashamed. They were alive and unhurt. That was something. They ate the meat; then Boyce took Patrick's knife and divided a granola bar into five slim servings. Amber chewed her portion slowly, savoring every sweet crumb. "Well, supper killed ten minutes," she said.

"How's your knee?"

She stretched it and winced. "Sore, but it'll be okay. Ruth fixed it."

Boyce looked toward the sun, which was beginning to set in the west. "We move in a half hour. I'll take Rosemary." He smoothed the child's matted hair. "You all right with that?"

"Very all right," the little girl said. She glanced back in the direction they'd come from. "I hope my mama and papa are well. I have prayed to Jesus to watch after them. And he will do it. I know he will. Jesus is with us, is he not, Mr. Boyce?"

Her question tugged at Amber's heart. She had no faith in heaven right now. They were on their own in a harsh and brutal place, like sailors cast overboard into a storm-tossed sea. A sea of dirt, rocks, heat, and danger. She tried to avert her eyes before Boyce read her feelings in them.

In the distance she heard a wild animal howl, and a new fear seized her. She had o__ read *The Call of the Wild* by Jack Lond__ now she recalled vividly the law o__ ness: *Kill or be killed. Eat or b__*

Boyce lifted Amber's chin so that she was forced to meet his gaze. "Yes, Rosemary. He is with us. God tells us, 'Fear not, I am with you. I will strengthen you. I will help you. I will uphold you with the right hand of my righteousness.' Don't ever forget that. We are *not* alone."

15

They moved forward under the cover of night, heading north, following Boyce's lead, stopping often to rest. Amber's thirst seemed unquenchable, but their stash of water bottles was so meager that she felt guilty even taking her allotted sips. She battled hunger, and images of food constantly flirted with her mind—fat waffles smothered in butter and syrup, crispy french fries with hamburgers, and slices of rich, red, juicy watermelon.

The night sounds of hunting animals frightened her, but when she mentioned it to Boyce he said, "They're more afraid of us than we are of them."

"Want to bet?" she countered.

They created a litter for Rosemary, similar to the ones villagers used to carry their sick to the hospital in Lwereo. Using sturdy tree limbs, strips of one of Boyce's cotton shirts, and grass that Ruth expertly wove into a mat, Boyce and Patrick carried the little girl by balancing the long poles on their shoulders. It was easier on her, and it helped them make better time.

Rosemary never once complained. Yet Amber knew the child hurt, because sometimes she heard her whimper. "Her bones are very fragile," Ruth explained during one of their rest breaks. "We must be careful not to break any of her bones."

By the time dawn approached on the fifth day, Amber was so weary that she had grown stuporous—absolutely numb. "I don't think I can go on," she confessed to Ruth once they'd settled beneath some concealing bushes and tall grass along the side of a hill to sleep.

"Yes, you can," Ruth said. "We are making good progress."

Amber didn't know how Ruth figured that. To her it seemed as if they were going around in circles. The scenery never seemed to change; the mountains in the distance never seemed to get closer. She recalled how Heather had gone off to some kind of boot camp before boarding the Mercy Ship. Amber had had no such preparation. Except for physical education class and a few paltry workouts in the gym at their house, she did little in the way of physical exercise. She vowed to herself that once she got home, she'd begin a training regime that would keep her in tip-top physical condition. *Home.* The thought of it made tears fill her eyes.

"Are you all right?" Ruth asked. The sun was rising, and the filmy grass had turned gold in the light.

Amber wiped her cheeks. "Sure. Just tired and hungry. This wasn't exactly how I planned to spend my time in Africa, you know."

"It is strange how things work out," Ruth said. She glanced toward Patrick, who, along with Rosemary, was sound asleep a few feet away. "I spent so much time thinking about my wedding night and how difficult it might be, I never thought that I might not have a wedding night at all."

"You never got to do *anything*?" Amber realized it was none of her business, but she couldn't stop herself from asking.

Ruth shook her head. "I dressed for bed, we lay in the dark talking for a long time. Then the runner came with the news about the rebels, so we had little time alone. And now we have no time at all." Ruth's smile looked sad and tired.

"Sometimes no matter how hard we try to plan our lives, the journey takes an unexpected road. The things we worry about never happen. The things that happen are the things we never think to worry about. It is a mystery."

Boyce squatted down beside them. "You both had better get some sleep before the sun gets too hot."

Ruth rubbed her eyes. "I will join my husband." She crawled to where he was lying and lay down next to him. She was sound asleep in seconds.

"I'm tired," Amber admitted. "But not sleepy."

"I know what you mean," Boyce said. "My eyes feel like sandpaper in a dust storm, but my mind won't shut off."

"I keep thinking about home. I'm supposed to graduate next month."

"You'll be back by then. Promise."

She shrugged wearily. "High school feels like part of another life. It's like I'm watching myself in a dream, except that it's not a dream. This is real and my other life is the dream." Her voice caught.

He put his arm around her. "You'll have a lot to tell your friends once you get back."

"We will get back, won't we, Boyce?"

"Never doubt it. I'll bet we're halfway there already."

She bent her head and started to cry. Hating herself for it, she crawled away to be alone but discovered that Boyce was right beside her. "Go get some sleep," she told him between sobs. "I'm just feeling sorry for myself. You don't need to waste time on me."

"You're not a waste of time, Amber. Not ever. And you can cry if you want to."

"Oh, as if crying's going to fix anything. And as if I don't look bad enough already. Now I'll have mud caked on my face." No matter how hard she tried, she couldn't shut off her tears. Her nose ran, and she wiped it unceremoniously on her sleeve.

"I think you're beautiful," he said.

"Oh, right!" She picked up a handful of dirt and tossed it on the ground, then scooted away from him. "How can you get near me? I haven't had a bath in days . . . my hair stinks . . . my clothes smell . . . I haven't brushed my teeth since the wedding . . . I—I hardly remember how I used to look." If she could just stop crying! She was going to wake up Ruth, Patrick, and Rosemary.

"I remember seeing you for the first time," Boyce said softly. "You wore pink. Pink shirt, pink shorts . . . even your toenails were pink. You looked like a cloud of cotton candy."

His reminiscence caught her off guard. "How did you remember that?" she asked in a quivery voice. "*I* don't even remember what I was wearing when we met."

"Because I thought you were the prettiest thing I'd ever laid eyes on."

Her insides turned to jelly, and more than anything, she wanted to curl up in his arms. "Well, close your eyes and envision that Amber, not this one. Okay?"

"But I like this one too."

"How could you?"

"Because this was the Amber who never thought twice about bringing a crippled child along when the easiest thing would have been to leave her behind."

Her tears had finally stopped, and she stared at him. "It was the only thing to do. You wanted to bring her too."

"Frankly, I never thought of it. But you did. And you thought of it instantaneously, without consideration for the risk, or the fear of her slowing us down. And without a single thought that we'd have to share our pitiful resources with her. And you know what that tells me?" She shook her head, too surprised to speak. "It tells me that you're beautiful, no matter what you look like on the outside. And it's made me a little bit ashamed of myself because I didn't think of it first."

"I—I didn't know what else to do."

His smile began slow, then broke across his face fully, lighting up his eyes. "I know. And that's what makes it good. It was spontaneous. And it was right."

Overwhelmed by his assessment, she drew away. He had a false picture of her and she knew it was time to set him straight. "Please don't go pinning any roses on me, Boyce." She took a deep breath. "Do you know why I really came to Africa?"

"Because Heather asked you to."

"That's what I told my parents and my friends. But mostly I came because I was bored. Isn't that the dumbest reason? Bored," she repeated. "At home I was bored with school, my friends, my boyfriend, my whole life. Now when I think about home, I can't remember one single reason I had for being bored."

"It's hard to appreciate what we have at times. The first time I came to Africa, I thought I'd pop in, do some good deeds, then roll back home and pick up where I left off. But when I got home, I couldn't get this place off my mind. The friends I made, the work we did together . . . well, it all counted for something. Nobody at home understood. They wanted me to be the same good ol' boy, Boyce Callahan. But I wasn't. I lost him over here."

"Is that why you came back? To find him again?"

"No. He wasn't worth much." He grinned. "I like the new one better anyhow."

"Heather told me the same thing about herself. She felt changed inside once she'd come here. But it's been hard for me to understand it. I mean, she was perfect before she came. When she got back all she did was disappear into herself. And preach to us about what we should be doing with our lives."

"You sound like you were mad at Heather."

The sun had risen fully by now and heat was building, like a fire being stoked.

"Maybe I was," she confessed. "Just a little. I love her, you know. She's my sister. But Mom and Dad are always on her side. She's the star of the family and always has been. Sometimes I feel invisible."

"I wish I was more invisible in my family. I'm the oldest. I have three kid brothers and for me, it's like I have to do everything right. And perfectly. They get to make mistakes, but I don't. They get to pick what they want to do with their lives. I get to carry on my father's business. It's expected of me."

"I thought you *wanted* to be an engineer."

"I do, but I want to work over here, not in my old man's office. I want to make the lives of people like Patrick and Ruth better. I want to help kids like Rosemary live where they don't have to worry about starving to death because it hasn't rained and the crops have all died."

"Can't you tell that to your dad?"

"I have. But he doesn't hear me."

Just like no one truly listened to Heather, Amber realized. All Heather had wanted was for Alice to have surgery so that the baby could have an easier life. But for a long time, no one had paid any attention to Heather's pleas. And Amber felt like the worst offender, insisting that their sisterly relationship return to the way things had been before Heather had made her trip. She saw now that Heather couldn't have returned to that image of herself—her experiences in Africa had irrevocably changed her.

Amber said, "If Heather hadn't gotten sick, I would never have come over here. And I'd never have met any of you all."

"And you'd never have been trudging through the bush trying to escape from bandits," he added without humor.

"Well, I'm not bored."

He laughed.

"If I hadn't come, if I hadn't met you all, it would have been a big loss, you know. My loss." She had leaned her head against his shoulder, and her eyes grew heavy. Heat blanketed the air. Insects buzzed. Sleep began to overtake her.

"There must be something you regret about this adventure," he said, his lips grazing her forehead.

Her stomach growled. She stifled a yawn. "One thing. That day we went to the lake . . . I wish I had eaten that chicken."

16

They'd walked six nights straight when Boyce and Patrick decided they might be close enough to the Ugandan border to change their pattern. They would walk during the day from that point on. "I figure we've covered maybe eight to ten miles a night since we left your uncle's village," Boyce said, nodding at Ruth. "That means we've traveled close to the distance we had to come. At this point, we'd *like* the Rwandan border police to find us. They could escort us into Uganda."

"Where's the border crossing?" Amber asked.

"No idea. But police units regularly patrol the countryside, especially near Bwindi National Park."

"To hold off poachers," Patrick explained.

They all looked at the mountains as Boyce

continued. "But getting closer to the park means a longer walk. I think we should just keep heading in this direction." He pointed north.

"What about the bandits?" Amber asked.

"It's unlikely they'd take the chance of operating this close to the border. They prefer to stay inland, farther away from the authorities."

"By now," Patrick added, "we have been reported overdue. Perhaps the police will be searching for us on both sides of the border."

Amber hadn't thought about that, but of course it made sense. She'd lost track of time. They were to have been gone only a week. She counted up the days and nights and realized they'd been away from Lwereo twelve days—most of those days spent walking through the bush. And she also realized that by now Paul would have contacted her mother at the hospital in Kampala to say that the wedding party had not returned and that their whereabouts were unknown. She groaned. "My mother's going to *kill* me when we get back."

Ruth looked startled. "But why? You've done nothing wrong."

"It's a long story," Amber said with a sigh. "I have a history of goofing up. I had to take a vow

I'd be on my best behavior to come to Africa. I didn't expect things to get so messed up." Then another thought occurred to her. She grabbed Boyce's arm. "Heather! What if Mom knows something about my sister? I have no way of finding out how she's doing. This is awful."

"All the more reason to get out into the open," Boyce said. "Plus, we're almost out of supplies. We need to be rescued, and the sooner the better."

During their arduous journey, they had found berry bushes, root vegetables, and edible plants that Ruth had discovered growing wild. Just the night before, Patrick had hunted and killed a rabbit. That morning they'd built a fire and roasted it. Amber had not been the least bit squeamish about eating it either. In fact, although it had been chewy, it had tasted delicious.

"We're tired now," Boyce said, "so I think we should all get some sleep. Especially through the heat of the day. First thing tomorrow morning, we start hiking again."

He must have known they were running out of energy to take both a day and a night to rest, Amber thought. With rationed food and water, everyone's energy reserves were low. By now she was used to falling asleep at dawn and rising in the late afternoon. Total exhaustion made it easy. *Good training for all-night cramming at college, Daddy*, she imagined saying to her father.

Her feet throbbed from all the walking. She'd loosened the laces on her boots as far as she could and still keep them on her feet, but she promised herself that once she returned home, she'd soak her aching feet in warm water for days and pamper them with gobs of cream and colorful polish. They deserved it.

"At least the scenery's better," she said as she stretched out on the ground. The weather wasn't as hot and the landscape was greener, more lush looking.

"We'll note that in the travelers' guide," Boyce said with a yawn. Seconds later he was snoring.

In minutes they were all asleep. Except for Amber. Despite her weariness, she couldn't make herself go to sleep. Thinking about Heather had upset her, and new worries assailed her as well. If their mother knew Amber was missing, so did their dad. Her family had no way of knowing she was all right. Just as she had no way of knowing how Heather might have taken the news of her disappearance. Would it cause her sister anxiety and harm her further?

Stupid, stupid, stupid, Amber told herself. *I did a really stupid thing by coming to the wedding.* And yet, even as she thought that, she dismissed it. Would it have been any easier to wait at the Children's Home in Uganda, sick with worry about Ruth, Patrick, and Boyce? And what about Rosemary? Would she even have been with them if Amber hadn't come along? The questions swirled in her head like a dog chasing its tail. By the time the sun was high in the sky, she had no answers. She also had not gotten any sleep.

Sweat poured off her. She felt sticky and itchy all over. Finally, at her wits' end, she stood and looked around. The others were dead to the world, and she didn't want to wake them with her restlessness. In the distance she saw a large clump of green and decided to explore it. If she found anything of interest, they could all return in the cool of the evening. She headed straight for the verdant patch of woods.

The area was farther away than it had appeared, and it took her fifteen minutes to get to it, but once there, she was glad she'd come. The air was cooler, the ground covered with a downy, soft grass. She stooped, ran her hand across the velvet blades, and sighed with pleasure. This would be easier to sleep on than the ground where they were sleeping now. She looked up at trees that grew tall and leafy, their branches webbing overhead like a sheltering canopy. And she heard the distinct sound of running water.

Her pulse quickened. A creek? She followed the sound and soon came to a gurgling stream trickling over rocks in a small gorge. Water! She had found water. She couldn't wait to tell the others. She told herself to get moving, but the siren sound of moving water rooted her to the spot. She knew better than to drink the stuff, but if she could just put her feet in it . . . Quickly she sat and tugged off her shoes and soggy socks. She half slid down the embankment and stepped into the stream—and felt as if she'd slipped into heaven. The cool water flowed up to her ankles, caressing her throbbing skin. "Wait till you see what I've found," she said aloud.

She turned, and a movement on the other side of the ravine caught her eye. She froze, her heart thudding. The foliage shook and she heard twigs snap. An animal? Realizing she was completely out in the open, she stooped, attempting to make herself smaller. Her heart pounded crazily as a shape emerged. She caught a glimpse of a man dressed in camouflage clothing. It couldn't be the Rwandan police because they wore dark blue. This man looked like a soldier. He carried a rifle. And Ruth's tales of her long-ago encounter with Rwandan rebel troops washed over Amber like scenes from a bad horror movie.

Bile rose in her throat. Maybe he wouldn't see her. Maybe he'd pass right by and never look down. She scrunched lower without taking her eyes off him. But he did look down. For an instant their gazes locked. His rifle came up. And in that split second Amber knew what she had to do. She ran.

"Simama! Simama!" he shouted.

She didn't know what he'd said. She didn't care. She only knew she had to lead him away from her sleeping friends. She scrambled up the embankment, oblivious of the sharp stones and dead branches that scraped and cut her hands and feet.

She heard the crack of the rifle, and a bullet

whizzed past her head. She dove over the top of the gully and dropped, crawling on all fours to the trunk of a tree, panting for breath. She heard him crashing behind her through the undergrowth. A second bullet fired, scraping bark off the trunk.

Terror tore at her insides. *I'm going to die!* He was going to kill her, shoot her to death when she could very well be a day's walk from safety. But if he killed her, it would be better than if he captured her. She was sure of that much. She wanted to get away but didn't know how. She wanted to hide but didn't know where. She wanted Boyce.

Another soldier materialized, then another. The woods were swarming with them. She'd foolishly fallen into a nest of hostile soldiers.

She saw two armed men coming straight toward her and struggled to cover herself under a heap of dead leaves. She lay flat, her face buried in a pile of moldy, rotting leaves, eyes shut tight, gasping like a cornered animal. She had nowhere to turn, no one to rescue her. They would kill her. Or worse.

A harsh male voice boomed down at her in a language she did not understand. Yet she knew the tone. It told her, *Get up. I've got you.* She heard the sound of a gun being cocked.

Amber sucked in her breath, opened her eyes, and saw the dark curved tops of military boots directly in front of her nose. *If you're real, God, help me.* The toe of the boot moved the rotting leaves around her face.

Time seemed to slow. " *'Fear not. I am with you. I will help you.'* " She heard Boyce's voice as clearly as if he'd been next to her. Defying all reason, a steely calm came over her. She gritted her teeth with determination. No matter what happened to her, she'd make them believe she was alone. And she wasn't going to die like some trapped, cowering animal, either. She raised one hand, reached inside her shirt with the other, and very slowly pulled out her American passport, still hanging on a dirty string tied around her neck. With both hands above her head, she held the booklet emblazoned with the American eagle aloft and staggered upright. She raised her eyes and stared up the long black barrel of the rifle.

"*Rafiki.*" Amber used the only word of Swahili that came to her mind. "Me, *rafiki.*"

17

"You are American?" the soldier asked in English.

"Yes," Amber said. The sound of her own heart pounded in her ears.

"But what are you doing in the bush?"

"I'm lost. I'm trying to get back to Uganda."

The soldier lowered his rifle. "But you are *in* Uganda."

"I am?" They had crossed the border and not known it. Tears welled in Amber's eyes.

"Are you the lost lady from Lwereo?"

She nodded, overcome with emotion.

"Where are your friends?"

She hesitated.

"We have been looking for you for many days, lady. You all must be very tired."

"Very tired," she echoed.

A grin split his face. "Welcome to Uganda."

* * *

Amber and her friends rode all the way into Kampala in a military convoy made up of Jeeps and two trucks full of Ugandan soldiers. The men made a great fuss over them, gave them food and water, and lavished candy on Rosemary, who'd tucked herself shyly under Ruth's arm. Against all odds, Amber fell asleep in the back of the truck, her head resting in Boyce's lap.

Once they arrived in the city, they were taken to the hospital, where a medical team checked them over and pronounced them dehydrated but in good condition considering their ordeal. Amber's cuts and scrapes were thoroughly cleaned and slathered with antibiotic ointment. She was also given a tetanus shot. When she got on the scale, she was shocked to see that she'd lost twelve pounds. "However, I don't recommend it as a weight-loss program," she told the nurse, who nodded in agreement. Amber also learned that her mother had returned to the Children's Home to await word from the soldiers who'd been sent out to search.

At the American Embassy, the five of them were greeted by photographers and newspeople. Amber felt overjoyed to be safe again, alarmed when she heard that their nighttime escape from invading marauders had captured world attention. That meant that everyone in Miami knew what had happened. There really would be no glossing it over to her parents.

"Almost a week in the bush—how did you do it?" one reporter asked.

Boyce told them that God had watched over them, protected them, and given them strength every day. But he also told them he'd once been a Boy Scout and had remembered his training. Patrick and Ruth had both been raised in the bush, so they too had survival skills. Only Amber felt as if she'd contributed nothing to the group's overall welfare.

When the session broke up, Ruth asked a reporter, "Can you tell us what happened to the village?"

"It defended itself bravely," he answered. "They had a stash of firearms the rebels weren't expecting. Rwandan military showed up the next day. Turned out they'd been trailing the rebels for weeks. These guys had already killed some tourists on safari, burned and looted a couple of smaller villages."

"How many deaths?"

"There were fifteen casualties, most of them on the rebel side."

"Do you have a list of the dead villagers?"

He handed her an Ugandan paper and she skimmed the article with a worried gaze while Patrick held her hand. Amber held her breath. Finally Ruth looked up with a trembling smile. "None of my family are on the list."

An embassy spokesperson arranged for a van to take them to Lwereo the following morning. "But first, a hot bath and clean clothes," he said. "We've made arrangements for you to stay the night at the Hilton."

By the time they reached the hotel it was almost nine in the evening, and Amber was dizzy with fatigue. "I don't know how I'll sleep tonight without you guys around," she told Boyce in the hall, while Ruth and Rosemary took the first showers. The girls had been given a sumptuous suite, Boyce and Patrick another down the hall.

"And I don't know how I'll fall asleep in a soft bed instead of on the hard ground."

"Well," she said thoughtfully, "I did want to talk to you about something."

"What now? You've got that look on your face."

"What look?"

"The one that tells me you're cooking up some wild plan."

"Not too wild. I'm too tired to think too wild. But I do I have an idea."

"Go on."

"First I'm going to take the longest hot bath on record. Then I'd like to bring myself and Rosemary to your room and put Patrick in our room with Ruth. They—um—never had that honeymoon night, you know."

An impish grin lit Boyce's face. "You'll give up your cushy bed for Patrick and Ruth?"

"No . . . you'll give up yours for me and Rosemary. Don't worry, we'll pitch you a pillow on the floor."

Boyce laughed. "I never guessed you were such a romantic."

"They deserve it, don't you think?"

"What I think is that you're pretty special." He drew her closer.

"Careful . . . I smell like the bottom of a compost heap."

Boyce shook his head and raised her chin with his forefinger. "I don't care."

Her breath caught as she realized he intended to kiss her. Her knees went weak, and her pulse quickened. "Um—can this wait until I'm more presentable?"

"No way." His mouth hovered above hers. "But I'll make you a promise: Once you *are* presentable, count on it happening again."

The following morning Amber, Rosemary, and Boyce went to the hotel restaurant for breakfast. "I told Patrick and Ruth to meet us here. But I told them not to hurry," Boyce said. His suggestive grin made Amber blush.

"No hurry for me," Amber said. "I only have to face my mother today. Come on, Rosemary, let's go check out the buffet."

The child had been given a new pair of crutches at the hospital, and she hobbled to the long table set with a banquet of food. Her eyes grew round. "Who is coming to eat with us?"

"Just the people in the hotel. What would you like?" Amber picked up a plate.

"Not the whole city of Kampala? There's enough for everyone, I think."

The realization that Rosemary had never seen so much abundance in her brief lifetime moved Amber. "Well, right now, there's only us, so let's try a few of my favorite things and see how you like them." She took another plate and proceeded to pile both with every kind of fruit on the table. Next she loaded up on scrambled eggs, rice, pancakes in warm syrup, bacon, ham, cheese and hash browns.

When she set the plates on the table, Boyce looked startled. "Did you leave any for me?"

"It's every man for himself," Amber said. She cut up the meat for Rosemary. "Try this." With much satisfaction, she watched Rosemary eat heartily.

"My turn," Boyce said, scooting out of the booth.

When Boyce returned, Amber asked him, "Do you realize this is the very same place Heather rested with baby Alice when she brought her out of Sudan?"

"I guess it is. Small world."

"It gives me a spooky feeling. Like we're both tied to this place somehow."

"It's possible."

Amber shook her head. "I hope not. Once I get home, I'm never leaving again."

"Heather couldn't wait to get back."

"I told you, my sister and I are different people. We want different things."

"You're not eating much." Boyce changed the subject.

She shoved her plate aside. "I dreamed of food when we were out in the bush. Now I'm not really hungry. I guess my stomach's shrunk."

"You're nervous about facing your mother, aren't you?"

Of course he'd figured it out. Amber said, "She's going to chew me out for taking off in the first place."

"She knew you were going. No one could have predicted the raid on the village."

"Yes, but I *may* have led her to think there were more people going than just the four of us."

"Well, if it will help, I'll tell her you were the hero that got us rescued. I'll tell her your bravery to go exploring by yourself made the difference."

She heard recrimination in his tone and knew it was justified. She'd put herself in life-threatening danger by wandering off on her own. "What you're saying is that if I'd stayed put, we'd still have been found, and I might not have gotten shot at and scared half out of my head."

"It gives me chills to think that you came so closed to being killed," he confessed. "But we can't go back and redo things, Amber. It worked out. Thank God you're alive."

She drummed her fingers on the table, then decided to tell him everything. "I prayed, you know. When I thought I was going to die, I asked God to help me. Inside my head, I heard you telling me not to be afraid, and suddenly I wasn't."

He put down his fork. "God's going to make a believer out of you yet."

"I think he already has. I just can't figure out why he's bothering with me."

"Maybe God's saved you to do something special for him."

His interpretation startled her, but before she could discuss it, Patrick and Ruth walked into the dining room. Amber jumped up and ran to them. "You two look wonderful!" she cried, hugging them both.

"We feel wonderful," Patrick said with a laugh.

Amber glanced anxiously at Ruth, wondering if she'd done the right thing by suggesting that they spend the night alone together. What if Ruth had not been ready? "Get the buffet.

Rosemary and Boyce are already chowing down."

Patrick kissed Ruth's cheek, then went to join Boyce, who'd returned to the buffet line when Amber had abruptly left the table. Amber hung back. She took Ruth's hand. "I—I have to see for myself that you're all right."

Ruth offered a beautiful smile. "I am a wife now in every way. There were no bad memories to hurt me, only the love of my husband to heal me."

Tears brimmed in Amber's eyes. "I'm happy for you both."

Ruth hooked her arm through Amber's. "Now, let us eat. Does this buffet have any roasted goat? I hardly got to taste it on my wedding day, you know."

It was afternoon when the van pulled into the town of Lwereo. Amber licked her lips nervously. Soon she'd be facing her mother's wrath. Soon she'd know all about Heather. She couldn't have one without the other.

Boyce put his hand on Amber's shoulder. "Remember, I'm here beside you."

"Thanks," she said gratefully.

But when the van pulled through the gates

of the compound, Amber couldn't believe her eyes. Throngs of cheering, waving people lined both sides of the dirt road, waving yellow ribbons. Every child, every family unit member, every worker on the irrigation project, even workers from the hospital had turned out to welcome them. Patrick and Ruth leaned out the windows and clasped hands with their friends. Boyce gave a high five to everyone he could touch. Rosemary stared at the crowd in awe.

The van slowed to a crawl and stopped in front of Paul and Jodene, standing out in their front yard. Their three sons pulled open the doors and, like overeager puppies, hurled themselves across the passengers' laps.

"We saw you on the news," Samuel, the youngest, yelled.

"Amber's mother bought us a TV!" Dennis shouted.

"And Dad turned on the generator so we could watch," Kevin finished.

Amber only half heard them. She was looking out at her mother, who stood off to the side, tears streaming down her cheeks. Suddenly Amber was crying too, apprehension over their reunion vanished. She jumped out of the van and ran into her mother's open arms.

"Oh, dear God, I thought I'd lost you," her mother sobbed.

Amber was crying so hard, she was shaking. "Mom . . . I—I'm sorry—"

"You're safe. That's all I care about. I was so worried, so scared." Her mother kissed her and hugged her until it hurt. "I don't know what I'd've done if . . ." She didn't finish the sentence.

"It's over, Mom. We made it out and it's over."

Her mother held her at arm's length. "No, it isn't. We've got to catch the first plane out of here."

Amber's heart constricted. Her mother's eyes changed from relief at seeing Amber to worried pools of grief. "What's wrong?" Amber asked urgently.

"Heather's critical."

18

"**Y**ou want some magazines for the trip?" Amber's mother asked. They stood in front of a newsstand inside London's Gatwick Airport, looking at its display of international newspapers. YOUTHS SURVIVE ORDEAL IN AFRICAN BUSH, *USA Today* declared in bold lettering. "Apparently you've made the news in seven languages."

"Do I care?" Amber said. She could hardly believe that the headline referred in part to her. All she cared about at the moment was getting home. She and her mother had packed and left Uganda in two days, boarding the already sold-out airplane to London via special arrangement by the American Embassy.

Amber had talked to her father on the satellite cell phone the night they returned to

Lwereo. "How's Heather?" had been Amber's
first words.

"Not good. How are *you?*" She heard so
much emotion in his voice that she almost dis-
solved into a puddle of tears.

"I'm all right, Daddy . . . just a few cuts and
bruises. Can I talk to Heather?"

"She's in ICU, and in isolation. She's very
weak."

"Tell her I'm coming. Tell her to hold on till I
get there."

"She's trying, baby. She's really trying."

"A good book might keep your mind busy."
Her mother tried again to interest Amber in
something from the newsstand.

"No, Mom. I'm going to try to sleep on the
plane." The long flight stretched ahead like an
eternity.

Her mother sighed wearily. "Me too. I sure
didn't get much sleep when I was in Africa,
and I'm sure we won't be getting much in
Miami."

"It feels weird to be back in civilization,"
Amber said. In the crowded London terminal,
she felt claustrophobic. The pressing crush of
bodies was a far cry from the lonely, sweeping

landscape of Africa. Cell phones rang, announcements crackled in several languages over the PA system, luggage on clattering wheels was pulled past them. Amber almost clamped her hands over her ears to shut out the racket.

"I felt the same way when I returned from my stint in the Peace Corps. A person gets used to all that quiet. Noise . . . it's one of the trade-offs for our modern lifestyle." Her mother paid for several newsmagazines. "Come on, they're boarding our flight."

They went to the gate and stood in line. Amber already missed her friends, unable to forget their tearful goodbyes at the Children's Home.

"Please let us know about Heather," Jodene had pleaded. "Tell her we're all praying for her. She can lick this thing. I know she can."

Patrick and Ruth had wept openly and without shame. "I will not forget you," Ruth said. "You have done so much for us, as well as for Rosemary. So much has happened. I wish that you could stay, but I know you need to go to your own family. *Rafiki*—girlfriend."

"I hope you and Patrick get your own church and start a healthy, beautiful family.

Ruth smiled through her tears. "And you and Heather will always be part of our family."

"Maybe someday the two of you can come visit America."

"I would like that."

Patrick had added, "I've gone to college in Boston, but I have never seen the South. Perhaps one day we will come calling."

"You'd better, because I won't be coming back to Africa, and I don't like thinking we won't see each other again."

"In the next life, we will," Ruth had said, giving Amber's hands a squeeze. "May God be with you, Amber."

Once aboard the plane, Amber shut her eyes and revisited her memory of saying goodbye to Boyce. The night before, he had walked with her into the field where he'd taken her on her first night. The change in the field had been dramatic—the irrigation canals were dug, the earth tilled and turned, the reservoir built and waiting for the rainy season. Moonlight spread across the waiting ground like golden cream. Boyce had said, "My work here is finished. By December this field will be planted and thick with crops. It gives me a good feeling."

"What will you do now?"

"Go back to school, I reckon. I still have several semesters before I graduate. After that, on to Dad's firm in Birmingham."

"Well, I'm sure this project will earn you the credits you wanted. What about our little side trip?"

"I expect it to earn me *extra* credit. How about you? What are you going to do?"

"After Africa, graduating and finding a college seems tame. I don't know what's going to happen if Heather—" She'd stopped herself, unable to say the words.

"No matter what happens to Heather, you have your life to lead, Amber. You'll go on."

"I don't know how. My first memories are of Heather. Of her holding my hand and playing with me." She started to cry, and Boyce held her against his chest. She heard his heart through the fabric of his shirt, felt her tears soak into the material.

"You tell that sister of yours to get well."

"If only she'll listen to me. She never has before."

"Take care of yourself," he said.

"No problem. I excel at some things."

He kissed her forehead.

"Not good enough," she'd told him. She'd put her hands on either side of his face and stood on tiptoe. "This is for taking care of us out there in the bush. We'd never have made it without you." She'd kissed him thoroughly, stepped away, and said, "I love you." Then, without letting him see her cry, she had turned and run back to the guest house. And out of his life.

The jet from London touched down at Miami International Airport just shy of three in the afternoon. It took another hour to get through customs, but once they were through the line, Ted Barlow was waiting for them at the baggage claim carousel. To Amber it looked as if her father had aged ten years since she'd last seen him. He was thinner and looked haggard.

He kissed them both. "Thank God you're home." He turned to Amber and ran his hands along her arms as if examining her for himself.

"I'm fine, Daddy. All my parts are still in working order."

"You're getting a complete physical as soon as I can arrange it."

"Whatever. Can we just go to the hospital?"

Janet fired questions during the drive through heavy traffic to the hospital. Amber tried to keep up, but her brain felt sluggish. She felt as if she'd been away years instead of just weeks, more like a visitor than a person returning home. The world she'd grown up in looked surreal—too hot, too bright, too noisy.

The colors were garish and cheap, the roads too wide, too crammed, an ocean of concrete instead of rich red earth studded with green.

At the hospital Ted took them up to the ICU, pausing at the forbidding door. "You're going to see Heather through a glass window. When she's awake she's coherent, and she can see you and talk to you through the speaker on the wall. Just push the button when you want to be heard."

"What does she know?" Janet asked.

"She knows it's bad."

Amber felt cold all over. "I want to hug her."

"Later. You have to go through sterility procedures. Her immune system is wiped out. Any germ can destroy her, even one from a common cold."

Amber walked to the window between her parents, holding their hands. Her knees went weak when she peered inside. Heather lay on a hospital bed, surrounded by equipment. She remained but a shadow of herself, wasted except for her abdomen—it was distended. Her hair had been cropped short, her skin was tinged yellow, several IVs ran into her arms, and clear tubing attached to a urine bag hung from below the sheets.

"Oh, my baby," Janet whispered. "Oh, my poor, poor baby."

Amber felt sick to her stomach. How could this be her sister? Heather resembled a limp, grotesque marionette. "Is she awake?"

"Push the button and talk to her." Ted motioned to the speaker box.

Amber pressed the button. "Hey, sis . . . guess who's here?"

Heather's eyelids fluttered open and she smiled. Only then did Amber see a flicker of her sister's former beauty. "Amber . . . Mom . . . can you come inside?"

"Dad says later." Amber's legs quivered from the strain of holding herself rigid. If she didn't, she feared she'd fall apart.

"Wasn't Africa wonderful? Did you have fun?"

Amber glanced at her father and he whispered, "I didn't tell her about your being lost."

"Wonderful," Amber said into the speaker. "Everybody there is praying for you."

"That's good. Can't have too many prayers." Heather's eyes closed, and Amber realized she was gathering her strength.

"I saw baby Alice right before we left. She's looking fine. Mom really did an awesome job of fixing her palate."

"I knew she would."

Janet stepped up to the box and relieved Amber's cramped finger. "Hi, honey. Mom here. You were right about getting back to my roots. I worked nonstop, but I fixed a lot of kids, corrected plenty of birth defects. And you know what? It felt good."

"I wish—" Heather stopped, then started again. "It would have been nice to go as a family."

"We can still do that."

"I don't know, Mom. I'm so tired."

"Well, I didn't mean right now."

Heather's eyes closed again, and Amber stepped away from the window. She couldn't bear to watch any longer. She didn't need a medical degree to know how sick Heather was. Or how useless it was to expect her to recover. Heather was dying. And all the medicine in the world, all the doctors and their expertise could not save her.

Amber went home with her parents for the night because they made her. She'd wanted to camp out at the hospital, but her father wouldn't hear of it. "Get some rest. Come back tomorrow," he said. "If you want to see any of your friends—"

"No." She interrupted him. "I don't want to see anyone. I'd just as soon not have them know I'm home."

"All right." He raked his hand through his hair and rotated his shoulders wearily. "Why don't we all get some sleep?" His suggestion made sense. Amber's internal clock was seven hours ahead of his, which made it one in the morning, Ugandan time. "Sleep in tomorrow, if you can. Drive to the hospital when you're rested. Your car's gassed and ready to go."

Amber agreed and went to her room, cool, quiet, spacious, awash in shades of lime and blue. After the bedroom of the guest house, it seemed obscenely huge. How much space did she really need? In Africa whole families lived in huts smaller than her room. "Quit it," she said to her reflection in the mirror. "You sound like Heather after she first came home." Her heart contracted as she remembered how sick her sister had looked that afternoon.

She wanted to talk to Boyce and actually picked up the telephone before she remembered he was three thousand miles away. *Bad idea anyway.* They'd already said their good-byes and gone their separate ways.

Without bothering to undress, Amber lay down on her bed. She felt as if the hard ground in Africa had been friendlier. There it had been only her body that was miserable. Here it was her very soul.

19

"I'm not afraid of dying, sis. I just regret not being able to do all the things I wanted to do with my life."

Heather's words did nothing to comfort Amber. She had stood at the window the next morning watching her sister sleep for a long time, and when Heather finally woke, Amber had complied with the necessary procedures and come into her isolation room. "Is this what I came home to hear you tell me?" Amber asked now. "I don't want you to die. Did you ever think about that?"

"We don't always get what we want."

"You're not giving up, are you? Because if you are—"

"What'll you do? Kill me?"

The absurdity of her anger made Amber pause. Heather was right. It wasn't as if Heather had any control over what was happening to her body. "Sorry," Amber said, hanging her head. "Let's start over, all right?"

"Okay . . . for starters, do you have any idea how silly you look in that getup?"

Amber wore a too-large paper gown. Latex gloves, a paper hat, and a special mask completed her ensemble. She twirled and struck a fashion pose. "I begged for something trendy, but this is all they had."

"That's better. Now, tell me all about Africa. Especially about you and Boyce."

"I'm crazy about him." Amber confessed her heart. "But what's the point? He has his whole life planned out. I still don't know where mine's going."

"Didn't anything in Africa get to you?"

"Of course it did. I haven't got a heart of stone." Amber told Heather about Ruth, Patrick, and Rosemary. She told her about their midnight run for their lives, about walking through the bush for six nights, looking for help and a way back into Uganda. Now that she was safe, she didn't see that Heather's knowing could cause any harm.

"And you thought you were going to be bored."

"No, boredom wasn't much of a problem. Except I can't say much good about the food."

"You nut!" Heather's eyes fairly glowed. "I wish I could have been with you."

"Don't think I didn't wish you were too. I figured I was going to be hanging around a hospital doing good deeds. Instead I was hanging around the bush eating strange life-forms."

Heather laughed, a sound that made Amber feel wonderful. "I kept asking Dad why you and Mom weren't home when you were supposed to be. Everyone thinks that just because I'm sick, I lose track of time. But I knew something was going on no one was telling me about. I thought Mom had gotten bogged down in an extended surgery schedule. I had no clue *you* were the one with the problem. So you had to make a run for it through the bush. And you did it. I'm impressed, sis."

Amber grinned, proud that she had pleased her sister. "The others get all the credit—especially Boyce. I just tagged along."

"Back to Boyce. Does he know how you feel about him?"

"Sure does—I made a fool of myself. I told him I loved him."

"Do you?"

Amber nodded. "I remembered what you told me about wishing you'd said it to Ian. I didn't want him to return to his real life without knowing how I felt. So I said it. And ran for cover."

"What if he feels the same way?"

"I'd be shocked. He's out of my league."

"I felt the same way about Ian. At least you laid your cards on the table."

Amber patted Heather's hand. She could tell that her sister's burst of energy was waning. "I'll come back later this afternoon."

"I'd rather you stayed. Until I go to sleep." Heather reached over to the morphine infusion pump and pressed a button. "My happy juice," she explained. "I hurt a lot inside. This stuff really helps."

Amber couldn't hold back the film of tears that glazed her eyes. Quickly she wiped them away. "I'll sit right here," she said, leaning back in a chair.

"Tell me more about Africa," Heather asked. "Tell me about the land, the people you met . . . Ruth's village. Tell me about . . . the Children's Home. Tell . . . me . . . please . . ." Her eyes drooped and closed.

Amber stroked Heather's thin hand and began to describe everything she could recall, no matter how insignificant. She continued to talk long after Heather was asleep. Long after her voice faded from the weight of emotion, while her heart trembled with memories.

Amber's high-school friends found out she was home and began to stop by the house in a steady stream. "I cut articles out of the newspaper about you being lost over there," Kelly burbled when she found Amber out by the pool. "I was so, like, totally scared. I mean, you could have died over there! So tell me, what was it like? I've got all afternoon."

"It wasn't so bad. The papers played it up. We ran from some rebel soldiers. We walked back to Uganda. End of story." Amber was reluctant to talk about Africa with any of her friends. She wasn't sure why. Her experiences ran deep, close to her heart. Her friends wanted a sensational story, and she wouldn't give it to them.

"That's all you've got to say?"

"I've got other things on my mind, okay?"

"You mean Heather. We're all really sorry about your sister, you know. Liz and Brooke and I tried to visit her in the hospital, but they wouldn't let us in the ICU because we weren't family."

"That was nice of you. I'll tell her you tried."

"Um—are you coming back to school?"

There were two more weeks of classes, but Amber wasn't about to return. "Don't need to. I passed all my finals before I left, remember?"

"Well, sure, but you could have lunch with us. Oh, and there's a party at Brooke's step-dad's lake place Saturday night. Why don't you come? Dylan's going to be there, and he's asking about you."

"Is that supposed to make me jump for joy? I could care less about Dylan."

"He and Jeannie broke up right after the prom."

Amber sighed. "Kelly, we've been friends for a zillion years, so I feel like I can be honest with you. Truth is, I don't want to party. I don't care what Dylan does with himself or who he dates. I don't want everybody hanging around asking me a bunch of questions. My sister's really sick, and she's the one I want to be with now. So please back off. And tell the others to give me lots of space."

Kelly looked shocked, then miffed. "Well—um—all right. I'll spread the word: Leave

Amber alone." She stood up. "See you at graduation."

"Whatever." Without regrets Amber watched Kelly leave, and as the door shut behind her, Amber felt as if the door to her once-perfect high-school life had also closed. She stood in a no-man's-land, unable to reconnect with her former world, unsure of how to live in her current one.

Amber went to the hospital with her parents every night, and after each visit she would say, "Heather looked stronger, don't you think?"

"About the same," her father would reply.

When he'd said it one too many times for Amber's liking, she erupted. They'd just walked into the kitchen together. Enraged, she flung her purse onto the kitchen counter. "You always say the same thing. I think she's looking better. Don't you, Mom?"

"I think having us with her again has helped her rally. It's lifted her spirits."

"See, Dad, Mom thinks so too."

He shook his head wearily. "Have it your way." He picked up a bag from the desk. "I keep forgetting to give these to you. It's your graduation announcements. The ceremony's been scheduled for next Sunday in the county auditorium. You've gotten some messages on the answering machine from your friends about all-night parties. If you want—"

"Would you and Mom be too disappointed if I didn't walk?"

Her parents exchanged glances. "Amber, high-school graduation is a major milestone," her mother said. "You've made it through twelve years of school, and we're proud of you. Not walking the aisle and getting your diploma won't influence what's happening to Heather."

"Is that what you think I'm doing? Sacrificing for Heather? Well, I'm not. I just don't want to go. The school can mail my diploma to me."

"Yes, but—"

Amber stamped her foot. Her nerves were on fire, stretched and ready to snap. "Didn't you listen? I don't want to go. It's not important to me. Please, don't make me!"

Her father moved swiftly to put his arms around her. She fought him but finally began to cry. "Shhh, baby," he said. "It's okay. Really. We're not going to make you do anything. Calm down. If you don't want to attend the ceremony, you don't have to."

She clung to him, sobbing, all her energy gone. "I don't want to, Daddy. I really don't."

He lifted her, cradled her as if she were a baby again. "How about if I tuck you into bed like I used to do when you were a little girl? Remember? You'd fall asleep on the floor next to your sister, and I'd have to carry you both."

Amber put her arms around her father's neck and burrowed against his shoulder. "Yes, I remember," she whispered, longing deep inside for those golden days of her childhood. She wanted him to take her back to a place where Mommy's kisses could banish boo-boos and Daddy's presence could vanquish the things that went bump in the night. A place where children played in magic forests, where there was no darkness, only light, and where sisters did not die.

The ringing of the front doorbell intruded into Amber's dreamless sleep. Her parents had already left for work, and she had planned to go to the hospital at noon. She put the pillow over her head to muffle the sound, hoping the person would give up and go away. But the idiot wouldn't stop ringing the blasted bell. "I'm coming!" she yelled, knowing she couldn't be heard from her second-floor bedroom. She struggled into a robe and padded down the winding carpeted stairway to the foyer.

The door was made up of geometric patterns of art glass, with thick glass-block sidelights. Light streamed through, but she couldn't make out the person's idenity. "Who is it? Can you come back later?"

"A hungry traveler," the visitor answered. "Hoping you might have some peanut butter to share."

20

Amber couldn't get the door open fast enough. "Boyce!" She flung herself into his arms. "How did you—? When—?"

He pressed his fingers against her lips. "I'll tell you everything. But first . . ." He held her against his chest and kissed her until her knees went weak. He tipped his head. "You ran off before I had a chance to say something to you."

"Wh-What?"

"I love you, too."

She almost melted, then remembered they were standing in an open doorway and she was in her bathrobe. "Come inside. Give me a minute to dress. The kitchen's that way." She pointed. "The peanut butter's in the pantry, the bread's in the bread box on the counter. I'll be right back."

She flew up the stairs, jerked on clothes,

quickly brushed her teeth, began to brush her hair, and then, realizing she was losing valuable time with Boyce, tossed the brush aside and ran down to the kitchen.

He was sitting at the counter, smearing peanut butter on a slice of bread. "Found it," he said.

She stood in front of him, braced her hands on the countertop, and caught her breath. "I can't believe you came all this way just to eat my peanut butter. Why *did* you come?"

"My project in Uganda was finished, and I'm headed home. I routed myself through Miami so I could see you and Heather. I grabbed a cab from the airport."

"How long can you stay?"

"I catch a plane tonight."

"Can't you stay longer? We have plenty of room—"

"I have finals starting Monday morning. And my family's expecting me."

"Oh." She felt let down. "Did you mean what you said about loving me?"

"If you'd hadn't taken off like a scared rabbit, I would have told you in Uganda."

"Sorry. I—I've never said that to a guy before."

"Here's a tip: Don't say it and then run away." He grinned. "I'm glad I was first."

She noticed he didn't say, *"You're also the first for me."* "Well, at least you're here now. Heather's going to be thrilled to see you."

"Tell me what's going on with her."

"She's in liver failure. She's on the transplant list, but—" Amber hated to tell him how hopeless it was. She stared down at his large rough hand covering hers and began to cry. "Sh-She's not going to make it, Boyce."

He was beside her in a second and holding her in his arms. "I want to tell her goodbye."

"We'll go to the hospital as soon as you're ready."

"I'm ready," he said. "Let's go."

She told the nurses in the ICU he was a cousin, just passing through. They gave her no argument. Amber helped him put on the protective clothing and took him inside Heather's room.

Heather's eyes widened when she saw him. "Boyce? I—I don't believe it."

If he was shocked by her appearance, he didn't show it. "I don't know how you recognized me in this outfit."

"I'd know those eyes anywhere."

"You look beautiful."

"Liar. I know how bad I look."

"You'll always be beautiful to me, Heather Barlow."

"Boyce is on his way home," Amber said. "He just came by to say . . . hello. Right, Boyce?" She'd almost slipped.

Heather's gaze softened. "Just passing through, huh?"

"I can catch a plane from Miami just as easily as from Atlanta. Except I didn't know anyone in Atlanta."

"I'm glad you came. Seeing you reminds me of last summer. It was the best time, the happiest time of my whole life."

"I think of Ian, too," Boyce said automatically, as if he'd read her mind. "He was my friend, and I miss him."

"I look forward to seeing him again. And I know I will. Soon." Heather's gaze drifted to Amber. "My family's the only reason I've been holding on so hard."

Amber felt a shiver of fear.

Boyce took Heather's hand. "Is there anything I can do for you?"

"Yes. Look after my sister."

"If she'll let me."

"She's stubborn."

"Hey, you two," Amber broke in. "I'm standing right here, you know. I'm hearing every word you're saying."

"She's also vocal." Boyce winked at Heather. "What else can I do for you?"

"Pray with me."

Still holding her hand and without hesitation, Boyce knelt on the floor and bowed his head. Self-consciously Amber dropped beside him. Certainly she'd prayed with him when they'd been on the run. They'd asked God for protection, and for deliverance, and had received both. Now she wanted Boyce to beg God for Heather's life. Perhaps Boyce had more clout with God than she did. Instead, he asked God to give Heather peace and comfort. And he asked God to give her family courage and strength.

When he had finished, he stood. "Put in a good word for me when you meet the Big Guy."

Heather nodded. "Only if you'll remove that stupid mask and kiss me goodbye."

Boyce lifted the mask and pressed his lips to her forehead. "Go with God, Heather."

"You too."

Amber choked back tears.

Heather looked at her and said, "Will you two please go have some fun? I need to get some sleep."

"I'll see you later, sis," Amber said.

"Later," Heather whispered, and closed her eyes.

Numbly Amber followed Boyce out of her sister's room.

Night fell like a purple veil, and Amber drove Boyce to the airport. Once he had checked in, she waited with him inside a restaurant for his flight to be called. They were tucked back in a corner booth that overlooked the tarmac, and she could see jets taking off in the distance. They reminded her of lumbering cows as they gathered speed, of svelte giant birds once they freed themselves from the bonds of Earth and rose skyward. Boyce ordered coffee for them both.

"I'm glad you stopped off," she said. "I'm glad you talked to Heather. I could see it meant a lot to her. And it meant a lot to me, too."

"I know it's hard to lose her. She's lucky to have such a good family around her during all this."

"If I could stop time, I would."

Boyce stirred his coffee. "Amber, stopping time would only prolong her suffering. Is that what you want?"

She shook her head, struggling to control her emotions.

"I've seen people die in Africa. In Kenya we buried a baby that was only days old. If that baby had gotten sick in this country, a pediatrician could have saved her with a phone call to a drugstore. That's not the way things are over there. I think that's why people like Paul and Jodene work so hard to spread the Gospel, so that the people have some kind of comfort when they face death day after day. Knowing that heaven is waiting makes it easier on everyone, especially on those left behind."

He paused, stared pensively out the window. Out on the tarmac, a jumbo jet coasted toward a docking gate. "Amber, the worst thing that can happen to a person isn't dying. Everybody dies. The worst thing is to be separated from the love of God."

"I know I'm being selfish," Amber confessed. "But I look at the future and I can't imagine it without her. I don't know what I'm going to do when she's gone."

"You'll find your way through it because you're strong. I know that because of the time we spent together in the bush. You showed a lot of determination, a lot of grit. You're smart, too."

"So smart that I ran from our rescuers and almost got shot."

"You had no way of knowing who those men were. And when they talked about it later, they said you ran in the opposite direction from where we were located. That's loyalty, Amber."

"I—I didn't want you all to get hurt."

He reached across the table and laced his fingers through hers. "It took courage."

"So what do I do after Heather's gone? Do you have any answers for me? Because I don't think loyalty, courage, and determination are worth much if there's nothing to focus them on."

"When you go to college, something will grab your attention and you'll go after it with the same kind of single-mindedness that you showed in Africa. It's out there waiting for you to discover."

She blew her nose on a paper napkin. "Are you telling me we won't see each other again?"

"I'm telling you that as much as I'd like that

right now, I'll only be in your way. I'd be a distraction. You have to work out your future for yourself. You're right on the edge, Amber. It's there. You're here." He drew imaginary lines on the table. "Go get it."

His green eyes bore into hers, challenging her to reach for something she still couldn't visualize. Her future might look shining to him, but she saw only a dark pit. She had no plans. She had no dreams. She didn't know where to find them. "Will you wait for me?"

He drew her hand to his lips and kissed the backs of her fingers. "I'll wait."

She felt as if her heart was breaking. She was losing her sister, losing him, too, in a way. He knew the path he was walking. She still had to find hers. What if it took too long? What if someone else came along he liked better? What if he got tired of waiting for her?

"It's time for me to go," Boyce said after glancing at his watch.

"I'll walk you to your gate."

"No. Go back to the hospital. You've got to finish this chapter of your life before you can move on to the next."

He stood, scooped up his backpack, and kissed her mouth. "Remember, I love you. I would have told you that in Uganda, but you beat me to it."

She followed him to the restaurant entrance, watched him step into the passing crowd. She watched until he melted into the flow of fellow travelers heading for the rest of their lives.

Twenty-four hours later, Heather slipped into a coma, where she lived for another day before God called her home and the doctor turned off her life support.

That afternoon Amber sent an old-fashioned telegram to Paul and Jodene in Uganda, since they had no fax, no phone, no Internet service. The message read:

```
Heather went to be with the
Lord this morning, 10 AM STOP
She hurts no more STOP
She is with Ian now STOP
I miss her STOP Forever END
```

21

Amber leaned out over the ship's railing and watched the bow of the great white ship cut through the water like a giant steel blade. The ship had been under way all day, leaving London in fog and drizzle. Out here on the high seas, the overcast skies were finally breaking up and sun was streaking through the billowing gray clouds like fingers raking through soil.

"Careful. It's a long way down."

Amber turned and saw a brown-eyed girl about her age. "Don't worry. I've got a grip on the rail."

The girl rested her elbows beside Amber's hands and lifted her face to the breeze. Her brown hair tumbled away from her face. "Don't you just love the smell of the sea? I think I've been looking forward to this more than actually getting to Africa." She turned toward Amber and smiled. "I'm Sherri Dickerson, from Greenbrier, Arkansas. I'd never seen the ocean until I got on this ship. I can't believe there's so much water! Just sky and water . . . everywhere you look."

Amber introduced herself. She didn't want to be impolite, but she wished Sherri would go away. She wanted to be alone.

"This is my first time on a Mercy Ship. How about you?" Sherri asked.

"First time for me, too."

"I've been wanting to travel to Africa all my life, and when the youth pastor at my church started telling us about how he went on this ship when he was a teenager, well, I knew that was just what I wanted to do." Sherri slapped the rail for emphasis. "You too?"

"I've been to Africa before."

"You have?" Sherri looked impressed. "When?"

"Last year. I went with my mother to Uganda. She's a doctor. I stayed for almost eight weeks. And I never thought I'd ever go back."

"Uganda! That's where I'm going as part of Dr. Henry's team." Sherri's smile widened.

Amber was part of the same team, but she didn't tell Sherri. The girl would find out soon enough when they had their first shipboard meeting as a group the next morning.

A year had passed since Heather's death. A tough year for Amber. She'd kept her promise to her father and enrolled in the local junior college in September because the freshman class was full at the University of Miami, her first choice. She hadn't minded. She lived at home, went to classes, worked part-time in a shoe store, saw a few high-school friends who had opted to remain in Miami.

"What's Uganda like?" Sherri asked. "I've read about it, but you're the first person I've actually talked to who's gone there."

"Uganda's beautiful. Lots of wide-open spaces. Except in Kampala. It's a big city with a million people and one traffic light."

"You're teasing me, aren't you?"

Amber wasn't, but she didn't want a long, drawn-out conversation with this girl, so she shrugged. "You'll see."

"How about the people? Did you like the people? Mama says I'm a people person, but I'm really sort of shy. I mean, what do you talk about with people who live so different from us?"

"The people are the best part," Amber said, thinking about Ruth and Patrick. "You'll never meet better people anyplace." She'd written them after Heather's funeral, telling them about her sorrow, that she felt like crying all the time. Ruth had responded, "God uses the tears of suffering to cause growth in the gardens of our lives. This is a strange thing, but it is true. I would not be the woman I am today if not for what I suffered in my past. God will be with you, *rafiki*. He will cause you to grow in your season."

"So why are you going back? Is it because you met someone over there?" Sherri brushed away the hair that blew into her eyes.

"I met lots of people. So will you, and you'll care about them even if you don't think you will."

Boyce had called Amber and sent numerous e-mails. He was doing well in school and expected to graduate at the end of the summer term. She would be in Uganda when he did. He would start work for his father immediately. His name would go on the door of the firm in gold letters. She was proud of him.

Proud to know him. Proud to have loved him. She did still.

"Is that why you're going back? To be with the people you met before?"

Along with the other members of Dr. Henry's team, Amber would stay with Paul and Jodene. She was pleased about that part. And they were really looking forward to her coming. But that wasn't why she was returning. "No," she told Sherri. "I'm going because I must."

Sherri looked puzzled. "I don't get it. Why must you?"

Her parents had asked the same question. They had begged her to rethink her decision. She was their only child. What if something happened to her? What about college? Was she just dropping out? She was only eighteen. What was she thinking?

She'd tried to explain to them how she'd been adrift for months and just going through the motions of living, of belonging. She loved them, but she wanted to fulfill her destiny. And somehow she knew it lay not in living in her sister's shadow, but in following in her footsteps and finding a path that belonged only to Amber.

She looked into Sherri's eyes. "My sister once told me, 'Sometimes you have to do it before you feel it.' That's why I went to Africa the first time—just to do it. Now I'm going because I feel it. More than anything, I want to go."

"Oh," Sherri said, her expression one of confusion. She brightened. "Well, I hope we can be friends."

"*Rafiki*. That's 'friend' in Swahili."

Sherri repeated the word. "Cool . . . now I know some Swahili." A bell sounded. "Dinner." Sherri stepped away from the rail. "You coming?"

"In a minute. Will you save me a seat?"

"Will do."

She left, and Amber turned back to the open sea. This dark blue water was much different from the pale green surf along the shores of Miami's beaches, but they were one and the same ocean. She breathed in the salty, briny scent and turned her face skyward, toward the lead-colored clouds shot through with shafts of sunlight.

All at once the clouds divided and, like stars falling from space, two gulls swooped downward. Amber thought it odd that the birds should be so far from land, but she watched them soar and dip and glide like graceful ballerinas, untethered to the earth as she was. And she envied them. They seemed so joyous as they danced with the wind, these feathered wind sprites, these wayward vagabonds. They were together, yet separate, a pair dancing in perfect unison to the music of a song only they knew.

Perhaps Heather and Ian were together in the same way in heaven, soaring with the angels. The thought gave Amber great comfort.

The gulls dipped low across the bow of the ship, so close she could almost reach out and touch them. Then their graceful wings began to flap and they rose through a shaft of sunlight into the bank of clouds and disappeared. She stared at the sky for a long time, but they did not reappear.

But their wind dance had moved something inside her heart. Like the lid of a hinged box, her heart seemed to open, and the heaviness that had weighed her down for months lifted. Surely the gulls had been an omen, a sign from God that she was not alone. The birds were free, just as she was free. Her childhood was over, but she was beginning the greatest adventure known to her kind—an adventure called *life*.

Amber opened her arms and lifted them heavenward, as if to hold the wind, as if to hug the sky.